ARTIFICIAL RESPIRATION

A Book in the Series

Latin America in Translation / En Traducción / Em Tradução

Sponsored by the Duke–University of North Carolina

Joint Program in Latin American Studies

ARTIFICIAL
RESPIRATION

·

Ricardo Piglia

·

Translated by Daniel Balderston

·

DUKE UNIVERSITY PRESS

Durham and London 1994

Second printing, 1998

© 1994 Duke University Press

All rights reserved

Printed in the United States of America on acid-free paper ∞

Typeset in Adobe Caslon by Keystone Typesetting, Inc.

Library of Congress Cataloging-in-Publication Data

appear on the last printed page of this book.

Translation of the books in the series

Latin America in Translation / En Traducción / Em Tradução,

a collaboration between the Duke–University of North Carolina

Joint Program in Latin American Studies and the university

presses of Duke and the University of North Carolina,

is supported by a grant from the Mellon Foundation.

To Elías and Rubén
who helped me to come to know
the truth of history

ARTIFICIAL RESPIRATION

INTRODUCTION

•

Daniel Balderston

Ricardo Piglia's *Artificial Respiration* was published in Argentina in 1981 and immediately became a strange sort of best seller: despite the considerable difficulty of the text, it became an essential reference point for readers hungry after years of violence and lies and repression. As was to happen at about the same time with Adolfo Aristarain's eloquent film *Time for Revenge*, the writing and publication, even the reading, of this novel seemed acts of incredible courage. Piglia impressed readers with his surpassing intelligence and immense personal valor, and despite a much different situation now, more than a decade later, his novel still speaks with authority and depth.

Up to that point, Piglia was known above all for a superb collection of short stories, *Nombre falso* (Assumed Name), published in 1975, which includes the highly ingenious novella "Homage to Roberto Arlt." He had published an earlier collection of stories, called *La invasión* in its Argentine edition and *Jaulario* in the Cuban edition, which won a coveted prize from the Casa de las Américas in Havana. "Homage to Roberto Arlt" revealed a complex literary genealogy, with its homages not only to Arlt but also to Onetti and Borges; it also showed Piglia's talent for writing fiction that doubles as literary criticism, updating a genre perhaps best exemplified in the Borges stories of the 1940s.

In an important interview with Marina Kaplan that appeared

in the *New Orleans Review* in 1989, Piglia argues that it is a mistake to read *Artificial Respiration* as a simple product of a period of state terror. "I believe," he says, "that coding is the work of fiction in any context. I don't believe that the ellipsis of political material performed by fiction depends on authoritarian situations. Perhaps the type of coding is different in the latter cases, and that would be interesting to research: whether there are different types of coding according to the different contexts within which the novelist works. I believe that fiction always codes and constructs hieroglyphs out of social reality. Literature is never direct. . . . What I do believe is that political contexts define ways of reading." This formulation is generous in leaving it to readers to make the connections that need making in a given situation.

The figure of Arocena in the first half of the novel is an ironic double to the ideal reader of this text. Inquisitive, endlessly inventive, Arocena hopes to find secret meanings in the letters from the future. Yet he is denied any knowledge of the context of those letters, so his hunches are always off, no matter how ingenious. The problem facing the reader of this novel is that it circles around horrors that are quite literally unspeakable. Tardewski recalls several times the famous sentence from Wittgenstein, "What we cannot speak about we must pass over in silence." Anguished voices from the past—Kafka, Wittgenstein, the disappeared—make themselves heard in this novel in their silence. If Renzi and Tardewski and Marconi talk endlessly in the latter half of the book, it is because there is so much they cannot speak about.

The title of the novel suggests, by a sort of anagram, that the theme is the Argentine Republic itself, in its tragic history. The two men to whom the novel is dedicated are among the thousands of the "disappeared," and the action begins in April 1976, just days after the military coup of March 24, 1976. Because many Argentine references of this sort are presumably beyond the ken of the readers of this translation, I have provided some notes, with indications of English-language bibliography for those desiring further information. Piglia studied history in college, and his references to Argentine history are fairly precise. I have not thought it necessary to provide notes on the other matters referred to—Wittgenstein, Hitler, Kafka, and so forth—as the reader can easily pursue the leads given in the novel itself.

Tardewski says near the end of the novel: "To read . . . one must know how to associate." To read this novel one must hone the skills necessary for that deadly serious game: the association of ideas. For reading is also a form of artificial respiration.

I would like to dedicate this translation to the memory of my mother, Judith Balderston, who didn't live to see it.

FIRST PART

•

If I Were the Dark Winter

We had the experience but missed the meaning,
And approach to the meaning restores the experience.
　　　　　　　　　　　　　—T. S. Eliot

I

1.

Is there a story? If there is a story it begins three years ago. In April 1976, when my first book is published, he sends me a letter. The letter arrives with a photo in which he is holding me in his arms: naked, smiling, I am three months old and look like a frog. But he looks good in that picture: a serge suit, a narrow-brimmed hat, a good-humored smile, he is a thirty-year-old man who looks at the world head on. In the background, blurred and almost out of focus, is my mother, so young that at first I had trouble recognizing her.

The photo is from 1941; on the back he had written the date and then, as if trying to guide me, had copied the two lines from the English poem that now serve as epigraph to this story.

There was no other tragedy in the history of my family, no other hero worth remembering. Several versions circulated in secret, confused, hypothetical. Married to a wealthy woman with the incredible name of Esperancita—they said she had a weak heart, always slept with the light on, and that she prayed out loud in her hours of melancholy for God to hear her—my mother's brother had disappeared six months after the wedding, taking with him all of his wife's money, to go off and live with a cabaret dancer who went by the name of Coca. Perfectly calm, never losing her icy courtesy, Esperancita reported the robbery and then pulled strings to force the police to find him—which they did some months later, living in luxury under an assumed name in a hotel in Río Hondo.

I remember the newspaper clippings about the case, concealed in a more or less secret closet drawer, the same place my father kept *Physiology of the Passions and Sexual Mechanics* by Professor T. E. Van de Velde (also the author of *The Perfect Marriage*), and Engels's book *The Origin of the Family, Private Property and the State,* along with various letters, papers and documents, including my birth certificate. After complicated stratagems that filled up the siesta periods of my childhood, I would open the drawer and secretly spy on the secrets of a man of whom everyone in the house spoke in hushed tones. Convicted and Confessed: that's how one of the headlines read, I remember, a headline that always moved me, as if it alluded to heroic and somewhat desperate acts. "Convicted and confessed": I repeated it over and over, getting worked up because I did not understand the proper meaning of the words and thought that *convicted* meant invincible.

My mother's brother was in prison for almost three years. From then on little is known of him: that's when the conjectures begin, along with the imagined sad stories about his fate and his extravagant life. It seems that he no longer wanted to have anything to do with the family; he refused to see anyone, as if he were getting even for some wrong done him. One afternoon, however, Coca came to our house. Proud and remote, she came to return part of the money and to promise that it would all be returned. I know the interpretations, the tales about the meeting, and I know that Esperancita called that woman "my child" although she was almost old enough to have been her mother, and that Coca used a perfume that my father could never forget. "All of you," they said she said before leaving, "will never know what kind of a man Marcelo is," and when the story reached that point, inevitably and almost without realizing it, I remembered the historic phrase uttered by Hipólito Yrigoyen about Alvear after the military coup of 1930, a strange association of ideas brought about in part by the fact that Esperancita was related to General Uriburu.

From then on, over a period of three years, Esperancita received a check every two months until the debt had been paid off. That is the period from which I have my first memories of her or rather an image that I have always thought is my first memory: a very beautiful fragile woman, her face expressing arrogance and reluctance, leaning toward me while my mother said: "Now, Emilio, what do you say to Aunt Esperancita?" You said "Thanks" to her more than to anyone else. An emblem of the family's remorse, she was like a rare and overly refined object that made us all feel uncomfortable and clumsy. I remember that whenever she came to visit, my mother brought out her best china and used starched tablecloths that crackled as if they were made of stiff paper. And that she preserved the habit of coming to our house for a visit once or twice a month, usually on Sundays or Thursdays, until she died.

My mother's brother did not discover that she had died. Vanished without a trace, some versions had it that he was still in jail, others that he was living in Colombia with Coca. The fact is that he did not find out about her death, did not learn that when Esperancita died they found a letter addressed to him in which she confessed that it was all a lie, that she had never been robbed, and that she spoke of justice and punishment but also of love, quite odd considering what she was like.

I could not but be attracted by the Faulknerian air of the story: the young man with a brilliant future, recently accepted into the bar, who leaves everything and disappears; the hatred of the woman who pretends that she has been robbed and has him sent to prison; his refusal to defend himself or bother to clear up the hoax. So I wrote a novel based on that story, using the tone of *The Wild Palms*, or rather, using the tone Faulkner acquires when translated by Borges, by which means the tale sounded more or less like a parody of Onetti. *"None of those of us present the night the secret of that old revenge finally got out, in the sad twilight after the funeral, could but think he was witness to the most perfect form of love a man can inspire in a woman: of that love unimaginable in character but not in intention, unknowable in the depths of the wounds it causes but not in the expected bliss."* That is how the novel began, and it continued like that for two hundred pages. To avoid the tendency toward an interest in the picturesque and in local color, and the tendency toward an oral style, both of which ravaged Argentine letters, I had (so to speak) fucked up royally. Some copies of the novel are still to be found on the remainder tables of the Corrientes Street bookstores, and now the only thing I like about that book is its title (*The Prolixity of the Real*) and the effect it produced on the man to whom it was unintentionally dedicated.

A strange effect, it must be said. The novel appeared in April. Some time later I received the first letter.

First corrections, practical lessons (the letter said). Nobody ever made good literature out of family stories. A golden rule for beginning writers: if the imagination fails, one must be true to the details. The details: the idiocy of my first wife, the frown on her little mouth, the veins visible under her translucent skin. A bad sign, transparent skin: a woman of glass, as I realized too late. Something else: who told all of you about my trip to Colombia? I have my suspicions. As for me: I have lost all scruples about my life, but I suppose that more instructive subjects must exist. For example: the British invasions. Popham, an Irish gentleman in the queen's service. "Let not the land once proud of him insult him now." Commodore Popham, bewitched by the silver of Bolivia, or by the terrified farmers fleeing their plots in Perdriel. The first defeat of the country's armed forces.

The history of defeat needs to be written. Nobody should lie at the moment of death. It is all apocryphal, my son. I made off with all the silver in Bolivia—and if she says I didn't it's because she's trying to deprive me of the only worthy act in my life. Only those who have money look down on it or confuse it with bad feelings. There were a million six hundred thousand and some odd pesos, minted in 1942, the product of various inheritances and of the sale of some lands in Bolívar (lands I made her sell with a particular purpose in mind, something for which she quite properly reproaches me, though I didn't go so far as to kill off the relatives she inherited them from). I tried to start a nightclub at Cangallo and Rodríguez Peña, but they found me first. (Where did they get the business about Río Hondo?) I paid back the money with interest: it is true that Coca went to see your family and almost gave your mother a heart attack. What they fail to tell is what she said—"I shit on your soul"—the first time that Esperancita said "my child" to her, and that they had to give Esperancita smelling salts. If I went to prison and the case came out in the papers it was because I am a Radical, a follower of Amadeo Sabattini, and at that time they wanted to finish us all off because the 1943 elections were approaching, though those were forestalled by Rawson's coup. (They didn't tell you that story either?) We Radicals were disoriented, lacking the energy of the heroic times when we fought in defense of the national honor and let ourselves be killed for the Cause. So she forgives me in her will? You can tell she's crazy; she always shat standing up—believe it or not—because someone told her it was more elegant. On her deathbed she says that I did not steal from her. How mysterious is the oligarchy and such are the daughters it engenders! Slender, illusory, inevitably defeated. They should not be allowed to change our past. "Let not the land once proud of him insult him now," Popham said. Coca set herself up on her own in Uruguay, around Salto. Sometimes I get news of her, and if I came to this place to live it was to be near that woman, to have her just across the river. She does not deign to see me because she is proud and silly, because she is old. I get up at dawn; at that hour you can still see the light of the street lamps on the other bank. I teach Argentine history at the high school and at night go to play chess at the Social Club. There is a Pole who is a real master, who used to play with Prince Alekhine and James Joyce in Zurich, and one of my most ardent desires is to stalemate him just once. When he is drunk he sings and talks in Polish; he notes down his thoughts in a notebook and claims to have been a student of Wittgenstein's. I gave him your novel to read; he read it attentively without suspecting that I am the fellow about whom the filthy dreams are told. He promised to write a review in *The Telegraph*, the local paper. He has already published several notes about chess and also some extracts from the notebook where he jots down his ideas. His fantasy is to write a book entirely made up of quotations. Your novel is not so different from that, being based entirely on family stories; sometimes I think I can hear your mother's voice; that you should have known how to disguise it with that loud style does not fail to be a sign of delicacy. The distortions, in any case, come from that direction. I should ask you—to change the subject—for utmost discretion with regard to my present situation. *Utmost discretion.* I have my suspicions: in that regard I am like everyone else. In any case, as I said already, at present I do not have a private life. I am a former lawyer who teaches Argentine history to incredulous young people, the sons of local merchants and farmers. This job is healthy: there is nothing like being in contact with youth if you want to learn how to grow old. You must avoid introspection, I tell my young students, and I teach them what I have called the *historical perspective*. We are but leaves floating on a river and must learn to look at what comes as if it had already happened. There will never be a Proust among the historians, which comforts me and should serve you as a lesson. You can write to me, for the moment, at the Social Club, Concordia, Entre Ríos Province. Greetings: Marcelo Maggi Popham. Educator. A Radical, a follower of Sabattini. An Irish gentleman in the queen's service. The man who loved Parnell all his life—did you read the biography? He was a worthless man but spoke twelve languages. He posed a single problem: how to narrate real events.

P.S. Of course we must talk. There are other versions you should learn. I hope you come see me. I barely move, having grown too fat. History is the only refuge I can find from a nightmare from which I would like to wake up.

That was the first letter, and with it the story really begins.

Almost a year later I was on my way to see him, dead tired in the shabby car of a train on its way to Paraguay. Some fellows who were playing cards on the top of a cardboard suitcase offered me some gin. For me it was like moving forward into the past, and at the end of that trip I understood to what extent Maggi had foreseen everything. But that was later on, when it was all over; first I received the letter and the photograph and we started writing to each other.

2.

Someone, a Russian critic, the Russian critic Yuri Tynianov, declares that literature evolves from uncle to nephew (and not from fathers to sons), an enigmatic expression that should be useful to us at this point, as it is the best summary of your letter that I can think of.

For my part, no interest in politics. What interests me about Yrigoyen is his *style:* Radical baroque. What hasn't anyone understood that the writing of Macedonio Fernández is born of his speeches? Nor do I share your passion for history. Since the discovery of the New World nothing has happened in these parts that deserves the slightest attention. Births, obituaries, military parades: that's all. Argentine history is the hallucinatory endless monologue of Sergeant Cabral at the moment of his death, as transcribed by Roberto Arlt.

Well then, shall we compose the great family saga in duo? Shall we tell each other the whole story all over again? What I can give you at the start is a summary of everything that was said about you:

1. That you courted Esperancita Ossorio when you discovered she was the great-granddaughter of Enrique Ossorio because you were interested in a trunk full of family papers.

2. That those papers were what really interested you, but that you couldn't get the one without the other.

3. That for years you have been working on a biography or something like it of that forgotten patriot, Rosas's private secretary but also a spy in the service of Lavalle.

4. That you became a follower of Yrigoyen in the thirties, at the wrong moment as usual, and that your politics are mysteriously linked to your flight with Coca.

5. That if you live in a border town like Concordia it is because you are involved in smuggling.

Of course other versions exist; some of them were actually invented during the wake for Esperancita, who looked like a china doll in her veils and orange blossoms. Nobody cried for her, poor thing; some say that before she died they heard her say "Buenos Aires, Buenos Aires" twice, just like José Hernández when he died in the arms of his brother Rafael. As you can see, I write to Maggi, she did not die with your name on her lips.

The only one who mentioned you was Don Luciano Ossorio, the father of the deceased, who is past ninety and goes about in a wheelchair. When he saw me arrive at the wake he crossed the room, the rubber wheels squeaking on the parquet floor. You, he told me, I write Maggi, you resemble Marcelo. A plaid blanket covered his legs and he raised his vulturelike face to ask me: Do you see Marcelo? Hasn't he asked after me?

So you have seen Don Luciano? Crippled and everything, he is the only worthy person in that whole band of nitwits. I don't know if you know his story. On May 25, 1931, in a ball court where the independence day ceremonies were being celebrated, he was shot by some drunkard. The old man was on the grandstand giving a speech when the drunkard said: Tell that SOB to shut up. Then he took out the revolver he was supposed to shoot off in honor of the British ambassador (who had come all the way to Bolívar at the invitation of the old man, the owner of almost the entire district) and shot the old man. After the clamor died down the old man grew pale but kept on speaking just the same, holding onto the railing of the flag-draped grandstand, and nobody would have known anything if curses hadn't started slipping into his speech. All of a sudden they heard him say very clearly into the microphone: They fucked me over. They fucked me over, he said. The ones from the Radical klan, the old man said, slumping to the floor. The guy who had wounded him was a former jockey who earned a living in the illegal horse races in the area; they beat him so hard that he ended up half-crazy and the truth of the matter never came out. The only thing the jockey managed to say before they started beating him was that he had been told that the revolver was loaded with blanks. The shot entered the old man in his side and grazed his spinal column, leaving him an invalid for the rest of his life. And to think, he would say to me, that the only things that really interest me in the world, apart from politics, are fucking and horseback riding. On seeing him one had a tendency to be metaphorical and he himself reflected in metaphorical terms. I am paralyzed, the same as this country, he would say. I am Argentina, shit, the old man would say, raving under the influence of the morphine they gave him to relieve his pain. He began identifying the history of the nation with his life, a temptation latent in anyone who owns more than seven thousand acres in the pampas. He was given shots all the time, and this gave him a strange lucidity, gradually changing his way of thinking, as shown for example by the fact that later on he wanted to give the land to the peasants. He had bought half of the Bolívar district in 1902 for eight pesos an acre in a judicial sale fixed by Ataliva Roca's gang. From time to time he would speak of that and how his conscience kept him from sleeping. The soldiers put all the foreigners in a freight train, he recounted, and sent them off to hell, somewhere in the area of the Caruhé salt marshes. What became of those poor people? The old man asked that, thinking that he had in fact deserved the shot in his back. I know better than anyone how savage one must be to get ahead in this country, the old man would say. His children had him confined to a wing of the house and gave him all the morphine he wanted so long as he would stop pestering them. I love that man, Maggi wrote to me, and if he confused you with me it's because I was your age when I started hanging around him. I always got along better with him than with his daughter Esperancita, may she rest in peace. Sometimes I would take him out in the sun and fresh air and the old man would be talking as calmly as could be and all of a sudden he would turn around, his face livid, and say: Never accept an invitation to give a speech on a grandstand even if it is May 25th. Do you hear me, Marcelo? Even if it is May 25th and the British ambassador is there with all his relations, don't accept, because that's when they slip in to put a bullet in your spine. The truth is that I started visiting him on an assignment from the party: we knew he was changing and wanted to see if he would sign a document against electoral fraud, because the old man had been one of the founders of the Conservative Union in the period of the break between Roca and Pellegrini; later on he was a senator with a lot of prestige. The old man signed just like that, and you know he was a first cousin of General Uriburu. But with all of these little pieces of paper we're not getting anywhere, he said. No matter how many secret ballots and dead children! The people must be armed! The people must be armed, the old man said, don't you people know that? Those fucking cowards have to be run off at gunpoint. The people, the old man said: which side are they on? That's how I started visiting him and how I met Esperancita. It was the old man, though, who first told me about Enrique Ossorio, his grandfather, and let me see the trunk with the family papers. The reading of those papers and the romance with the daughter happened at the same time. I don't know how my feelings worked at the time, but she seemed very sweet and was very young. The truth is that at first I would go to the house to talk to the old man and all of a sudden he would bring up the story of the suicide, traitor, and gold miner. But that's another story, one I'll tell you later, because who knows, maybe you'll be able to help me with all of that, Maggi wrote to me. What is certain is that I have been working on those papers for years now and sometimes I think that Don Luciano is still alive because he's waiting for me to finish and doesn't want to be disappointed. Of course everyone thinks the old bird is crazy, but everyone thought the same of Enrique Ossorio, to say nothing of me.

So I'm involved in smuggling? Why not? When all is said and done this country owes its independence to smuggling. Everyone here is devoted to that pursuit, no big deal, but I, as you will see, traffic in other illusions.

Last night, for example, I stayed up until dawn discussing certain changes that could be made in the chess game with my Polish friend Tardewski. A game must be invented, he tells me, in which the functions of the pieces change after they stay in the same spot for a while; they should become stronger or weaker. Under the present rules, he tells me, Maggi writes, the game does not develop, but always remains identical to itself. Only what changes and is transformed, Tardewski says, has meaning.

In these feigned arguments we pass the idle provincial hours, because life in the provinces is famous for its monotony. Greetings. Yours ever, Professor Marcelo Maggi.

3.

We began writing to each other and kept on for some months. It makes no sense for me to reproduce all of those letters. I have read them all over again, and do not find the least bit of clear evidence that could have made me foresee what happened. At first it was all like a game: he accentuated his professorial air and had a lark. He recounted his provincial life in a slow ironic way, described his conversations with Tardewski in some detail, asked unenthusiastically for information about my existence and situation, and pushed forward with a sort of peaceful assault on my tendency to second-guess his life. Your letters amuse me, he wrote, too many questions, as if there were a secret. There is a secret, but it is of no importance. At my age I have learned that I do not need to hide anything; I have learned, I mean, Maggi wrote, what I already knew, that I don't need to justify myself. I don't write to you, then, Maggi wrote to me, because I wish to preserve something amidst this desolation, I write to you because the years have been depositing memories like tartar on the teeth, because for me the past has turned into an old cripple. Perhaps for that very reason I need a witness, someone, in short, who will listen to me attentively and from afar. As you can see I try to be sincere, Maggi wrote to me from Concordia, Province of Entre Ríos.

He also devoted himself with waning enthusiasm to disproving or correcting some of the facts about his past that I had at my disposal. For instance, he wrote to me once, where did you get that version about Coca? She wholeheartedly enjoyed the night time but was not the least bit perverse. At most she had that quota of perversity necessary to make life bearable, but no more than that. She was happy as she was: she never wanted to have a child, never repented of anything she had done. Those who cannot accept their desires, Coca would say, they should be called cowards. I met her in 1933 because I was hidden for a while in a Rosario nightclub run by a fellow Radical who had been police chief. Coca worked there and I seemed like a strange creature to her. The truth is that unwittingly I had the air of a conspirator in some Dostoevsky novel; she thought I was an anarchist, some sort of mystic or nihilist, and I suppose that's why she noticed me. I spent two months hidden in a little room in the attic of the cabaret, reading Sommariva's *History of the Federal Interventions* and doing crossword puzzles. At dawn, when she was out from under all of the customers, Coca would come see me to have some yerba mate with me and listen to me talk about Leandro Alem.

Sometimes he included references to his Radical past, but he seemed to have little enthusiasm for this and did so less and less. Nobody can imagine what 1945 was for us Radicals. To make matters worse I spent most of the game in jail, so you can just imagine. I got out in 1946 and the country was so different that I seemed like an eccentric, a sort of 1880s dandy just disembarked from the time machine. My people met at the Plaza Hotel and we would listen to "Chino" Balbín, who recommended that we "dig deep in the furrows of Argentine hope" (that man always liked agrarian imagery). When I was starting to understand a little it was all over already and we were involved in another circus with Captain Gandhi, the Consultative Board, the "Fugitive Tyrant" and all of that.

He was always elusive; if you wanted to claim that in a sense he tried to anticipate what happened later, all that you would find would be this frail sort of image. I am convinced that nothing ever happens to us that we have not foreseen, nothing for which we are not prepared. It has been our luck to live at a bad time, like everyone else, and we must learn to live without illusions. A friend of a friend once had an accident: a fellow who was half-crazy attacked him with a razor and held him hostage in the bathroom of a bar for almost three hours. He wanted to be given a car and a passport and to be allowed to cross into Brazil, otherwise he was going to kill him (my friend's friend). The madman trembled like one possessed and put the razor to his throat and at one point made him kneel and say the Lord's Prayer. Things were getting worse and worse when all of a sudden the madman recovered from his fit and dropped the weapon and started begging for everyone's forgiveness. Anyone can have a case of jangled nerves, he said. My friend's friend came out of the bathroom walking as if in his sleep and leaned against a wall and said: something has finally happened to me. Something has finally happened to me—isn't that wonderful?—Maggi wrote to me.

To tell the truth, beyond these bits of news, beyond the arguments we pretended to have from time to time, what emerged as the focus of Maggi's correspondence with me was his work on Enrique Ossorio. He had been writing that book for a long time and the problems he was having began cropping up in his letters. I am like someone lost in his memory, he wrote me, lost in a forest, trying to find a path, tracing what remains of that life besides the proliferation of fragments and testimonies and notes, all the machinery of oblivion. I suffer the classic misfortune of the historian, Maggi wrote, although I am no more than an amateur. I suffer that classic misfortune: to desire possession of those documents so as to decipher the truth of a life in them, only to discover that the documents have ended up taking possession of me, imposing their rhythms and chronology and peculiar truths on me. I dream about that man, he writes to me. I see him in accord with the lithography of the period: magnanimous, desperate, with the feverish glow in his eyes that carried him to his death. He sank deeper and deeper into that suicidal obsession, which nevertheless somehow contained the whole truth about his time. They say he was a traitor; there are men destined by history to commit treason and he was one of that number. But he always knew it, Maggi wrote; he knew it from the very beginning and up to the very end, as if he understood that such was his destiny, his way of taking part in the nation's struggle.

In fact, Enrique Ossorio's story began to come together for me bit by bit, fragmentarily, in the jumble of Marcelo's letters. For he never told me explicitly, I want you to become familiar with this story, I want you to know what meaning it has for me and what I intend to do with it. He never told me directly but he let me know, as if in a sense he had already named me his executor, as if he foresaw (or feared) what was going to happen. What is certain is that I gradually reconstructed the fragments of the life of Enrique Ossorio.

The son of a colonel in the independence wars, Ossorio is one of the founders of the Literary Society of Buenos Aires. He studies law and is accepted into the bar at the same time as Alberdi, Vicente Fidel López, Frías, and Carlos Tejedor. While studying at the university he becomes interested in philosophy and takes private courses on Vico and Hegel with Pedro de Angelis. His gifts are such that de Angelis persuades him to continue his studies and writes a personal letter of recommendation to his friend Jules Michelet. At the last moment and for unknown reasons Ossorio decides not to go and remains in Buenos Aires. Toward the end of 1837 he is assigned a job as Rosas's private secretary and becomes one of the men in the dictator's confidence. In mid-1838 he establishes links to Maza's clandestine group in their conspiracy against Rosas. From his office, Ossorio maintains a correspondence in code with Félix Frías, exiled in Montevideo, to whom he sends secret information and documents. When the plot is discovered no one suspects him and he remains close to Rosas for a while, then decides to flee, even though his life is not really in danger; he takes refuge in the house of his cousin Amparo Escalada. He lives hidden in the cellar of her house for some six months. The woman will have a son by him, a child Ossorio will never know. In 1842 he crosses to Montevideo. The exiles are fearful; they think he is a double agent. Isolated and disillusioned with politics, he goes to Brazil, where he settles in Rio Grande do Sul, lives with a black woman slave, and devotes himself to writing poetry and contracting syphilis. The woman dies of malaria, and Ossorio, ill himself, embarks for Chile. In Santiago he offers to give private classes and has cards printed: *Enrique Ossorio. Maître de Philosophie.* His only student is a Jesuit priest who works for Rosas, informing on the activities of the exiles. At the same time Ossorio lays out the project of an *Encyclopedia of American Ideas* and tries to interest Sarmiento, Alberdi, Echeverría, and Juan María Gutiérrez in writing parts of it. The project fails and Ossorio devotes himself to journalism. In 1848 he embarks for California, attracted by the gold fever. He wanders around San Francisco and then through the uninhabited Sierras in the company of tramps, adventurers and prostitutes, German and Chilean miners. In less than six months he amasses a fortune and leaves California for Boston, where he frequents the company of Nathaniel Hawthorne, just married to a sister of Mary Mann, Sarmiento's friend. Later he settles in New York, ready to devote himself to literature. He passes entire nights closeted in a room on the East River writing various texts (among them a utopian novel). At the same time he initiates a copious correspondence with Rosas, de Angelis, Sarmiento, Alberdi, and Urquiza (whom he sees as the key to future national unity). He has begun to show signs of the strangeness that will turn to madness. One night, terribly drunk, he provokes a disturbance in a Harlem bawdy house in which a woman ends up dead. Even though he cannot be proved responsible for the crime, he is deported to Chile. He lives for two months in Copiapó, isolated, alone, consumed by insomnia and hallucinations, all the while engrossed in feverish activity, rewriting his papers and organizing his personal archive. One afternoon, after wandering around the port until dusk, he goes to the graveyard; lying down on the tomb of a famous actress, he smokes a cigar and watches the night fall. Then he shoots himself in the head. Two weeks later Rosas is defeated by Urquiza at Caseros.

Maggi had at hand the unpublished documents preserved by the Ossorio family for almost a hundred years. These are the papers Esperancita's father handed over: writings, letters, reports, and a diary written by Ossorio in the United States. They had kept the trunk closed since the 1870s, Maggi writes to me. The papers arrived from Copiapó together with the gold Ossorio had gathered in California. The history of the family, we might say, forks here. On the one hand, a fortune sufficient (according to Ossorio's own calculations) to free five thousand black slaves, should anyone think of using such wealth to buy the freedom of five thousand slaves. On the other, the trunk, the papers, the memories of the disgrace. Amparo, the cousin, received both at the same time. Disconsolate at the news of the suicide, she remains in a perpetual state of widowhood, never marrying. She would wander around the house like a ghost, they say, and from time to time would shut herself in the basement where once and forevermore she had been seduced and made love to by Enrique Ossorio; she would close herself in to read what he had written in the years of his exile. It was really she who charged herself with preserving those documents, for she was more interested in the dead man's words than in all the gold in California. She read those papers as if they were the signs that would allow her to understand the misfortune that was her life; there, sheltered in those letters, she could see the outlines of the barely remembered but always desired body of the suicide. As for the son, that is, Don Luciano's father, he became heir to it all, and what he did was invest the fortune well. Investing it well and at the right moment, taking advantage of a period in the country's history when, with gold in hand and good contacts, one could buy all the land one cared to imagine. So that in 1862 Esperancita's grandfather was already one of the most powerful landowners in the group of men who supported the candidacy of General Mitre for president. If he had had his way his father's papers would have been burnt. And if he did not do so, it was because his mother survived him so as to prevent it. In any case, before dying that man made the whole family swear upon the trunk itself that no one would let those documents be publicly revealed until at least a hundred years had gone by. And that, Maggi wrote me, was how they survived for me to receive them. Actually, Maggi wrote to me, I try to use those materials to reveal the other side of history, remaining faithful to the facts while at the same time showing the exemplary character of the life of this Rimbaud-like figure who departed from the main avenues of history so as to bear better witness to it. I face difficulties of various kinds. First and foremost, it is clear that I do not intend to write what is called, in the classic sense, a Biography. I am instead trying to show the movement of history contained in an essentially *eccentric* life. For example: doesn't Ossorio exhibit in a dramatic way a tendency latent in the entire history of the Argentine intelligentsia, increasingly autonomous in the Rosas period? Aren't his writings the other side of Sarmiento's? Besides, there are various enigmas. Was he really a traitor? That is, did he always keep in touch with Rosas? I have several working hypotheses, each implying a different way of organizing the material and ordering the discussion. It is necessary, above all, to reproduce the *evolution* that defines Ossorio's existence, something very hard to capture. Opposed in *appearance* to the movement of history. His life is marked by a kind of excess, a utopian trace. But, as Ossorio himself wrote (Maggi writes to me), what is exile but a form of utopia? The exile is the utopian man par excellence, Ossorio wrote, Maggi writes to me; he lives in a constant state of homesickness for the future.

I am sure, besides, that the only way of capturing the sense that defines his destiny is to alter the chronology, to go backwards from the final madness to the moment when Ossorio takes part with the rest of the generation of Argentine romantics in founding the principles and bases of what we call the national culture. In that way, perhaps, by means of that inversion, it may be possible to capture what that man's *misfortunes* express. Thus, that life (Maggi seems to be trying to convince me) might be written with the suicide at the beginning, and so the book should start with the words that Ossorio wrote before killing himself. *Listen, my dear Alberdi: with death already in me I have special knowledge. A hateful, very dangerous, road: that of solitude. To all of my countrymen or compatriots: I did nothing in the course of this war except from conviction. Must we always remain far from our native land? Even the echoes of my mother tongue are dying out for me. Exile is like a long wakefulness. I know that apart from myself nobody in the world will believe in me. Many acts of disloyalty will still be discovered. Ah, scoundrels! Goodbye, my brother. I want to be buried in the city of Buenos Aires: this is my strongest desire, and I ask by the Sun of the May Revolution that you see to it. May you all remain passionate, for passion is the only link we have with truth. Treat my writings with respect; they have been put in proper order and I call them my Annals. Who will write this history? No matter how much shame covers me, I would not surrender either my despair or my decency. I like and have always liked your way of signing a letter, so allow me to imitate you: For country and freedom. And I must call you by your first name this once, with your permission, Juan Bautista. Yours: your brother, Enrique Ossorio, the one who is about to die.*

4.

I spent an almost sleepless night because of the heat, and now the fresh air from the open window is blowing on my face. The light of dawn quivers, fragile, and you can see the river flowing by among the willows; the water sometimes rises, carrying everything away. People here learn to live at the edge of misfortune. The tourists call this misery local color. Border towns are apparently picturesque. Tardewski says that nature does not exist except in dreams. Nature only makes itself manifest, he says, in catastrophes and in lyric poetry. Everything that surrounds us, he says, is artificial, bearing the mark of human life. And what other landscape deserves to be admired? I was thinking about this just now, before starting to write to you. Various complications, difficult to explain in a letter, make me believe that for a time you will not have any news of me. Letter writing is a truly anachronistic genre, a sort of tardy inheritance from the eighteenth century; those who lived at that time believed in the pure truth of the written word. And we? Times have changed; words are lost with ever greater ease; you can see them float on the waters of history, sink, come up again, mixed in by the current with the water hyacinths. We'll have to find a way of meeting each other soon.

Some setbacks have forced me to change my plans. In any case I would like you to come see me in the near future. I will let you know how and when. In the meantime, would you do me the favor of visiting Don Luciano Ossorio and giving him my regards? I don't know if I will be able to write to him. I have told you more than once, no doubt in an emphatic or comic way, that for me history is the motor of these plots. However, we should not doubt the resistance of the real or its opacity. The dove that feels the resistance of the air, says my friend Tardewski quoting Kant: The dove that feels the resistance of the air thinks that it could fly better in the void.

Our misfortunes are woven on the loom of those false illusions. Warmest regards. Marcelo Maggi.

I received your letter a while ago. First point: of course I will come see you whenever you want. Second point: what is the meaning of the *warning* that for a time I will have no news of you? I want to make clear that you have no obligation to write to me at any particular time, no obligation to answer me by the next mail or anything like that. It's not a matter of playing one card right after another as in a game of *truco*. It doesn't seem to me that letter writing need be confused with a bank debt, even if it is true that they are somewhat related: letters are like scrip, received and owed. One always has a feeling of some remorse toward a friend to whom one *owes* a letter, while the joy of receiving them does not always compensate for the feeling of obligation to answer them. However, letter writing is a perverse genre: it requires distance and absence to prosper. People only write to others nearby in epistolary novels, in which they send letters instead of talking to each other even when living under the same roof, forced by the rhetoric of the genre, a genre of which one might say that it (the epistolary genre) was wiped out by the telephone, rendered totally anachronistic. (It could be said that with Hemingway we pass from the epistolary to the telephonic genre: not because the characters talk on the phone a lot in his stories, but because the conversations, even when the characters are sitting face to face, for example in a bar or in bed, always have the dry, choppy style of telephone conversations, that way of establishing the relation between speakers that the linguist Roman Jakobson—to make use of *my* academic knowledge and, in passing, to contrast the imperial science of our time with the anachronistic handicraft of the discipline you practice, which lingers in the twilight after the splendor it possessed in the nineteenth century when it turned, with Hegel, into the lay substitute for religion, and with the dashes I bring to a close this digression on linguistics and history—calls the phatic function of language, represented in the case of Hemingway in more or less the following form: Are you all right? Yes, fine. And you? Fine, just fine. A beer? Why not? Cold? What? Your beer—cold? Yes, cold, and so forth and so on.) So the epistolary genre

31 •

has aged, and yet I must confess that one of my dearest fancies is someday to write a novel wholly composed of letters. In fact, now that I think about it, there are no epistolary novels in Argentine literature, which is of course due (to confirm one of the theories hinted at in the recent rather melancholy letter I received from you) to the fact that Argentina had no eighteenth century. In any case, beyond the fantasy of someday writing a story entirely consisting of letters, apart from that, sometimes at night, when the dampness of Buenos Aires is what keeps *me* from falling asleep, I start thinking about all the letters I have written in my lifetime, letters that, if one could only read them over, would doubtless turn out to be chock full of projects, fantasies, bits of news of that other self I was at the time I wrote them. What better autobiography could one imagine than the sets of letters one has written, sent to a variety of addresses, women, relatives, old friends, in different situations and moods? But what—it might be objected—might one find in those letters? Or at the very least what would I find in them? Changes in my handwriting, first of all, but also changes in my style, the history of certain changes of style and of ways of using the written language. And what is the biography of a writer in the last instance but the history of the transformations of his style? What else, besides these modulations, might one find after following this trajectory? I do not believe, for instance, that one could find experiences worth mentioning in those letters. No doubt one would find or remember events, petty facts, even passions long since forgotten, details, the story, perhaps, of those events, written while they were occurring, but nothing more. Ultimately, as was said so well by that friend of yours held hostage by the madman with the knife, ultimately nothing extraordinary can happen to us, nothing worth recounting. It is in fact true that nothing ever happens to us. All the experiences we can speak of are no more than fantasies. And anyway what can one *have* in one's life but two or three experiences? Two or three experiences, no more (and sometimes not even that). Nobody has experiences any more (did they have them in the nineteenth century?); there are only fantasies. All of us invent a variety of stories (ultimately versions of the same story) so as to imagine that something has happened to us in the course of our lives: a story or series of stories that ultimately are all that we really have lived, stories we tell ourselves so as to imagine that we have had experiences or that something meaningful has happened to us. But who can guarantee that the order of the story is that of life? We are made of those illusions, dear master, as you know better than I. For instance, I always remember with nostalgia the period when I was a student. I lived alone, in a boarding house in La Plata, alone for the first time in my life; I was eighteen and had the feeling that adventures happened one after another. Adventures (or at least I thought they were adventures) happened to me in quick succession at that time. Not only with women, although during that period things started going very well for me. (For no particular reason, no special talent at seduction: in the School of Humanities, there were more or less thirty-eight women for every man, so that if you didn't pick any up there you must have suffered from a peculiar leprosy that only women can perceive.) Not only with women, as I said, did things happen. I was free and *available:* in that consisted the fascinating feeling of living in the middle of an adventure. I could get up in the middle of the night or go out at dawn, board a train and get off somewhere, go to an unknown town, spend the night in a hotel, dine among strangers or traveling salesmen or murderers, walk through empty streets, without a history, an unknown, a stranger who observes or imagines the adventures that develop around him. At that time, that sort of thing represented for me the fascinating possibility of adventure. Now I realize that as soon as mama's boys leave home, reality instantly becomes a sort of imaginative representation for them of what, for instance, whaling in the high seas must have been for Herman Melville.

The bars are our whaling ports, which is at once comic and pathetic. To cap it all off, at that time I was convinced that I was going to be a great writer. Sooner or later, I thought, I am going to become a great writer, but in the meantime I should have adventures. And I thought that everything that happened to me, no matter how idiotic, was a way of accumulating that depth of experience on which I assumed great writers built their great works. At that time, at the age of eighteen or nineteen, I thought that when I reached thirty-five I would have exhausted all of experience and at the same time have produced a finished body of work, work so varied and of such high quality that I would be able to go to Paris for four or five months of the easy life (which I suppose was for me the most spectacular model of success). To arrive in Paris at the age of thirty-five, saturated with experience and author of a whole body of written work, to then wander through the boulevards like a real man about town, like someone who has no more illusions: that's how I imagined myself wandering around the boulevards of Paris. I dreamed of that at eighteen and look at me now, past thirty, the author of a book I am less and less proud of, and all of that would not matter if it were not for the fact that for a year now I cannot write, I mean everything I write feels like shit. That exasperates me, to be frank. My present life, in keeping with the tone of your last letter, seems quite ridiculous to me at those times when I think about it all of a sudden. I go to the paper to write bullshit (to make matters worse, bullshit about literature) and then come here and shut myself in to write, but after a while find myself doodling lines, circles, figures, little pictures—maps of my soul— or if not I write things that the next day I cannot even brush against with my fingertips without getting sick.

Today, as you can see, instead of that I have been sitting here for more than two hours, writing you this letter that seemingly will never end, as if this were my way of responding to (or making up for) that enigmatic sort of farewell that was your last letter. So I am writing these interminable pages to you, *mon oncle* Marcel, who have appeared from so far away, from such an ancient place, from such a remote period of my life: your (epistolary) reappearance in these last few months has been the purest triumph of fiction that I can boast of (not to say the only one). In sum, I am advancing with a dizzying slowness in that so-called novel I am trying to write. I hear a tune and I cannot play it, said Coleman Hawkins, I think it was. I hear a tune and I cannot play it: I don't know a better summation of the state I'm in. I know well enough what it's about; in a sense, from time to time, I can hear that tune, but when I start to write what comes out is the same old shit, without the slightest hint of music. Yesterday, when things had gotten really bad, in the early morning, I went out and stood in the street watching some guys from the Water Works (or the State Gas Company) digging a tunnel in the middle of the night; the guys were working, digging their tunnel, and I crossed the street to the Ramos Bar and ordered a beer and a double shot of gin because that mixture is the prescription Dickens advises for those on the verge of suicide. Not because I had decided to commit suicide or anything like that, but because I like the idea: to think I was a suicide who walks (or better still, drifts along) through the city in the early morning while some guys dig a tunnel in the darkness, lit by the yellow light of the street lamps. It all seemed like an adventure to me (just the same as when I was eighteen). Wasn't it an adventure, one of those adventures I had had without trying when I was eighteen? Had my adventures been reduced to this wretched state? Then I went into the Ramos Bar, empty at that hour except for one table where these guys who were blind drunk had joined some low-class nightclub dancers. It was some sort of celebration or private event and they proceeded with all due solemnity. Especially one of them, dressed in a checkered suit and a tie with a big knot, his hair dyed a sort of mouse color: standing and swaying slightly, holding onto the back of a chair in an attempt to maintain his dignity, he raised his glass to make a speech, to toast to one of the ladies present (Miss Giselle), who apparently was celebrating a birthday or some similar anniversary that night. "I raise my cup and toast," said the drunk, "the flower who graces this *petite fête,* the lovely Miss Giselle, because in her the springtimes have joined together through the years, because in her the springtimes have joined together, one after another, the springtimes have joined together in her," (he spoke half in verse), "until turning the fragrant years of her life into a bouquet of roses. I drink to her," he continued, "and not to us or to me, for whom the years are like a death notice, like a sword of Themistocles hanging over our hearts" (he said sword of Themistocles, isn't that wonderful?). After which all the drunken men and the ladies applauded and Miss Giselle, dressed in satin, leaned across the table to embrace him and said, "Thanks, Marquitos. Thanks, my dear, I am so moved, you are the artist who will always be the favorite of all the girls." And she gave him a kiss and everybody was very touched and Giselle sat back down, but Marquitos remained standing, holding with utmost dignity onto the back of the chair so as not to sway too noticeably, and then he started the same speech all over again. "I want to toast and raise my cup once more," he said. "I want to toast again and raise this cup because I too am deeply moved on this unforgettable night," and he wiped his eyes with the back of his hand, "deeply moved, and I toast," said Marquitos, "the ladies and the friends here present and especially," he said, stopping for a moment, "especially." "It would be especially good if you finished; finish the toast, Marquitos," one of the guys said, and Marcos turned around very slowly until he faced Miss Giselle, greeted her with a slight nod, and then very carefully sat down at the table once more, he too like a misunderstood artist who hears a tune and cannot play it, while I was finishing the beer mixed with gin prescribed by Charles Dickens and, right then, with the guys outside still digging the tunnel under the yellow light, I began thinking about the painting by Franz Hals, *If I Were the Dark Winter*. And so I go on writing to you until dawn, writing a letter that has kept me company for a whole night, a letter that has lasted until dawn, when I can go out on the street and see if Marquitos is still at the Ramos Bar toasting Miss Giselle, despite the threat of the terrible sword of Themistocles hanging over his heart. Warmest regards, Marcelo, in the hopes of hearing from you soon.

Emilio

P.S. I will of course try to see Luciano Ossorio. Soon I will write to you about that and about my trip to Concordia (when you let me know the manner and means of meeting you).

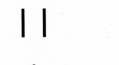

1.

"You can call me Senator," said the Senator. "Or former Senator. You can call me former Senator," said the former Senator. "I held the office from 1912 to 1916 and was elected under the Sáenz Peña Law, and at that time the office was practically for life, so in fact you ought to call me Senator," said the Senator. "But given the present situation it would perhaps be preferable and not just preferable but, moreover, in closer accord with the facts and the general course of Argentine history if you would call me former Senator," said the former Senator. "Because strictly speaking, what is a senator if not someone who makes laws and speeches? But—what happens when he does not make laws? When he does not make laws he turns automatically into a former senator. So then, if, having held that office, or rather, having fulfilled that function, someone preserves the characteristic of making speeches, even if no one hears him and no one contradicts him, then, in a sense, he continues being a senator. For which reason, I prefer that you call me Senator," said the Senator.

"Please don't think that in what I am telling you there is any trace of malice or irony, some underhanded maneuver connected with what came into fashion in the twenties, especially with Leopoldo Lugones, with the poet Leopoldo Lugones. Because exactly what does that fashion or peculiarity consist of? It consists in looking down on those who make speeches, on those who use language. It consists of making speeches to deny or reject the virtues of those who have been chosen to express in words the truths of their time. It is said then," said the Senator, "that it is only a question of empty, hollow words, and that the only worthy realm is that of deeds. I agree, to some extent, as long as we consider what sort of deeds are at issue. For example, there are millions of people who have no access to words, that is to say, who have no chance to express their ideas in public in a speech that could be heard and transcribed in print. On the other hand there exist those who act, those who exist even before they speak, because the discourse of action is spoken with the body. The discourse of action," said the Senator, "is spoken with the body. As you can see I am paralyzed. I have been sitting in this chair for almost fifty years. So that, in my case, of whom could I be considered the representative? Of whom except myself? And yet," he said, "it was not always that way. It is true," he said, "that if I make speeches it is because I am alone and I roll around this room, on this machine, speaking, because that has become for me the only possible mode of thinking. Words are my only possession. And I will say, besides," said the Senator, "that words are my only activity. So that, summing up, I should not be considered a representative, since the other functions that might help me sustain my words with my body have atrophied."

"Now then," he said later, "they would not let me see Marcelo when he was in prison. What is more, I suspect that he himself refused to see me. He sent me word that for the moment he saw no reason for anyone to consider him a martyr. I study and think and exercise, he informed me," the Senator said that Marcelo had had them tell him. "I found a Piedmontese Italian, Cosme, an anarchist from the word go, who is teaching me to cook *bagna cauda*. Also I play *tute* with the boys in the cellblock: we organized a tournament and I didn't do all that badly. I have no reason to claim mistreatment, he let me know. One feels the lack of women, to be sure, but to compensate for that there is a good deal of intellectual exchange. You could say that he jumped right into life in jail," said the Senator. "I told him," he said, "let the storm pass. This thing will last quite a while, I told him. I know them well, I told him, I know these people well: they have come to stay. Don't believe a word they say. They are cynical, they lie. They are the sons and grandsons and great-grandsons of murderers. They are proud to belong to that line of scoundrels and anyone who believes what they say, I told him," said the Senator, "anyone who believes even a single word is lost. But he—what did he do? He wanted to see things close up and they caught him right away. What better place than my house to hide?" said the Senator. "But no. He went out on the street and was put in jail. There he was ruined. He came out disenchanted. Don't you think he was disenchanted when he came out? I came to the conclusion during those days, those nights, while the country was coming apart, that it was necessary to resist." He said that he was not an optimist himself at all, that it was more a matter of conviction: that it was necessary to learn to resist. "Has he resisted?" asked the Senator. "Do you think he has resisted? I do," he said. "I have resisted. Here you see me," he said, "shrunken, almost a corpse, but resisting. Surely I am not the only one. Messages, news reach me from outside, but sometimes I wonder whether they have in fact left me completely alone. They cannot come in here. First of all because I hardly sleep and would hear them arrive. Second because I have invented a system of vigilance that I cannot describe in detail." He said he received messages, letters, telegrams. "I receive messages. Letters in code. Some are intercepted. Others arrive: they are threats, anonymous letters. Letters written by Arocena to terrify me. He, Arocena, is the only one who writes to me: to threaten me, insult me, laugh at me; his letters come through, defying my system of vigilance. It's harder for the other ones. Some are intercepted. I am aware," he said, "in spite of everything I am aware." When he was a senator, he said, he also received them. "What is a senator? Someone who receives and interprets the messages of the sovereign people." He was not sure, now, whether he received them or imagined them. "Do I imagine them, dream them? Those letters? They are not addressed to me. I am not sure, sometimes, whether I perhaps am not dictating them myself. Nevertheless," he said, "there they are, on that table, don't you see them?" That bundle of letters—did I see them?—on the table. "Don't touch them," he said. "There is someone who intercepts the messages that reach me. An expert," he said, "a man named Arocena. Francisco José Arocena. He reads letters. Just like me. He reads letters that are not addressed to him. Like me, he tries to decipher them. He tries," he said, "like me to decipher the secret message of history."

Later he told me that, from the pit of weariness in which he found himself, he never stopped calling on the Fatherland in defense of an Idea that people always told him could not be thought because, "strictly speaking," said the Senator, "it was not an Idea that could be thought on an individual basis. Now then: I am alone, I am isolated and nevertheless I *try* to think it, I try to conceive of it, and when I draw closer, I *know* what it is: it's like a line of continuity, a sort of voice that comes down from colonial times; those who pay attention to it, who listen to and decipher it, can convert this chaos into something transparent as crystal. Yet there is something else I have understood: that thing, let's call it, that line of continuity, the reason that explains the disorder in which we have found ourselves for the last hundred years, that meaning," said the Senator, "that meaning could be expressed in a *single* sentence. Not in a single word, because it's not a matter of a magical charm, but surely in a single sentence that, once expressed, would reveal to all the Truth of this country. I cannot say how many words that sentence would have. I cannot say. I don't know. But I do know," the Senator said, "that it's a matter of a single sentence. As if one were to say: 'Infinite movement, the point that exceeds everything, the moment of repose: infinity without quantity, indivisible and infinite.' Not that sentence. That sentence is just an example to help you see that many words would not be required. Do you realize how close I have gotten, how much I know about all of this? But nevertheless I cannot conceive of it, of the Idea, I cannot, nevertheless, conceive of it, even though that's what I'm here for and why I *survive*, that's why I do not fade away, why I remain. But I have just one fear," said the Senator. "Just one fear and it is this." That in the successive atrophy of his functions, year after year, at some point he might lose the ability to speak. That, he said, was his fear. "Finally grasping it," he said, "and being unable to express it."

"What am I?" the Senator asked later. "What are you seeing when you see me? You are seeing the inactive survivor of a fairly patriotic life, a disabled man paralyzed in both legs, who is *enduring*. A jockey shot me on the 25th of May of 1931 to avenge an injustice," said the Senator. "Now I survive and my sleep is so close to wakefulness that it can barely be called sleep. Am I not something like a brutal performance of death? And yet," he said. "*And yet.*" He rocked in his wheelchair, his vulturelike face lit up by the silky glow of drugs. "I have that mission, among others," he said. "That mission. Do you see? On the table. Why me? They are not necessarily addressed to me. They reach me. Do I dream them? I have never been able to distinguish dreaming from waking life. And yet, there they are." Did I see them? I should take them, he said. "Those are the ones I have received today. Leave them here now." That I should leave them. Soon I would be able to read them. "Everyone will be able to read them," he said, "at the appointed time. All readers of history will be able to read them at the appointed time," said the Senator. "Arocena," he said later. "I see him: closed in like I am, closed in

45 •

among the words, hemmed in by the walls of an office perpetually lit up by fluorescent lights: reading." And what about him? "And what about me?" He said that for him the world had become much too small a space. "I never leave this place. I reduced my properties to this room. From time to time I look out that window. What do I see? Trees. I see trees. Are those trees reality? For me Marcelo was the companion I had always searched for. For me he was the air that made me live while he was here. He spent long nights with me going over papers and speaking of the past and the future. Never of the present: of the past and the future. It was, of course, a ridiculous marriage," said the Senator. "It probably didn't last a month, as a marriage, I mean. You see," he said, "I am telling you the family secrets. And then what happened? All of a sudden he left. Suddenly, without saying a word to anybody, without saying goodbye to me. He was with another woman. And so? He would tell me: Don Luciano, your daughter makes me melancholy. That woman, he would say, referring to my daughter Esperancita, that woman is in her entirety an incomprehensible mistake. And then, suddenly, he left," said the Senator. "And I think about him," he said. "I think about him. Not once, in contrast," he said, "do I think of my daughter," although he said that she was the being who inspired in him the greatest pity he had ever felt. He had thought sometimes of why he did not think about her, and said: "Nor have I dreamt of my daughter in many years. I dream about bonfires lit on the swampy shores of a lagoon. They would build bonfires so that we could find our way in the water, when I was a kid, because when you swim at night you can get lost," said the Senator. "For me dreams," he said. "For me dreams have come to occupy the place of memories." He said that he now lived on without memories, without waiting for death. "Without memories," he said, "because now nothing is a memory for me. Nothing is now a memory for me: everything is present, everything here. And only when I dream can I remember or feel remorse."

As for the waiting, he said, he was convinced that it was a fallacy to say that one waits for death. "It's a lie that one waits for death," he said. "A lie." He said that he was convinced; that rationally speaking that was the only thing that we are incapable of waiting for. "It's a fallacy," said the Senator. "Nobody waits for it, nobody can wait for it. Not even me. Especially not me," he said. "For death flows, multiplies, overflows around me; I am a castaway, isolated on this rocky isle. How many people have I seen die?" asked the Senator. "Motionless, dry, trying to preserve my lucidity and the use of speech while death sails around me. How many have I seen die?" Perhaps he had turned into someone who should bear witness to the endless proliferation of death, to its *floods*. If that were the case, "how could anyone say that I am waiting for death," asked the Senator. "How can anyone say that when in fact I AM death; I am its witness, its memory, its fullest incarnation." A soft brightness in his glance, the Senator raised his hand: "Listen," he said, sitting motionless, his face looking up, as if looking for something in the air. "Listen," said the Senator. "Don't you see? Not a sound. Nothing. Not a sound. Everything is still, suspended: in suspense. The presence of so many dead oppresses me. Do they write to me? The dead? Am I the one who receives the messages of the dead?"

"My father," said the Senator later on. "My father, for instance, died in a duel." Two months before he was born his father had died in a duel. "So that," said the Senator, "I am what is called a posthumous son. But note that by some strange coincidence my father was also what could be called a posthumous son. *Another* posthumous son. That is to say, both of us, my father and I, each in his own way, have been unfortunate posthumous sons. In his case," he said, of his father, "not because my grandfather, Enrique Ossorio, had actually died when my father was born, but because he had been exiled and my father would never know him. And yet it was in defense of that man he never knew, that father he had never known, that my father accepted—or, strictly speaking, provoked—that duel. He provoked that duel to defend his father's honor, my grandfather's honor—a father he had never seen, and who had, in a sense, *abandoned* him, who had conceived him in a basement, on a cot, as it were in the very bosom of the earth, after having seduced his own cousin, who had given him sanctuary," said the Senator. Not that he wanted to discredit anyone with what he was saying. The Senator said: "I am not trying to discredit anyone. In truth all sons should be abandoned, left on the steps of the church, in a doorway, in a wicker basket. We should all," said the Senator, "be posthumous or foundling children because *that* is what we are *in fact*. That's what we are. Why care about the basement where we were conceived? Marcelo, for instance," the Senator said suddenly. "Marcelo, for instance, is my son. That's why my father died in a duel. To defend his father's memory, besmirched by a scribbler. Blood ties are blood ties. Above all ties. Of blood. The family is a bloody institution, an always abject amputation of the spirit. Marcelo, for example," said the Senator, "Marcelo, for example, is my son."

"So my father died in a duel, to defend his father's honor," said the Senator. In the Varela newspaper, *La Tribuna,* the memory of Enrique Ossorio had, he said, been stained when they wrote that he had always been, and was until his death, a spy in the service of Rosas, a traitor, a madman and a savage. "He dressed in black and went to a country house near the river to fight. He had never handled a pistol, was a follower of Mitre, was pale, had been conceived in a cellar. He had never seen the face of the man whose face would be the last he would see in his life." The Senator's father had left a note that read: "*It's five in the morning. I have not gone out all day. All the news I have had of the coward who is the protegé of those who serve him as seconds in this business,*" said the Senator quoting from what his father had written, "*confirm for me the certainty that he is less than nothing to me, although these gentlemen speak of him as if he were someone,* that's what my father wrote," said the Senator. "*Sweetheart,* he wrote to my mother, *if misfortune is what awaits me on the field of honor, I know that you will find an honorable way to raise the son* (that is, me) *you carry in your loins, to raise him loving God, the Fatherland, and General Mitre,*" said the Senator. "One bright morning in 1879 my father died." An icy breeze was coming from the river, the only sound the smooth rustle of the wind in the trees. "My father raised the lapels of his frock coat, but then fearing that that might be taken for a sign of fear, he took off his coat and his white shirt stood out sharply against the dark background of the carob trees." The duel had been set at ten paces. "My father did not cross himself because he did not want them to see that his hands were shaking. The two pistols were raised to the heavens and before the shots had finished ringing out my father was dead," said the Senator.

"In those days, in this country," he said, "Argentine gentlemen were Hegelians without knowing it. Freedom is only preserved at the risk of one's life; someone who is willing to face the risk of death proves himself capable of being a Master, a self-aware being. Those men killed each other, you could say, because none of them wanted to be a Slave. They killed one another, then, these men, to prove that they were Argentine gentlemen and men of honor, by which means there were ever fewer Argentine gentlemen and men of honor. Which, looked at from my present vantage point, and leaving aside all filial loyalty, looks most emphatically like a plus. Had they continued with that custom, perhaps they would all have disappeared, one after another, all those gentlemen who helped turn this country into what it is today. It was a sort of seigneurial genocide: any difference of opinion, any expression of less than total enthusiasm, was immediate cause for a duel. A custom had to be ended that forced the gentlemen to kill one another to prove that they were Argentine gentlemen, that their fathers, grandfathers and great-grandfathers had been Argentine gentlemen. Now then, notice that my father died in that duel in 1879 and that it was the first case of a crime of honor brought before a jury in a public court. The trial in which the man who killed my father in a duel was brought to judgment was an *event*. An event," said the Senator. But what was, he said, an event, what, he said, in that case, was *the* event? "Not the duel," he said, "but the event of that trial. An event like that was not, generally speaking, preserved by historians and yet, he said, those who want to know the meaning of our modern world, those who desire to know what was opening up in this country about 1880, to be precise, need to be able to decipher in that event the first sign of change, of transformation." That was more or less what the Senator said about the duel that had taken his father to the grave. "For the first time, in a trial held to judge the duelist who had killed my father, in the case of that coward in the pay of the Varelas, justice became something in and of itself, independent of a literary and moral mythology of honor that had served as norm and truth. For the first time the norm of passion and that of honor do not coincide," said the Senator, "and an ethic of true passion emerges. Because in truth those men, those gentlemen, those Masters had learned that it was when they were facing others, when they were *with* those others facing them, that they had to prove who was the Slave. They had discovered," said the Senator, "that they had another means of proving their manliness and chivalry, that they could go on living in the face of death without the need to kill one another; instead, they could *unite* among themselves to kill those who were not disposed to recognize them as their Lords and Masters. As in the cases," he said, "of immigrants, gauchos and Indians. So that," the Senator concluded, "the death of my father in a duel and the subsequent trial is an *event* that in a sense is linked, or rather, I should say," said the Senator, "that accompanies and helps explain the conditions and changes that brought to power General Julio Argentino Roca."

2.

"Sometimes," he said later, "I think that all of that coherence, all of that rigor and its implacable consequences, is, I think, sometimes," said the Senator, "all of that is present in my life, not just anywhere in my life, not for instance in my past, but *ici même,* as if on a stage before me. An empty stage where one can breathe the icy air of the high mountains. The icy, frigid air," he said, "of the high mountains that, as you can see, blows through this room where I spend my existence." And one of his diversions, he said, was "to wander around in my wheelchair, my rattletrap, my stagecoach, from one place to another, from one wall to the opposite one, in my wheelchair in this empty room. Because my body is now no more than a machine made of metal, wheels, spokes, tires, nickel-covered tubes, which transports me from one end of this empty room to the other. Sometimes here in this kingdom of silence there is no noise other than the smooth metallic hum that keeps me company on my excursions, back and forth, back and forth. The emptiness is absolute: by now I have managed to give up everything. And yet one must be prepared for the thin air, otherwise one runs the risk of *freezing* in it. The ice is close by, the solitude is immense: only someone who has managed, as I have, to turn his body into a metallic object can risk living at these altitudes. The cold, or rather," said the Senator, "*coldness* is for me propitious for thought. Prolonged experience and the desire to slip between the nickel spokes of my body have granted me the possibility of glimpsing the order that rules the polyhedral machine of history. Drawing closer, contemplating it in the distance, even if less than what one might desire, but in any case getting closer for a few moments, *drawing near,* with my metallic body, to that factory of meaning, dragging myself toward it as if swimming in the Sargasso Sea. And what do I see when I catch a glimpse of it? I glimpse," he said, "in the distance, on the opposite shore: the *construction.* Remote, solitary, its high walls looking somehow lost in the snow, I see it: *the great construction,*" said the Senator.

To come closer he had had to give up everything and yet to retain it all. "Giving up everything and reducing myself," he said, "to this hole, this cave," but at the same time being astute enough to preserve those possessions that, from the *outside,* guaranteed him the greatest amount of freedom and preserved him from possible attacks. It had thus been necessary, he said, to carry out an extremely delicate operation, "a dangerous logical operation," which consisted of holding onto his possessions and giving them up. That logical exercise was, he said, "a representation and a result" of his general state of being. Had he not given up all the functions of his body, turning into "a sort of metallic vegetable," all in order to acquire the ability to reason "up to the freezing point"? He said that all of his intelligence was due to his illness, his paralysis. In his ascetic state, bound to his sedentary flesh, he nonetheless knew that his external possessions provided the measure of his freedom and of his isolation. "Might this be the method of reaching the unimaginable Ideal? Disintegration, however," said the Senator, "is one of the persistent forms of truth."

"My luck," he had been thinking, the Senator said later, "*that thing* that could be called *my luck,* has, for me, something of the abstract quality of death. For death also flows around and beats against this awesome rock, trying to wash it away. I find there," said the Senator, "there I find the matter that memory is made of. *Another* memory: not this memory of mine, made of words and coded messages, *another* memory that reaches me accompanied always by the desolation of insomnia. I try to free myself," he said. "I try, in vain, to *get loose* of this ballast that for years has bound me to the tides of the past, to its subterranean currents. In order not to drown in the tides of the past I am forced to reflect: not to see what floats on the surface and what sinks, not to let any of it come near. I have to make an effort to separate myself, to draw away from those things I must say no to again and again. Rejecting, not letting *that* come too close is an *expenditure,* of that I am sure, a force *wasted* for negative ends. I know what I am risking, but there is no other way. It's not a matter of chance but an ironclad design. I am not mistaken. I know that simply from the constant need to defend myself I can become so weak that there is no longer any possibility of self-defense. For me, at those moments, thought is something like a floating mast; a castaway clings to it hoping to survive, crying for help, waving his arms in the immensity of the sea, praying that someone might rescue him." In such cases, in the middle of the most utter desolation, he had been able to understand, said the Senator. "I have understood, for instance, that for me death and money are made of the same corrupting matter." Not just, thinks the Senator, because money and death corrupt human beings, "that analogy would be too trivial and besides I do not buy the dubious morality that makes indifference the mark of spirituality and turns poverty into the fleshly raiment of pure souls. In any case, it is untrue that money corrupts; corruption and death have produced money and turned it into the King of men. Its arbitrary, fictitious character, the fact that it, an abstract sign, grants the possession of *any* object one might desire, that universal logic of equivalence that is incarnated in money, is what has forced reason to adapt to a spirit of abstraction that is at the very origin of thought, at the very origin of the logos," the Senator said he had thought. "As you know," he said, "for the Greeks the word *ousia,* which signifies *being, essence,* the *thing itself* in philosophical language, also signifies wealth, money. My asceticism, then," said the Senator, "my asceticism, if it is such, is not a moral act; it is different in that I give up everything in the same way that I have given up my whole body. Only those things are mine whose history I know. Something is *really* mine," said the Senator, "when I know its history, its origin. It exists," he said. "Something exists, however, an extension of my body, something outside, beyond these walls of ice, something that reproduces and proliferates as if it were death; I know its history but choose not to think about it, though others trouble themselves with it, those who I think function as undertakers, as grave diggers. Thus, so as not to think about that, I speak about something else," said the Senator, "something else whose history I *should* tell, because only those things are mine whose history I have not forgotten. And as I speak of it, I believe it dissolves, erased from my memory: for whatever we speak of is lost, goes away. Speaking is thus a means of my erasing from the branches of my memory those things that I always want to keep far away from my body."

Then the Senator told the story of that tradition, of that chain by which his memory firmly joined the golden links of death and wealth. "Death, wealth, and what the Greeks in their musical language called *ousia*," he said, "that's what all of that stuff about the links of history is about, the first rungs in the ascent to a height that frees me from the swampy rivers of memory. A first definition," he said, "exists, and it is necessary to begin there." One had to begin there, he said, if the story one wanted to tell could be understood, even if that beginning was really a result. "That beginning, that result was this: for us blood ties or more precisely filiation have always been economic ties above all else, and death is a way of making property *flow*, a way to make it reproduce and circulate." He knew, he said, that that chain of succession was what he, the Senator, had come to break. In a sense, he said, "I am the link that is *not* missing, that will never be missing." That was why, he said, his situation was that of a false syllogism, that of a paradox. "I," said the Senator, "am a paradox. And some people," he said, "will do anything to re-establish that logical coherence, that lost property that comes from the past. For example," said the Senator, "how can I fail to know that my children desire my death, so as to gain their inheritance?" He said that he was acquainted with that equation. He was acquainted, he said, with that equation, that alchemy, not because he had ever desired the death of his father, since his father, after all, had died before he, the Senator, was born, "but because when my father died," the Senator recounted, "in that duel destined to safeguard the honor of my grandfather, when he, my father, died, I, even *before* my birth, became the lone recipient of the family fortune. Thus I," said the Senator, "*know* what it is to be an heir, I know what it is to inherit. Genealogies and filiation are founded on the corpse planted in the ground," said the Senator, "and for a son what is inherited is the future, a mother tongue whose verbs one must learn to conjugate, or better still," said the Senator, "a *father* tongue whose verbs one must learn to conjugate. Upon these territorial conjugations," he said, "miles and miles of open country that lasts and *endures* long after one's ancestors, over this deathly expanse, family memory is erected. That *other* memory invades and gnaws away at me during the insomniac's white nights. For I," said the Senator, "am guilty of a death. I am guilty of a death: my own. I am a debtor, the debtor, I am the one who is in debt to death. With me, as I grow old endlessly, as I grow even *older*, for I am old and have always been old, with me, those properties are as immobile as am I myself. Thus I am someone whose broken body is made of the earth, of the enduring, perpetually calm earth. I, the rootless one, am that land," said the Senator. "Because as long as I live I am its owner. That is my domain. My children may administer it, *walk* on it, use it, but they are not the owners; they *will be* the owners but for that to happen I must die first, but I, like those fields, grow older and older, endlessly. Miles and miles of open country, miles and miles, against the motionless background of the ponds, and simultaneously this metallic object—myself—made of flesh and stainless steel, able only to move back and forth across this empty room," said the Senator. "That, then, is the paradox," he said. "The modification of a Law, violence imposed on a tradition: that is the paradox that is myself, that is what allows me to think." He said that that violence, that "twisting" is what allowed him to think. "My reasoning as a whole is the result of a break in that chain that rules filiation and makes of death the safest guardian of family succession. For I know," said the Senator, "that it has always been like that, even in my own case. Always. Even for me. For example, my father was also an heir, and his fortune, which increased into my own, was the inevitable result of another death, in this case better termed a suicide. And so? A circle. One death after another. Now then, where is the beginning of this chain that links the years together, coming to a close with me? How does it begin? Where does it begin? Shouldn't that be the matter of my story? The origin? Because if not, why bother to tell a story? What use, young man, does telling stories have, if not that of erasing from memory all that is not origin or end? Nothing between the origin and the end, nothing at all—an arid plain, a salt flat—between him and me, nothing, a most inhospitable emptiness, lying between the suicide and the survivor. That is why I can *see* him, despite the enormous distance: because nothing stands between us, each on one bank of the river, the current flowing gently between us, between him and me, gently, the current of history."

"*So*," said the Senator, "*that's why* there is no certain origin. An origin from which everything follows. And that origin is a *secret*, or better still, *the* secret that they have all tried to hide. Or at least the secret that they have hidden far from where it should be, so as to collapse all of the mystery in the name, in the life, of a man, what should have been concealed, to the extent possible, like a crime. That man, Enrique Ossorio, is a Hero. *The* hero.

The only one who forged himself, the only one who did not inherit anything from anyone, the only one to whom we are *all* in debt. Because he owes nothing to anyone: he owes it all to himself, to that fever that took him to the alkali deserts beyond the Sacramento River, up there to the dry river bed where, in the sand between the rocks, there was *Gold.* Everything starts there. It starts with the gold that my father's father had, so to speak, imagined he might find in the state of California in the year 1849. It starts with the gold that the deluded, pitiless, feverish man dreamed he found and that he did in fact find. Therein lies the origin of the story that I am reconstructing, in order to forget, in the solitary nights of insomnia," said the Senator. "Gold, the gold that he left almost intact when he died because he was in no hurry to spend it, given that he had not inherited it; that gold, of no concern to him except knowing he had it, that he was carrying it concealed on his person, around his waist, like a belt, a golden saddle-girth of metal against the skin of his waist. And all that I see," said the Senator, "in the distance, beyond the plains, all open because there is nothing, nothing but the unending increase of death, lying between him and me, nothing lies in between, we are alone, one at either end of history, that's why I can see him, for nothing lies between us, that's why I can imagine him as I slip over the translucent edge that separates my sleep from my waking. The belt, the weight of the gold that impedes him from walking and makes him move with an illusory dignity, a bit stiff, ramrod straight, feeling on his skin the *hard substance* of dreams come true. Such are the images I can see: the tin-roofed hotels on the Mexican border where proud, sallow men speak to him in bastard Spanish, some kind of rude dialect, while our hero thinks of *something else,* thinks of the silky glow of the metal he carries against his skin, in its infinite power to become whatever he may desire or want. In that alchemy, in the feverish chemistry of his fantasy, I am able to think. Everything he did I can imagine. Especially the final seclusion: that almost empty room on the East River where he shut himself in for weeks and weeks, to write, at last," said the Senator, "one word after another, letters, fragments, to say, at last, what he had suddenly understood. And sometimes, especially at night, I hear him pace around that room, from one side to the other, back and forth; I hear his voice as he speaks to himself; he forges metallic sentences, trying, all alone, isolated, lost in New York City, in a country whose language he barely understands, trying to take hold of the vertigo that was his life, a vertigo surprising and unexpected even to him: to capture in words the vertigo of his life. And I hear him pacing back and forth, back and forth, in a dreary room on the East River, while he writes," said the Senator. "Exile helps us capture an aspect of history, the leftovers, the trash, because the past's truth is what condemns us to this exile, that is what he writes," said the Senator. "The best thing about extreme situations is that they always lead us to extreme positions, he writes," said the Senator. "The main thing about situations as extreme as this one is to learn to think in crude terms. Crude, unpolished thought: such is the thought of the great. That is what he was writing," said the Senator. "I confess that I have no hope. Blind men speak of a way out; there is *no* way out possible. We should learn from the water: in time its movement wears away the hardness of the rocks. The tough are always beaten by the soft movement of the waters of history. That is what he writes, secluded in a room by the East River. I can hear him, see him: he is there, enclosed in that empty room, and nothing lies between us, we are alone, he and I, nothing lies in between; I can hear him, I am Ossorio, I am the foreigner, the exile, I am Rosas, I was Rosas, I am Rosas's clown, I am all the names in history, I am the sea bird that flies over dry land. Below, far from the clear air I push aside with my wings as I fly, there below, on the frozen plains, to the left, at the very edge of the foothills, far from the world, from its noise, from its dismal clarity, there are great masses, masses that seem petrified but that *nevertheless* are slipping forward, moving, overcoming all resistance, advancing, creaking as they slip forward, like great icebergs. To take stock of the slowness, the pace of that march, depends on the altitude that the sea bird has reached in its flight; the higher the sea bird, the albatross, flies, the more it risks while flying over dry land, the better it can see the unceasing movement, the advance of those masses. Their pace cannot be guessed by an isolated man, by one individual. Why should we demand that they move faster if their time is not our own? Why hurry in the face of the unyielding firmness of that advance? Does not the hero also seek to *approach,* despite everything? Crippled, he slides, dragging himself forward; the metallic sound of his body as he approaches is the only music that can be heard on the alkali deserts of the present. On the other side, on the other front, what our enemies always thought identical to themselves is revealed in its diversity. What they thought unified, solid, begins to splinter, to dissolve, eroded by the water of history. Their defeat is as inevitable as is our task of bearing the burden that weighs in our memory, thanks to their maniacal presence, their cynicism, their deliberate perversity. Or has the ceaseless increase of death from the past to now stopped even once for a moment?" asked the Senator. "They, our enemies, what belief will enable them to resist? What belief will aid them to resist? They cannot resist. They waver, confined to the dryness of the future. And we, we have learned to survive; we know the crystalline substance, unending, almost liquid, that forms our capacity to resist. Patience is an art that takes centuries to learn. And we only value a virtue when we note its total absence in our enemies." That is what the Senator said.

3.
"You, young man," he said later, "you will go see Marcelo. You should tell him this: That he should take care of himself. That I only barely receive his letters. There are interferences, grave

risks. Tell him to take care and protect himself. Arocena, that good-for-nothing, interrupts our communication, intercepts the messages. He tries to decipher them. Or is it my children who guard the door and do not allow some words to reach this place? Do they, my children, filter the messages that I receive, even those of which I am not the intended recipient? Tell him to take care: that's what you should tell Marcelo, young man, when you go see him. That I, Ossorio, the Senator, am thinking about him. And Marcelo will be able to guess, despite all the dead bodies that float on the waters of history, he, Marcelo, will be able to guess," said the Senator, "what matter *that* thought is made of." That thought was made, he said, of leftovers, of fragments, of splinters, also of the memory of old conversations. "Fragments of those coded letters I receive or dream about or imagine that I receive, letters I perhaps dictate myself when I cannot write. Because I must tell you that I cannot write any-more. My hands—can't you see?—are claws; I am the albatross, flying peacefully over the edges of the *cimetière marin;* at that height my hands have become the claws of a bird that can only come to rest on the sea, on the rock that sticks up in the middle of the ocean. I can no longer write; these hands cannot write anymore; I have lost," he said, "the priestly elegance of my handwriting. Only my voice persists, each day closer to the croaking of a bird; only my voice persists and with it I dictate my reply to the messages I receive. But—to whom? Alone, isolated, balancing my wings on that rock—to whom can I dictate my words?" Then the Senator asked me whether he might dictate to me a reply that he wished to write. Would I be his secretary? "Wouldn't you like, young man, to be my secretary, to turn my croaking into written words?" There was something, he said, that I should know. "My secretary must *enclose* himself with me. Never go out. Live on these snowy heights." How could he then ask, said the Senator, that I be his secretary? He said that in any case he would dictate at least one letter to me. "I, the Senator, am going to dictate a letter to you," said the Senator, and he began to roll his wheelchair around the room. "Mr. Juan Cruz Baigorria," the Senator dictated. "Beloved compatriot and friend. I know of your situation and you may rest assured of my solidarity. I have received a letter of yours that was not addressed to me and that is how I know of your misfortune," the Senator dictated as he wandered in his wheelchair around the room. "The loss of a son is the greatest sorrow a man can suffer. But has your son died or been lost? I cannot believe: the nation, the Nation with a capital letter," the Senator dictated from the other end of the room, "the Nation does not forget its finest sons. Watch out for Arocena. He does not allow your words to reach their intended recipient. I will try to have one of my secretaries or my manservant Juan Nepomuceno Quiroga bring you a small sum of money, something that will not in any way lessen your grief, of that I am sure," the Senator dictated. "This present should not be seen as an affront to your great dignity or to your decency, but as a means of helping you resist. I, the Senator, know what my countrymen in this land are going through. Resist, my friend Don Juan Cruz Baigorria, my countryman, and in your misfortune please feel my solidarity, sincerely, Senator Luciano Ossorio," the Senator dictated. Then he said: "Bring me that paper and pen and I will sign my name to it."

4.

The Senator said later that that was all he could do. "That," said the Senator, "is all I can do. Isolated, alone, never sleeping, that is all I can do. Sitting here, dictating words of consolation, wandering back and forth, thinking about the letters, the replies, all of that grief." He rolled back and forth in his wheelchair across the empty room. "I go back and forth, thinking of the words I could dictate, wandering, pushing my sedentary body, imagining what I must write, pushing, back and forth, sliding, from one side to the other, my crippled body, around this empty room. And so I will go on, moving from one side to the other, sometimes in circles, sometimes in a straight line, from one wall to the other, always working with words, trying to make the fog lift that keeps us from seeing the construction clearly, the construction that is being built, on the opposite shore, on the rocks of the future. And perhaps words will allow me to catch, as in a net, the paradoxical quality of that Idea, of that concept that comes from the very depths of history, from that voice," he said, "that plural voice that comes from the past and that is so difficult for a man who is alone to capture. And nevertheless," said the Senator, "no deception will prevent me from making every effort to draw my body's wheels closer and closer. No deception can hold it off. No threat. Not even tolerance or pity. Because I," said the Senator, "know my luck. Sedentary, decayed, artificial, my metallic flesh rusts, confined by walls, consumed by the whiteness of electric lamps, yet I will never despair of being able to think beyond the limits of my self and my origins."

"Sometimes," he said later, "I think I understand it all. To understand the years and years that a body, for instance, waits before beginning to fall apart. Sometimes I even think I understand my own fate. For a moment. The understanding lasts but a moment and in that moment no doubt what has happened is that I have fallen asleep when I thought I was thinking or understanding. But we need so little to sustain the illusions we are made of; I emerge from those moments, from those dreams, renewed, with a renewed belief. That's why, now, I must try to define the illusion I seek, to be able to grasp it in words. To explain the distant glow I seem to see all of a sudden: the memory of some huts tucked beneath the willows by Laguna Negra when I was a boy, there where the bonfires blazed, as I like to imagine, as if in memory, the nights I cannot sleep. To explain," he said, "the meaning those papers, written by a man in a room by the East River, had for me. Or to explain what emerges from the very depths of this nation's history, at once unique and multiple. But how could I explain that? How would I—how could I—do that? That's why I must stop talking now. I, the Senator, should, for a moment, stop talking. What I cannot explain without words I prefer to keep silent," said the Senator, "as I am unable to explain without words."

III

.

1.

New York. July 4, 1850.

My fellow countrymen:

I am Enrique Ossorio, who struggled tirelessly for Freedom and who now resides in New York City, in a house by the East River. I deserve being called all of the names in history. They all fit in this drawer where I keep my writings. I came here having decided to finish this work of mine. I go out walking in the city at dawn and sometimes I spend the afternoon at Miss Rebba's bordello in Harlem, where there is a young whore born in Martinique who knows how to speak Spanish. I speak with her of our miserable future and she nods her sweet kittenish head. Naked in bed, as the night cools off the air in the room, we can give each other full attention. Kitten was born a slave and has dedicated herself to the oldest profession for ten years (she is now seventeen) in exchange for her freedom. Isn't that the same as what I have done with these last few years of my life? Debasing myself as no one else has been debased in the history of the fatherland, all in the search for freedom. But what have I achieved? I, the traitor, have I won my freedom? You who see the liberation of the Republic at hand, you who see the fall of Rosas within reach, have illusions of a freedom that will however never come. You are now all united with Justo José, seeking strength in the very heart of the country, so as to achieve what we have all dreamed of. But will it work out that way? I foresee: dissension, differences of opinion, new struggles. Interminably. Murders, massacres, fratricidal wars. I am alone in New York City and I ask myself: what has changed? Justo José—wasn't he once the Tiger's closest ally? My life has consisted of one mistake after another: not my life's objectives, which have always been the progress and happiness of my country, but something different and much worse. We can no longer go back. The Entre Ríos cavalry, gauchos who once followed Pancho Ramírez—are they going to give us freedom? I think all of our lives have been nothing more than a single senseless mistake. We can no longer go back. What we have done is done.

I have thought of writing a utopia: there I will narrate what I imagine the country's future to be. I am in the best possible position to do so: removed from everything, outside of time, a foreigner, caught up in the webs of exile. What will the country be like in a hundred years? Who will remember us? Those of us now—who will remember us? I am writing about those dreams.

Thus, I will write of the future, not wanting to remember the past. One thinks about what will happen when one says to oneself: How can it be that I wasn't able to see *then* what seems so obvious now. And what can I do to see in the present the signs that announce the course of the future? I have begun reflecting on all of that and also upon my life and that is why I am writing to you.

Very soon I will send you my Autobiography. Every man should write his life story when he approaches the age of forty.

Where does this horror of solitude come from? I am familiar with the invincible vice of prostitution. My friend, the young whore, is named Lisette Gazel. She knows how to read the future in the flight of seabirds: she is as superstitious as a cat. Her skin is like black silk. I pay her to hear her speak in Spanish of Martinique. Perverse words, a confusing creole.

My dear Don Luciano:
I always think of you and if I have not written these last few months it's because I have had some mishaps (nice word that, so metaphorical). It appears to me that I will soon have to begin moving. The truth is I have been comfortable here in Concordia, a town I chose (among other things) because of its peaceful name. I got along well here, felt well established (as they say), but I know that I am not a man who can live for long in one place, and the times we are living in don't help us form sedentary habits either. Lucky for you, Senator, and I really mean it, you who suffer alone and can survive anything, and are closed in alone where you can see what you choose to remember. The closer one is involved in events, the more complicated and distant they seem. And yet, in this country everything is as clear as spring water.

I have continued working on the Enrique Ossorio volume: I'm quite fascinated with the New York period, when he was alone and isolated, he too, trying to discover where and how he had gone wrong. There is a letter he writes to Alberdi in August 1850 that has made a deep impression on me. I don't know if you remember it: "To mistrust: that much I know," he writes. "And I know well that the best among you, namely you, Juan Bautista, more than anyone, you who are a man of principles, can expect nothing but despair and exile all over again. I see only too clearly the tragic destiny that awaits us, especially you, Juan Bautista, especially you, because I know you well enough to know that you will never compromise. You are the kind of man who does not compromise and that kind of man, in the coming days, will have two roads: exile or death. The others, and among them some who today call themselves your friends, will of course be successful. This country is ready for that. How can they fail to be successful if they have an open horizon, all the pampa to themselves? Those who run quickest will win, not the best, not the most honest, not those who think most clearly or most love their country. As for you: no glory will be denied you, Juan Bautista, nor will any misfortune." That's what he wrote in his strange lucidity. Nobody listened to him, and he was alone: perhaps because of that he had learned to think as one should think, the way those with nothing to lose think.

Anyway, what I wanted to tell you is that given the new circumstances in which this country finds itself, I am feeling rather uncertain about my immediate future. Various complications are in store for me and I anticipate a number of changes of address. I was thinking that for the moment the best thing would be to pass on the Archive (with the documents and notes and the chapters that I have already written) to someone in whom I have complete confidence. That person could even, if necessary, carry on with the work, finish writing it, give it the last touches, publish it and so forth. It's a question for me (above all) of guaranteeing that these documents are preserved, not only because they will be useful (to anyone who knows how to read them properly), casting a light on the past of our unfortunate republic, but also in order to understand some things that are happening in our time and not very far from here.

I have wanted to write to you to keep you informed about all of these matters, Senator. I have tried to put everything as bluntly as possible, because we know each other well and because I know that you will not worry about me in the future any more than you have worried up to now. These bad times will pass; in the long run they always pass.

That's all for the moment; these lines will also serve to let you know that I am thinking of you. We will see each other soon, because we both desire it so much. Take care, Don Luciano, with my love.

Yours:

Marcelo Maggi

P.S. In a few days a nephew of mine will go to see you. I will no doubt meet up with him soon and he will bring me news of you. Fondly.

July 6, 1850. I continue. My Autobiography.

Ancestors 1. One of my grandfathers got rich in the humanitarian business of buying sick slaves and helping them recover enough so that they could be sold again (at a better price) as healthy slaves. This business, which combined profit with philanthropy, allowed him to get rich at the expense of the health of others. I have seen engravings of emaciated slaves, all skin and bones and covered with pustules, and other engravings in which the same slaves are depicted as strong, emaciated and covered with pustules, next to my grandfather who points to them with a whip handle, glowing with satisfaction. When he was seventy years old this grandfather of mine abandoned the family and shacked up with a fourteen-year-old Jamaican black woman nicknamed The Empress. In my youth, they say my grandfather used to say, a man of seventy was not an old man: it was the French Revolution that brought old age into the world.

Ancestors 2. My father was a disillusioned man. He was a soldier because that is what the times demanded. He fought against the British during the Invasions and later marched with Belgrano in the expedition to the north. He came back sick and badly wounded, never having known victory; the persistent fevers made it impossible for him to take part in the Campaign of Liberation and in the civil wars, and he always felt indebted to the province of Santa Fe. He sued the government until his services were finally recognized and he was granted a pension, something he in any case did not need. At home, the servants called him My General, but he never attained that rank. At night his pain or remorse kept him from sleeping and he paced up and down the hallways waiting for the light of dawn. In his insomnia he amused himself writing a work that he called "Maxims on the Art of War." I remember a few of them and reproduce them here:

1. I, war, think. We have put up a sign—"Thinking takes place here"—above the devastation that war brings the nation.

2. There is no baptism like a baptism of fire.

3. War cannot be humanized; its violence reveals in man a quality that is older than any civilized feelings.

I heard him say that the people of Entre Ríos (when mounted on horseback) are the best soldiers in the world and that General Manuel Belgrano never sweat and that the worst thing about battle was the way the gunpowder stank like shit.

Ancestors 3. My mother was of the proud and restless race of the bohemians of this world, though she never knew it. From her I have inherited *mal du siècle* and an affected way of lengthening the vowels when speaking. My mother did not love my father and told him so. She was cruel but also innocent: she believed in the merciful power of truth over the humiliations inflicted by lying. That soldier who was the living image of defeat knew nothing of the manners that were expected by a woman desiring romantic passion. For several months she was courted and pursued by Count Walewski, the French consul in Buenos Aires, a natural son of Napoleon Bonaparte (by the Polish woman Maria Walewska). Everything took place in plain sight of my father, who felt such disdain for bastards and for Europeans that he didn't even bother to feel jealous. The count, a perverse and refined man, would invite my mother to the theater and send her notes written in his treacherous hand in a Gothic script that accentuated and rendered more rarefied his erotic demands. He wrote them in French, a language my father did not know how to read. One night I caught my mother by surprise as she alighted from a horse carriage in the alley across from the Piedad Church: she wrapped her black mantilla around her and that gesture was meant to signify that I had not recognized her. I think that she had managed, at last, by force of despair (but also, perhaps, with shame) to shroud herself in a secret life worthy of her illusions and hopes. She read Alfred de Musset and George Sand and dreamed of living in Paris and frequenting the salon of Madame de Staël, not knowing that that worthy lady had already died some years before, the victim of the scorn heaped on her by the father of the bastard to whom my mother now surrendered her body.

Ancestors 4. As for me, I was born Enrique *de* Ossorio, but I have given up that preposition because it offends the spirit of the times with its resonances: the virtues of illustrious lineage do not stand up to the times, or to my ambitions, and I prefer to give myself full credit.

As for me, Enrique Ossorio, I have been a traitor and a spy and a disloyal friend and I will be so judged by history, even as I am now judged by my contemporaries.

You have let some of the news I have sent you slip through. Suspicions mount in this house. How can we know whether they have not already guessed something and if they intend to discover who is the traitor (as they put it)? This is not fear, I want you to know. But you should await a better opportunity so as not to compromise my position. I am alone here; I am staying in the same hideout in Tigre.

I reread my private papers. More than ten years have gone by since then and yet I feel once again that I have put myself in the position of traitor. Or is that not the case? It is the case, you may be sure of that. Might this not be my natural position? Why? you will ask. A traitor? Again? Now I am traitor to my past in much the way that before I was traitor to my future. You may prefer to be ever faithful to your mistakes, to act as if what is happening now is what was foreseen and premeditated at that time. But I know it was not that way: I was where one had to be to know that.

Someone named J. R. Rey (or Reyf) has written a letter to a resident here that reveals what only an informer and a spy could reveal. They asked me to make a copy of that letter and that's how I got a chance to see it. How evil is this Rey person? But what Rey or King is not that way? I would like to have utmost confidence in your prudence, making sure that these messages are favorable to our cause so as to avoid problems that could make anyone sorry in the future.

So long. I will write my letters in the code you request, and can promise that in my conduct as in everything else I will maintain the complete reserve that you have asked of me (without needing to).

2.

One of the letters was in code. Or all of them. Arocena re-arranged those he had opened on his desk. He examined the envelopes and quickly established a first system of classification. Caracas. New York. Bogotá. A letter from Ohio, another from London; from Buenos Aires, from Concordia, from Buenos Aires. He numbered the letters: there were eight of them. He left aside the letter from Marcelo Maggi to Ossorio that he had just read. He took a slip of paper, jotting down some of the following names: Juan Cruz Baigorria, Angélica Echevarne, Emilio Renzi, Enrique Ossorio. The light of the fluorescent bulbs was not sufficient. He turned on the lamp, trying to make it light up the center of the desk. At an equal distance from the edges, he thought, barely moving the shade. He took a typed envelope. The return address read: Orinoco Publishers, 687

Simón Bolívar Avenue, Caracas (4563), Venezuela. He picked up the sheet of paper and examined it against the light. Then he set it down on the desk again and began reading.

Little news here, much heat; to think that Miguel Cané wrote *Juvenilia* in this place. All the better reason to leave, as Alfredo says. But where? Mexico City is the same story. I spend all day shut in translating (right now a quite interesting book by Thomas Bernhard). I only go out to go to the movies; I have a Venezuelan girlfriend, I don't remember if I told you (I am teaching her to sip *mate*). The dead and some friends (you among them) appear in my dreams. That's how things are these days: to meet up with the people you care about you have to go to sleep.

One who showed up here was Raúl. He wants the Argentines "on the outside" (as he says) to all contribute some money so we can buy an island in the Pacific (hopefully Juan Fernández). We will plant wheat, raise cows, never forgetting to protect the handicrafts of the interior. We will become independent of the Spanish crown, but without becoming Frenchified. We will nationalize customs duties and will reject the emphyteusis that is Rivadavia, cutting off large landholding at the roots. Mariano Moreno will remain in the country, leading the Supreme Junta, without traveling to Europe, so as not to die at sea, etc. It will be, according to him, the first nationalist utopia.

One yearns for the land of one's birth; the news that reaches us here is confused and quite depressing. Nobody understands what you are still doing there. Who do you see? Can you publish? You are like the last of the Mohicans. You ought to know that at times one's faithfulness to one's tribe is not necessarily expressed in geographic terms. The Chilean lyric poets and philosophers, I have heard tell (according to that Brecht you admire so much) used to go into exile the way ours go into the Academy. A worthy custom. Many fled several times and it seems to have been a question of honor to write in such a way that one had to shake off the dust of the native soil at least once.

All of the friends here think of you. Greetings to Magdalena and the kids. I look forward to news of you. I miss you.

Roque

P.S. Sometimes (no joke) I think that we are the generation of 1837. Lost in the diaspora. Who among us will write the *Facundo?*

July 14, 1850

Now then, today I have been thinking: What is utopia? The perfect place? It's nothing like that. Above all, for me, exile is utopia. *There is no such place.* Banishment, exodus, a space suspended in time, between two times. We have memories that remain of the country; we imagine what the country to which we will return must be like (how it will be). That dead time, between the past and the future, is utopia for me. Thus: exile is utopia.

Besides the emptiness that exile brings, I have had another personal experience of utopia that helps me imagine the romance I would like to write. The gold of California—that feverish march of the adventurers who eagerly advanced westward—what was that but a search for the ultimate utopia—gold? Utopian metal, treasure to be found, a fortune waiting to be picked up in river beds: alchemical utopia. The soft sand runs between the fingers. *We shall be rich at once now, with California gold, Sir,* sang the men on the brave Wells Fargo coaches. So I know what the fuss is all about. Every night before going to sleep I feel the weight of that golden illusion against the skin of my waist. A personal secret, hidden like a crime. Not even Lisette knows about this. What do you carry there? she has asked me. A bronze sash, I have replied; a doctor recommended that I wear it to correct a curvature of the spine. And I don't lie: didn't I walk bent over double like a slave for years? Nobody can be surprised now if in order to combat the effects of the uncomfortable posture prescribed for me by history I should have to use a sort of corset made of solid gold. Only gold cures the memory of subjection and betrayal.

Besides, on those caravans to utopia that crossed the alkali deserts of New Mexico I have seen horrors and crimes that I would never have been able to imagine in my wildest nightmares. A man cut off his friend's hand with the edge of a shovel so as to be able to reach a river bed first, a river bed where, it should be said in passing, no gold was found. What lessons have I learned from that other experience I underwent in the hallucinatory world of utopia? That in its quest all crimes are possible. And that the only ones to reach the happy, gentle realm of pure utopia are those (like me) who are willing to drag themselves down into the most utter depravity. Only in the minds of traitors and evildoers, of men like myself, can the beautiful dreams we call utopias flourish.

Thus the third experience that serves as material for my imagination is betrayal. The traitor occupies the classic position of the utopian hero: a man from nowhere, the traitor lives *in between* two sets of loyalties; he lives in duplicity, in disguise. He must pretend, remain in the wasteland of perfidy, sustained by impossible dreams of a future where his evil deeds will at last be rewarded. But—how can the traitor's evil deeds be rewarded in the future?

Greetings—
I don't know whether I told you before that material interest has never been the motive of my actions. You prick me deep and surprise me when you offer me money. Money, to me? For the sake of the allegiance we both profess to the same cause I will conceal my sorrow and indignation. I am faithful to the dignity that never abandons me even in the difficult moments I must endure. Satan conjures up

perverse situations for a man of honor to withstand. Be that as it may, do not repeat, sir, those unworthy offers that offend not only me but also yourself. You should know that I have nothing personal at stake, nor do I hope to get anything out of this, quite the contrary.

I reread my papers from the past to write my romance of the future. Nothing between the past and the future: this present (this emptiness, this uncharted territory) is also utopia.

July 15, 1850

The utopia of the present-day dreamer departs from the classic laws of the genre in one essential respect: one must refuse to reconstruct a nonexistent space. Thus—*a key distinction*—one must not situate the utopia in an imaginary or unknown place (most commonly on an island). One must instead make an appointment with one's own country, on a date (*1979*) that is itself fabulously distant. There is no such place: in time. There is *still* no such place. As I see it, this is the equivalent of the utopian perspective. To imagine Argentina as it will be in a hundred and thirty years: the routine exercise of nostalgia, a *roman philosophique*.

Title: *1979*
Epigraph: *Every period dreams of the one before.* Jules Michelet

I have spoken of the theme of my story with Lisette. She asks me: Will you include a woman like me who knows you to read the future in the night flight of birds? Perhaps I will include a seer in my story, I tell her, a woman who knows, as you do, how to look where no one can see.

Dear Sir:

I am sure that we met at Maestro Pizurno School in the 900 block of Segurola Street. I studied there from first to sixth grade.

My name is Echevarne Angélica Inés, they call me Anahí. I was the girl who in fifth and sixth grade sat at the end of the row, Mr. Mayor, and when I saw your picture in the paper, I thought right away of getting in touch with you. Do you remember? At the end of the row, almost at the back of the room, in the second term of sixth grade. Once, Your Excellency, you sent me a lovesick note that unfortunately for reasons of health I have not saved. I wanted to take the opportunity offered by memory, evoked by seeing your picture in the newspaper *Crónica*, to communicate the following to you. Your Excellency and Other Authorities and Officials: several visions have recently taken up residence at the address indicated, from north to south and from south-southeast to west. For instance: the twins. One of them is named Farnos and the other is The Japanese Man (the Japanese Man from Tokyo). Despite your many activities I am sure that you will be able to recognize them right away thanks to the fact that both of them use black patent-leather boots. Be careful to pay attention to the location indicated: south-southeast to the west (that is to say, in the direction of Munro). What is occurring is the following, Mr. Mayor: they made an incision and hid a transmitter among the branching veins and arteries around my heart. While I was asleep they installed a tiny device, as tiny as this, in order to be able to transmit. It is a glass capsule, like a charm from a charm bracelet, made of crystal, and the images are reflected there. I see everything through the device they installed in me, like a TV screen. I see that vacant lot and cannot imagine what I have seen: so much suffering. At first I could only see the dear departed. Lying on an iron bedstead, covered with newspapers. There are others there, at the end of a hallway; the floor is of tamped earth. I close my eyes in order not to see his wounds. And then I sing so as not to see him suffer. I do not want to see him suffer so I sing, because I am the official singer. If I speak of the images that pass through the crystal charm nobody believes me. Why me? Why does it have to be me who sees everything? For instance, there is that boy who is looking for me, who wants to see me. And there is the Pole. Poland. I saw the photographs: they killed the Jews with baling wire. The crematoria are in Bethlehem, Palestine. In the north, way up north, in Bethlehem, in the province of Catamarca. The birds fly over the ashes. Or isn't that what Evita Perón said? She saw everything the way I do and they took out her innards and filled her with rags, like a doll. Metastasis, like a blue spider web, on his skin. Lying on an iron bedstead: why must I be the one to see him suffer? I have been designated the witness to all that pain. I cannot bear it any longer, Your Excellency. I close my eyes so as not to see the wounds. And then I sing so as not to see all the suffering. I am the official Singer and when I sing I don't see the wretchedness of the world. I am going to sing an Anthem. *High in the sky, a bold warlike eagle rises up in triumphal flight.* That's how I, Anahí, the Queen of the River Region, sing; I sing, must sing, otherwise I will go mad. That's why I must sing, why I must sing once more. I must be the official Singer. Could I be named official Singer? Sir, with all due respect, I would like to request that appointment. Can I ask you for that favor? Singer, Vocalist, Diva: call me whatever you wish, Your Honor. I recall most fondly the little note you sent me by means of Chola, your neighbor in the row, at Maestro Pizurno School, second term of sixth grade. I wish you, Mr. Mayor, my most sincere greetings, with all best regards and highest respect, in memory of those distant days we shared on the 900 block of Segurola Street, the second term of sixth grade (at the end of the row), when you, Mr. Mayor, sent to me a little letter with the sweetest words, words I have never forgotten, despite all the horrors that this life as a seer has brought me. The sixth grade teacher was named Miss Olga and she was quite short but had light blue eyes. When she entered the room she would always say to us in the morning: "Good morning, children." And we would answer her in unison (even you, Excellency, when you were a boy): "Good morning, ma'am." Of course before that, while the flag was being raised, we all sang *Dawn* and luckily, despite everything that has happened over the years, I have never forgotten that patriotic song, so when I can't stand it anymore I sing once again—*A wing the blue of the color of the sky, a wing the blue of the color of the sea*—that's what I, Anahí, sing. With all due respect, and greetings to the Governor, yours truly: Echevarne Angélica Inés.

One of those was always reaching him. Addressed to the Mayor, the Prefect, the Vice-Consul or the Minister of whatever Ministry and of Authority in General. Sometimes they would photocopy them and take them home to enjoy them some more. Some day, thought Arocena, I am going to receive a letter that is addressed to me. Or I will write it myself. He put this one aside, apart from the others. Then he picked up the next one. It was written by hand, in pencil, in clumsy handwriting, on a sheet torn from a notebook. Shit, thought Arocena as soon as he started reading, and where does this Juan Cruz Baigorria come from?

July 17, 1850
Another difference between the novel I want to write and the utopias I am acquainted with (More, Campanella, Bacon): in my case it's not a matter of trying to narrate (or describe) that other period, that other place, but of constructing a story in which the future only presents itself to possible witnesses in its most trivial and ordinary form, just as a historian is presented with documents of the past. The Hero will be face to face with written texts in that future time.

A historian who works with documents of the future (that is the project). The model: the trunk where I keep my papers. What would someone reading them in a hundred years infer from them, without access to anything else, without any other knowledge of the life being reconstructed?

July 23, 1850

Old aches and pains return. Aches in the bones of the skull. An icy object, like a piece of metal, driven *in between* the bones of the skull: the pain spreads and penetrates into the cracks and masses of the brain. I increase the dose of Lichenin without feeling any relief. The tea is only effective in the morning. *Sitting* the least amount of time possible. So I have started pacing around my room. I must continue, in spite of everything, thinking about a story that lives up to my hopes.

The "real" time of the novel will go from March 1837 to June 1838 (the French blockade, the Terror). During this period, by means of a device still to be resolved, the Hero finds (comes into possession of) documents written in the Argentina of 1979. He reconstructs (imagines) what that future time will be like as he reads.

A discovery. I was pacing around the room, from one side to the other, trying to forget the pain, when I suddenly understood what *form* my utopian story should take. The Hero receives letters from the future (not addressed to him).

An epistolary novel, then. Why this anachronistic genre? Because by now utopia is itself a literary form that belongs to the past. For us, men of the nineteenth century, it's an archaic form, just as the epistolary novel is archaic. None of the contemporary novelists (not Balzac, for instance, or Stendhal, or Dickens) would think of writing a utopian novel. For my part I try not to read current writers. I look for inspiration in books that are out of fashion (L. Mercier's *The Year 2440*, Montesquieu's *Persian Letters*, Voltaire's *Candide or Optimism*, Diderot's *Rameau's*

Nephew, Sade's *Aline and Valcour or the Philosophical Novel*, Laclos's *Dangerous Liaisons*).

Several hours each day spent lying in bed. A damp cloth over my eyes. This crisis must pass.

July 24, 1850
How have I discovered that my utopian novel must be epistolary in form? First: correspondence is already in itself a form of utopia. To write a letter is to send a message to the future; to speak of the present with an addressee who is not there, knowing nothing about how that person is (in what spirits, with whom) *while* we write and, above all, *later:* while reading over what we have written. Correspondence is the utopian form of conversation because it annihilates the present and turns the future into the only possible place for dialogue.

But there is also a second reason. What is exile but a situation that forces us to substitute words for the relation among close friends, now far away, absent, scattered in different places and cities? And besides, what relation can we maintain with the country we have lost, the country that we have been forced to leave? What other presence can that absent place have besides the testimony that letters (sporadic, elusive, trivial letters) bring us, full of family news?

Thus I have done well in choosing the form of that novel written in exile and *by it.*

My dearest son:
We, your mother and I, are well, same as always. I hope this letter finds you in good health. Your mother is more and more nervous. At night she barely closes her eyes. She is afraid that something might happen to you. Are you still in Winnesburg, Ohio? Here everybody is working harder than ever and earning less and less. Since the General died nobody remembers the

poor. But just in case I better not write about that. I planted potatoes and also a bit of squash and beets, I'll see about planting some eggplant and tomatoes, which is what grows best, though if a frost comes, that's all, folks. I always remember my late father, he always said that, that's all, folks, as if to say I'm through, and another saying of his that I remember is when we were in Mendoza in 1921: The stars in the sky, the thorns in the field and in my heart Carlos Washington Lencinas, that's a politician who was later shot to death by someone from Corrientes. Here, much concern; I hope you are well in Winnesburg, Ohio. It doesn't appear on the map: we were at Mr. Crespo's house, we saw the United States of North America, we saw the province of Ohio, but we couldn't find that place. Your mother doesn't sleep much from worry. The oldest of the Weber kids asks after you whenever he sees me: he is the only one who dares do so and who comes up to me in the street: his sister finally got married to Ortigosa the cripple. It's no use trying to work the fields: the harvest isn't even enough to pay the lease. I am going to write to my buddy Anselmo Arnaldo Maidana: he is the official baker in Espeleta, in the province of Buenos Aires. Who knows, maybe I'll get a new start, a new life: I'll move to the capital. I would have gone in '46, those were happy times indeed, I think everything would have gone better, you wouldn't have gone through what you did. In this shithole who can hide? They haunted all of you as if you were rabid dogs: nothing remains of the Leagues. The poor have been getting fucked over since the time of Mitre, as my late father would say. Even so, the last thing one should lose is Hope, make them respect you and don't bow your head, my son. The world turns, turns some more, and eventually things come out right. I feel like a kid, 63 and as healthy as I've ever been, never tired, always looking things straight in the face, but honestly who will give me work at my age? Not long ago a circus came near here in Pila. Clowns, lions, and a guy walking on a tightrope so high up that it made you dizzy just watching him, up there in the air, looking like a little bird, his arms out to keep his balance. The best part, to my mind, was a guy from the countryside who recited *The Gaucho Martín Fierro*, with lots of feeling and all dressed in black. "To heat properly the fire has to come from below," he said, and I remembered General Perón. Are there cattle in Winnesburg, Ohio? I must say you went far away, it looks like the veritable asshole of the world. You did the right thing, even so, there was reason enough. No one should let himself get squashed. I think: how in the process you are seeing the world. That's what I wanted to do in 1946 and '47, when I wanted to go to the capital, but I stayed here and sometimes I look over toward Bolívar and think that the land would not let me go. What for? That's what I say even though the only land a man can have is what he gets when they bury him. Your mother always misses you and sometimes I find her crying in the kitchen but I pretend not to notice and she wipes her eyes with her hand, as if the smoke from the fire got the better of her. As ever, all best wishes, your father,

Juan Cruz Baigorria

Naïve writing, Arocena thought. Winnesburg, Ohio: repeated three times. He understood that there was a certain pattern in the misspelled words. He jotted them down separately on a slip of paper. After that he counted the letters: he connected that number with the total number of words in the letter: he analyzed that number: he classified the vowels in the alphabet according to that number. He was working from the hypothesis that the code must be included in the letter itself. Anything could be a sign, allowing him to find the clue to discover the secret message.

July 25, 1850
That *icy* pain has returned. Little icebergs are floating in the blood in my brain.

My enemies are willing to do anything. They would forge documents, verify them using false witnesses and apocryphal letters; they would deform what I have written and what others have written about what I have written: they would pay people in the underworld to burn the places where I hide and where I conceal my archives, all of this would not be hard for them to do, even if I pay someone I trust a modest sum to guard me all night long.

Safe haven: this room on the East River, where I hide away with Kitten in the afternoon. And if she were a spy? Isn't it odd that a black whore from Martinique should speak Spanish so well and pay so much attention to everything I say? I know how informers work, the way they have to pretend. I know from experience. Have I confided too much in her? Today Lisette—to whom I spoke of my suspicions—said: What do you know? Lying in bed, one knee up, a hand curled sweetly on the blue foliage between her legs, she said: What do you believe? No woman will ever be as loyal to you as Lisette. But didn't I tell you that in a dream I saw that something evil was going to happen between the two of us? I have told you (she said) yet here I am with you, afraid but with you anyway, even though I haven't been able to find out what the evil thing is that is going to happen to us or when it will happen. What do you think? Lisette asked me in her gentle damp voice, as if frightened by the forebodings she sees in her dreams, forebodings she always believes. What do you think, my child? Kitten said while beginning—slowly, lazily—to massage the tight skin of her regal breasts. That I don't know the bad thing that will happen to me because of you?

(Early morning)
I continue. In the oppressive heat of night. Here in the room, a deathly silence—only the sound of my pen scratching the paper—but I like to think as I write, because a machine has not yet

been invented to reproduce the thoughts we have not expressed in any medium. Before me there is an inkwell for my heart to drown in; a pair of scissors; the white sheets that await my words. I write:

Not far from this house a good religious woman lives, a nun I sometimes visit because I find her purity soothing. I will write down her exact name: Lisette Gazel. I know her from head to toe, better than I know myself. Not long ago she was a slender, graceful nun; I was a doctor; all of a sudden I managed to turn her skin dark and have her grow fat and learn to speak Spanish. Her sister Miss Rebba lives with her in incest (Lesbos): she (the sister) is too fat for my taste: now I can make her skinny, skin and bones, cadaverous— like a corpse. I am a doctor. One of these days she is going to die—and what gives me pleasure is that I will perform the autopsy.

Before me I see the scissors, the inkwell, the white sheets waiting for my words. I write:

Those papers from the past, buried in the trunk, are my private zoo. Shrunken animals are locked in there: lizards, rats, snakes with cold flesh. I have only to open the cover to see them seething in there, tiny, like the tiny icebergs that float in my blood. In the sheepfold of history I take to pasture the animals in the herd: I feed them with the flesh of my thoughts.

Before me I see the white sheets that are waiting at night for my words. I write. The only sound is my pen scratching the paper.

Last night, when I dipped my right hand into the trunk where I keep my papers, the beasts climbed up my forearm, their legs waving, their antennas, trying to come out into the fresh air. The reptiles that crawl on my skin every time I decide to sink my hand into the past produce in me a feeling of infinite repugnance, but I know that the scaly feel of their bellies, the sharp contact of their feet, is the price I must pay whenever I want to confirm who I have been.

Before me, a pair of scissors:

When black silk is torn it makes a strange snap similar to the sound of paper when it burns.

Arocena rearranged the text, dividing the letter into paragraphs. The code did not match. There was nothing there. Was there nothing there? He worked a bit more but finally decided to give up on those scrawled pages. He looked for the next letter. Emilio Renzi, Sarmiento 1516, to Marcelo Maggi, P.O. Box 12, Concordia, Entre Ríos. He adjusted the lamp and began, once more, to read.

Dear Marcelo:
I had a visit from young Angela, your beautiful envoy and/or pupil (strangely erotic word, *pupil,* as if expressing at once the discipline of teaching and that of prostitution), and I shall follow your mysterious (and exciting) instructions. One always has the sense that behind your life there is something hidden, a secret you cultivate as others care for the flowers in their garden. An effect, I think, not so much of History properly speaking, as you imply, but rather of the profession of the historian: dedicated as you are to prying into the mystery of the life of other men (of one other man, Enrique Ossorio), you have ended up resembling the object you investigate.

Well, I will arrive in Concordia on the 27th, at ten in the morning; I am traveling by train. I have the numbers, addresses and so forth, but don't think I need them. These lines, then, are only to confirm the date and the hour: soon we shall see each other (at last), will talk interminably until we have clarified our respective versions of the story. I feel tempted to say to you: Marcelo, I am going to stand on the steps of the station (surely there must be steps at the Concordia train station), I am fairly short, curly hair, I wear glasses, I will be carrying a canvas bag and in the other hand (the free one) I will hold a book with black covers tightly against my chest: an edition of the complete short stories of Martínez Estrada that I just bought to read on the journey. Did you ever reflect on the fact that we have never seen each other, that we are not acquainted, that in fact this is an *appointment* between two strangers? Fondly, dear uncle.

Le neveu de Rameau, alias Emilio Renzi

P.S. I am also going to meet the Senator. I arranged to see him on Saturday, I almost forgot to tell you, so I am adding this today, the 12th, the day after I wrote you the preceding letter. It was hellish beyond words (to arrange the meeting). I called on the phone. First a sort of butler who seemed to have come out of some Agatha Christie novel answered and didn't pay me much mind, although he did pass the phone to Agatha Christie herself, that is, to an old woman (or to a woman with an old woman's voice) who said she was the wife of one of the Senator's sons, to whom I repeated what I had already told the butler. (That is, that I wanted to speak personally with Dr. Luciano Ossorio.) Which she answered by asking me to hold for a moment: an instant that lasted about half an hour until finally the voice of one of the sons (Javier, I believe) appeared on the telephone and starting interrogating me not as if I were a nephew of yours— which is what I told him I was and thus, if you think about it, a sort of in-law of Esperancita and hence of all of them—but as if I were actually an agent of the KGB (if not of the CIA, though in that case they would have been more understanding). I told him I wanted to speak with the Senator, that you had asked me to see him, and so on, and the guy at first didn't want to have anything to do with me. (For what purpose? How? No, better let him rest—that sort of thing.) But suddenly and without giving the slightest hint in advance he changed his mind, abruptly changing in a way that, beyond a doubt, must be a peculiarity of the way of thinking of the upper classes, (all at once) becoming sweet tempered as could be, telling me to wait for a moment while he transferred the call to the other side of the house, where, as he put it, the rooms were located where his father "resided." I waited some seven hours, more or less, as if the guy with the telephone had had to cross all of the hallways, staircases and passages of Elsinore Castle so as to put me in direct touch by telephone with the ghost of the father of Prince Hamlet, until at last, out of that labyrinthine silence, there appeared the voice of the Senator, an incredible voice, as if he were speaking from another world; a sort of distant tone, at once ironic and ostentatious, so Argentine (so precisely what I suppose an Argentine voice is like) that I suddenly felt like I was speaking on the phone with Juan Martín de Pueyrredón or some other founding father. Then I told him that I was calling him on your behalf, that you sent him warm greetings and that I would like to visit him in person, if that were possible, and the old man seemed enchanted to have news of you, but after that fleeting moment of joy he became serious and began giving me a series of minute and extremely detailed instructions about how to reach the wing of the Castle of Elsinore where he was said to "reside." How it was important to come up the side staircase at the end of an entry hall and under *no* circumstances to take the elevator and above all *not* to permit any of his sons or relatives to accompany me. "I don't want any of my sons around, or their wives, or my grandchildren, is that clear? You are to come up by yourself, have them stay far away. All of those people from time to time," he told me, "feel moved by filial piety and burst in here to find out whether I have died yet," said the Senator. "Do you understand, young man? So," he told me, "first you go down the hallway and then you come up the stairs to where I will be waiting for you in my reception area." So that, after the simple negotiation I have summed up for you, the day after tomorrow I am going to meet the Senator and I will tell you all about it when at last we meet on the 27th, you and I (in your reception area). Greetings.

Emilio

The crisis passed. I am returning from what they call my illness.

My tale continues. I keep on thinking about it. To reconstruct a period in all of its density from those random letters arriving from a different time. The Hero works with those documents as if he were the historian of the future. Why does he receive them? In what fashion? No explanation: the tale does not clarify the means by which this suddenly begins to happen. Everything will be taken for granted from the start: fantastic literature. (Have any of you read the stories of Edgar Poe in the *Baltimore Herald?*) Some isolated, almost trivial, letters exchanged by future Argentines. Letters that seem to have gotten lost in time. Little by little the Hero begins to understand. He tries, using almost invisible signals, to decipher what is going to happen.

(If only one could read the letters from the future!)

You appeared in the newspaper. All of us were *so* proud: at the club, on Saturday, no one spoke of anything else. I am sending you the clipping; the picture is small but you look the same as ever. Cute as can be. Mom has a surprise for you, so act surprised. You'll never guess what happened? Mom and dad started having an argument. Mom practically ate him alive. She says that he never liked the fact that you studied physics—is that true?—that he was against it from the start and now pretends to have forgotten. That he wanted you to be a lawyer and take charge of the company—think of what a future that would be!— the very thought makes me sick. By the way, *terrible* news reaches us of the cold wave in Europe. Alejandra, poor thing, is a wreck. Why don't you write to her? Don't fall in love with a foreigner, don't be a cad. (Is it true that there are *black* prostitutes in London?) In any case I've lived life, such as I can: I'm a sort of sleepwalker. Everything here is awfully dull. Buenos Aires is like Catamarca. (The scum in the capital is more than I can stand any more. Was it Spinetta who said that?) Do you go to the theater, the cabarets and so on—or do you *study* all the time? We have a young and *extremely handsome* history teacher; all the girls study the first Triumvirate and raise their hands right away. The other day dad said that if things stay this way all year we'll spend the summer in Europe. (Another secret: it *appears* that he wants to buy a house in Paris.) Prepare yourself because you're going to have to take me *everywhere*. I should tell you that I have thought *seriously* about leaving this house. Dad is positively unbearable: You young people (that's me) have empty heads, you need to be put on tight reins (he uses equestrian metaphors); we (the young people, especially me) are going to be the ruination of the world. You can just imagine, if it were up to him we would have to install a monarchy, decree the reopening of the Inquisition, that kind of thing. The history teacher, cute as can be, prattles on endlessly: according to him San Martín was a monarchist, the troubles began in this country when we had the bloody idea of throwing out the English at the time of the invasions, etc., etc., etc. There's nothing like listening to my elders to make me feel better. Speaking of that (this letter is coming out rather scattered), speaking of that, *I repeat:* how are you making out with the English language? *I am the sister. This is a pencil.* I envy you *enormously.* Why wasn't I born a man? I am reading a huge amount, by the way: fifteen or sixteen hours a day I read psychology, psychoanalysis, all of that (Sigmund Freud and company). I think that's what I'm going to major in. What do you think? (*Important:* I urgently need to ask you something. Do I seem intelligent to you? For quite a while I've been feeling slightly dim-witted. *Would you be capable* once in your life of giving a serious answer to something I ask you? It's terribly important to me, fundamental, etc. Answer me frankly: if it seems to you that I am of below average intelligence, tell me so directly in all candor; don't be afraid that I'll commit suicide or anything like that.) For a while now I've had the feeling that I'm becoming slightly idiotic. For instance: I spend the whole day counting the cars with odd-numbered plates that go by the house. The impulse is stronger than I. It impels me. I cannot resist it: suddenly I find myself at the window calculating how many cars with odd-numbered plates pass the house every five minutes (about twenty on average). Doesn't that seem strange to you? Answer me about this because it is very important. I cannot spend my whole life counting cars with odd-numbered plates and reading Sigmund Freud. (I understand twelve point five percent of what I read.) (I am reading *The Psychopathology of Everyday Life:* it's *wild.* Have you read it? It's fairly hard though. This business about the cars with odd-numbered plates is peculiarly *psychopathological,* don't you think?) To top it all off, guess what dad wants me to do: to study *court stenography!* There are times when I think that he is a monster, impossible, unbearable and so on. He acts as though we were living in the time of the first Triumvirate (they would even seem too modern to him, I think). Court stenography! Even if I were to squeeze my head for twelve hours in a row I couldn't possibly think of anything more totally idiotic than studying that. So I am now *completely* decided that I'm going to be a psychologist. As soon as I graduate, we'll get married. Incest seems *very* interesting to me, modern, sinful, and so forth. (I should tell you, *dearest,* that in Oceania or Australia or somewhere around there, according to Sigmund Freud, siblings can marry without any problems.) Answer me right away about everything I am asking you because otherwise I think I'll throw myself beneath the first car with an odd-numbered plate that passes beneath my *fenêtre.* Oh, that boy with a catlike face came looking for you (Ernesto or something like that, I never catch his name), the one who was your classmate at the university. I almost fainted, he is *such* a sinful looking dude, he looks at you out of the corner of his eye with an air of such *virile* sinfulness that you feel faint. He says that Angela is sick, that they admitted her suddenly and that you shouldn't write to her; that's why he came. (He repeated it to me at least two dozen times—he seems convinced that I am dimwitted—that they admitted her on the fourteenth and that you shouldn't write.) So you had a hidden Angela? I hate you. You're never going to marry your sister, of that much I'm sure. Men are horrible. I'm going to stay celibate. *Adieu, mon semblable, mon frère.* (I started at the Alliance Française again to get ready for France.) It's eleven o'clock; the time has come for me to obey my psychopathological instinct and go to the window: about noon (for unknown reasons) there is a sudden increase in the statistical frequency of cars with odd-numbered plates; the frequency increases from an average of twenty (every five minutes) and in moments of odd-numbered frenzy goes up to *almost* twenty seven (every five minutes). I'm on my way. Farewell, cruel brother. Of course I love you even unto madness, I adore and idolize you. Bye, you rascal. Signed: Crazy Jane

Arocena picked up the clipping that was folded up in the envelope. *London—the 9th—AP. Yesterday Martín Carranza, a graduate student in physics at Oxford University, was awarded by his department the prize for the best paper of the year in the category of doctoral research.* Prizes, he thought, progress. Now mom's spoiled brats devote themselves to physics while their sisters masturbate to *Les fleurs du mal.* He worked on that letter for about an hour. First he divided it up into segments and each segment into sentences and each sentence into words and letters. He looked for anagrammatic constructions, repeated letters. By the end he knew the text almost by heart and could perceive its logic with clarity. *Paris:* five letters. *London:* six letters. He reread it. Suddenly he understood that there was a repetition *among* the underlined words, a sort of stationary repetition. The code might be in the letters that came after the end of each segment. He reconstructed the letter in accord with these units and reorganized it, but didn't find the code. There was something there that did not come out right. How then to decipher those letters? By what means to understand what they announced? They are in code: they conceal secret messages. Because that is what letters from the future are: coded messages to which no one has the key.

How to understand what is coming, what is foretold? The Hero is suspicious, insistent, blundering in the dark.

There were still two more letters. One was addressed to a strange address in Buenos Aires: it was written in longhand on a piece of stationery from a hotel in Bogotá. The author was desperate: in a Church they had robbed him of everything he had; he asked for an urgent mail order from the import-export company where he worked.

I am stuck in this fucking city where there's nothing but thieves and the smell of shit. Four guys stuck a knife in my kidneys and took away my last penny while the priest went on saying mass. I have no documents, no money, not even my address book, so I have to write to you because the office is the only address I know by heart. Do something, please. Please make a collection or say something to Mr. Peralta so he sends me the salary for April in advance.

It was important to check where that office was. The street was odd; Arocena had never heard its name. It was like stumbling in the dark, trying to grasp a fact that was going to happen somewhere else, something that would happen in the future and that was foretold in such an enigmatic way that one could never be sure of having understood. The hardest thing always consisted of avoiding the content, the literal sense of the words, and in looking for the coded message that underlay what was written, that was hidden *between* the letters, like a discourse of which only snatches could be heard, isolated sentences, occasional words in an unknown language, from which one had to reconstruct the meaning. One had, however, to be able (he thought) to discover the code, even in a message that was not coded. So that when he finally devoted himself to reading the final letter and discovered the code almost at first sight and saw another text appear in the text, Arocena felt at once satisfied and disappointed. Too easy, he thought, as if they had put it there for me to see. He opened the letter, which was written in New York, in a street by the East River, in blue ink on yellow paper.

Something so strange has happened to me that I will spare you other personal news (except to say that I am well, visiting museums). I was reading a novel by Bellow (*Mr. Sammler's Planet*) about a week ago. I had bought it at a drugstore because I had time to waste while they renewed my visa. I took a bus that goes along 42d Street; I sat down and starting reading. All of a sudden I look up and see a pickpocket robbing a woman. He was stocky, wore dark glasses with tortoiseshell rims, was dressed with extraordinary elegance. I was fascinated watching him in action but suddenly the guy turned his head and looked at me, almost calmly, through the smoked glass of his shades; I got frightened and almost involuntarily lowered my eyes and went back to my reading. It took me a minute to realize that what I was reading was exactly what was happening on the bus. You can look at page 3 of the Random House edition of the novel. There you will find the description of a stocky guy wearing dark tortoiseshell glasses who dresses with extraordinary elegance, who robs a woman on a bus that goes down 42d Street.

I ended up so confused that I could not react, and when I tried to call attention to what was happening it was already over. The guy with the dark glasses wasn't there any more and I started thinking that it had all been a hallucination. Later, while I was in line at immigration, I thought it was a mere coincidence; the pickpocket probably always worked on that line, Bellow had seen him working once and had reproduced the scene. Nature imitates art; the excessive realism of U.S. writers; etc. I forgot (or almost forgot) the episode. Four days later I was in a movie theater on Broadway; they were showing a strange film about dolls and gangsters. It was one of those theaters that is open 24 hours: it was about 10:00 A.M. and I went in to get away from the cold. The theater was almost empty; there was a strange diffuse glow as if they hadn't turned the lights all the way down. On the screen the dolls were torn apart and the gangsters died. Suddenly a tall guy came in and sat down near me in the third row. He started talking to someone else I hadn't noticed before, sitting in front of him in the first row, a bit to the left. Their whispered voices reached me, confused with the sound and music of the film. "Don't bother to visit Mr. Brown," the guy who was sitting in the front row said without turning his head. I looked at them, standing out in silhouette against the images in the film, as if in a dream. "Mr. Brown has been so kind," said the one seated in the front row, ever intent on the film. They sat in silence for a minute and then crossed in front of the screen and went out through a side door that had an acrylic sign, illuminated in red light, that said Exit. I believe I was left alone in the theater, watching the dolls spinning on the screen, and then I remembered. I went home and spent a while looking around until I found the book by Donald Barthelme, *Come Back, Dr. Caligari:* there's a story in there, you can look it up, called "Movie" (on page 176 of the 1970 Scribner's edition). I remember that I sat still, quiet, watching the street through the window. Sometimes I get excited about what I am reading and I feel like living it right then. Years ago, for instance, when I finished *The Great Gatsby,* I felt the desire to be proud and passionate and worthy of my illusions. I also felt elegant and a bit desperate but ready for anything. It's like a climate, an atmosphere, or better still like a feeling, and that impression lasts as long as the echoes of a melody, it's always been something fleeting. This is different. It's not an illusion. The events are reproduced exactly. That's why I decided to do an experiment. I took a book at random (*An Accidental Man*, by Grace Paley), and opened it. In Central Park, a girl dressed in light blue is playing with a hoop and singing, "One of these days, you'll miss me honey." A boy comes to skate on the lake. He is carrying his skates over his shoulder; they are tied to a strap. They start talking. (Hi, Raquel, how do you do, and so forth.) Off to one side a woman is kissing an old man; the girl sees them and without knowing why feels like crying. It's almost dusk, and the light is soft and dirty. I went out, took the subway, and got off at Central Park West and 81st. I crossed the street and went into the park, finding my way to the lake. I looked for a bench and sat down. Everything was quiet. All of a sudden I saw the girl on the gravel path, dressed in light blue, playing with a hoop and singing "One of These Days." The boy came walking along, with his skates hanging on a strap over his shoulder. Off to one side a woman is kissing an old man and the girl, singing, fights off tears.

I am calm. I think: I have discovered an incomprehensible relation between literature and the future, a strange connection between books and reality. I have only one doubt: Can I modify those scenes? Is there some way of intervening or can I only be a spectator? In any case I would not want to give up the joy I felt just now, sitting on a bench in Central Park, watching the girl sing "One of These Days" and play with a hoop, knowing at the same time that soon I would see her crying when the woman and the old man began kissing.

From the outset he understood two things. First: that the code could not be hidden in the titles of those books or in the books themselves: that would be too obvious. Second: that they were trying to distract him with that story. The code was somewhere else. The first words of the paragraphs referred to had eleven letters each, all starting with a different letter. The eleven letters marked the order of the sentences and concealed the code at work in the secret message. Arocena worked calmly and an hour later had reconstructed the hidden text.

> *There's no news. I am waiting for the contact. I will stay at the Central Park Hotel at 42d and Broadway. If there is any news before the tenth, I will follow instruction 9.8. If there are problems and I have to come back I will wait for a telegram. It should say: Congratulations, Raquel.*

He sat down at his typewriter. He wrote: "*Coded letter from New York. From Enrique Ossorio to Marcelo Maggi.*" He transcribed the message he had deciphered. Beneath it he wrote: "*Send a telegram to Enrique Ossorio. Central Park Hotel, New York. It should say: Congratulations, Raquel.*"

Pretty imaginative guy, Arocena thought. All that's lacking is for them to devote themselves now to fantastic literature.

He got up and collected the other letters. On one card he wrote: ["Angela 'admitted' on the 14th. Concordia. Renzi arrives on the 27th. (Maggi.)"] Martín Carranza: graduate study in Oxford. Soon new messages would arrive speaking of quantum physics or of brightly colored fish. He looked at the one from Colombia. This won't work, he decided, and amused himself for a moment thinking about the office clerk stuck in a ratty rooming house in Bogotá. He deserves to get screwed for acting like such a fool, he thought, going to mass with all of his cash on him. Then, as if the image of the thieves at work in a church had helped him, he realized that a code might also be coded. A code is also a message, he thought.

He reread the message he had just deciphered. (There's no news. I am waiting for the contact. I will stay at the Central Park Hotel at 42d and Broadway. If there is any news before the tenth, I will follow instruction 9.8. If there are problems and I have to come back I will wait for a telegram. It should say: Congratulations, Raquel.) He counted the letters, put the words in columns. $3 \times 2 + 5 = 11$. Eleven. The same number. Were the vowels scrambled? The consonants? In two hours he had reconstructed the message hidden in the code he had just cracked.

Raquel arrives at Ezeiza on the 10th on the 10:03 P.M. flight.

He looked at the sentence. There it was, written on the piece of paper. Raquel arrives at Ezeiza on the 10th on the 10:03 P.M. flight. And if that's not right either? Who could be believed? Raquel: a code for *Aquel* (So-and-So). He wrote "*Aquel*" on a card. He put it aside. Ezeiza: e/e/i/a. Double z. An alliteration? There were the numbers: 10.0310. The *e* is repeated six times in the entire sentence. The *a* is repeated four times. There are two *O*'s and three *I*'s. Each word could be a message. Each letter. Who is arriving? Who is about to arrive? The numbers: 1.00.31.0. E/e/a/i/u/o. Double z. Raquel: an anagram. Who is arriving? Who is about to arrive? Me, thought Arocena, they'll never fool me.

July 30, 1850
I am writing the first letter from the future.

SECOND PART

•

Descartes

IV

1.

He was seen getting off the morning train from Buenos Aires at ten. He paused on the stairs of the station, a bit disoriented; he asked which way was the river. We will meet at six. We arranged it by phone. I am Emilio Renzi, he tells me. He has come to Concordia especially. Mr. Tardowski. Tardewski, I tell him. It's pronounced Tardewski, with the stress on the second syllable. I explain to him how to get to the club, where to find me, then say goodbye. It's been a pleasure and so forth. Who called you? Elvira asks me. A nephew of the Professor. He came to pick up some papers that were left here, I tell her. She doesn't believe me. It's hard to tell the truth when one has given up one's mother tongue. Be careful, please, don't get involved, she tells me. The liquid clarity of her eyes is truly extraordinary. Liquid clarity? One of the first things one loses on switching languages is the ability to describe. That I shouldn't get involved? Why did he come? she asks. Who? I ask her. That boy, why did he come? It's simple; the Professor decided to go on a trip. He spoke with his nephew, told him to look me up. Perhaps, I tell her, the Professor will return today. Then Elvira asked me not to lie. Don't lie, she said. Please, don't lie to me.

And yet I am not lying. Perhaps it's worth showing that I am not lying.

I met Professor Marcelo Maggi at the Social Club; we saw

each other regularly to have dinner or play chess. I should say that he was not open with me (or I with him); I know of his life what he wanted me to know. Did he have a secret life? We all have secret lives.

One afternoon, about ten days ago, the Professor came looking for me here, an unusual thing. He said that he had to request something, but preferred that I not ask questions. If I wanted to ask him any questions, he said, that was the moment, before he asked me for anything. I had no questions for him. Then he asked to spend the night at my house.

He spent the night at my house. We talked until dawn. What can you talk about until dawn?

At some point, that night, the Professor told me that he wanted to leave me the rough drafts and notes of a book he was writing. We had already spoken of that book on several occasions. He preferred that I take charge of those folders, he said, until he should ask me for them or send someone for them.

He also told me that he might cross the Uruguay River that afternoon to say goodbye to a woman with whom he had lived at some other period in his life. He wanted to say goodbye to her, he said, because he was planning to go on a trip and he was not sure that he would be able to see her again.

We agreed to meet two days later, at the usual hour, at the club. If for some reason he did not arrive he would try, he said, to be back by the 27th at the latest.

Two days later he did not come to the Club, nor did he show up any of the following days. Since then (today is the 27th) I have had no news of him.

That, more or less, is what I explain to Renzi when we meet at the club at six that afternoon. And then? he says to me. Nothing, I say. Let's wait for him. As soon as he arrives, I'm sure he'll come here. If he arrives, he says. Of course, I tell him, if he can return today. So then, he says. It's strange. From one day to the next. He seemed to know exactly, I tell him, what he was doing.

On the other hand, I say to him, he was not the sort of man interested in explaining very much. And why, after all, should he explain anything? He decided to go away, I tell him. That's all. I see, he says. But why that night, Marcelo? Renzi starts to say. Maybe a way, I interrupt, of having company. To have someone with whom to talk as morning approaches. We were good chess mates, the Professor and I, during all those years. He did not have many friends; he taught his classes, sometimes met up with his students, they went to visit him. For some time, I tell him, he had been living at a hotel, one that is on the riverbank, on the other side of the square; perhaps you saw it when you came here. He seemed to want to forget himself; he did not like sharing intimacies. On the other hand, who could want to share intimacies at times like these?

Renzi thought that in any case I must have some hunch. What did I think had happened? I am not the most appropriate person, I want you to know, I tell him, to have hunches or give explanations for the behavior of others. I live—how shall I put it?—a bit removed. Sometimes I even think that he cultivated my friendship, if we can call it that, I tell him, that he cultivated my friendship all of this time because he was preparing for this departure and needed me, Vladimir Tardewski, or someone like me, an exile, a foreigner. For years now no one has paid much attention to me and—to tell the truth—you are the first person to visit me, to put it that way, since the consul came to see me and asked that I become a naturalized citizen, which I refused.

Afterward I told him that I was not like him, like the Professor; I, I told him, do not like to change. Besides, changing is very difficult, don't you think? Things should change, be transformed, but oneself? I told him that changing was much more difficult and risky than people could ever imagine.

Then Renzi wanted to know what we had talked about, that night, the Professor and I. He thought that perhaps that night Marcelo had said or hinted at something that would help us, he said, understand why he decided to go away. I also think, said Renzi, that he knew from the start what he was doing, what he wanted to do, and that if he began writing to me it was because in a sense he was also preparing me, Renzi said, for his departure and that he wanted me, at that moment, when that happened, to be here, as I am here now, he said, with you, ready, intent on waiting for him. That is why he believed that if it were possible to reconstruct, even if only in part, what we had said that night, perhaps some clue could be found, or at least, he said, the beginning of an explanation.

I told him that it was better not to try to explain in words what a man had decided to do with his life. In any case, I said, we could speak of that afterward, when the two of us were also a bit better acquainted. I asked him if he wanted to have another gin and called the waiter.

In this club, I told Renzi, one can drink and drink without anyone getting upset. Look at that man over there, the fat one with the jacket on: he gets drunk every night, always by himself, and yet preserves a strange dignity. There's a story about him, I tell Renzi, a painful story. While cleaning a shotgun he killed his wife of just three months. I told him that it was doubtless an accident and not a crime, for nobody kills his wife of three months in that fashion, with a shotgun blast in the face, unless he's crazy. And besides, I tell him, the man has been literally broken since the accident. He does nothing but get drunk and says that firearms are the work of the devil. Two glasses of gin, that's right, I tell the waiter. Oh, and please bring a bit more ice. You, I say to Renzi, have no doubt read my compatriot Korzeniowski, the Polish novelist who wrote in English. A renegade, to tell the truth, a romantic of the worst sort. He spent his life fascinated by that sort of character. The man has a secret. But which of us does not have a secret? Even the most insignificant person, I say to him, if he had some listeners, could fascinate them with the mystery of his life. It's not even necessary to have killed a woman with a shotgun blast. That other fellow—see?—the one over there, next to that column. His name is Iriarte; he has a watch shop, is the classic type of insignificant person, and yet I am sure that when he has had enough to drink he also dreams of the great man he almost became. At some moment in his life he must have witnessed something that he needs to keep hidden. That happens to all of us. Each one of us, I tell him, has his own repertory of extraordinary moments and heroic illusions. Everyone, Renzi says to me; the difference lies in that only some are able to realize those illusions. Illusions? That depends on one's age. After one's thirtieth birthday, I tell him, we are nothing but a sad collection of illusions and of women we have killed with shotgun blasts. Besides, I tell Renzi, what a man thinks of himself is of absolutely no importance.

Renzi then told me that the Professor was not like that. He was not sure that he knew him well, he said, but he could imagine exactly how he thought. And how did he think—I ask him—according to you? Against himself, always against himself, Renzi said; that method seemed to him like an almost infallible guarantee of lucidity. That's an excellent method of thinking, he said to me. To think against, I tell him, yes, that's not bad. Because he, Marcelo, Renzi told me, mistrusted himself. They train us for so long to be stupid and finally it becomes second nature to us, Marcelo would say, Renzi says to me. The first thing that we think is always mistaken, he would say, it's a conditioned reflex.

One must think against oneself and live in the third person. That—Renzi says—is what Professor Maggi told him in his letters. Let's drink to him then, I say. To Professor Marcelo Maggi, who learned to live against himself. Cheers, says Renzi. Cheers, I say.

And yet you see the Professor also did what he could, like the rest of the world, I tell Renzi now. One day, it seems, he decided to go away on a trip, to change his life, to begin again—who knows?—somewhere else. And what's that, after all, I tell him, if not a modern illusion? It happens to all of us eventually. We all want, I say, to have adventures. Renzi told me that he was convinced that neither experiences nor adventures existed any longer. There are no more adventures, he told me, only parodies. He thought, he said, that today adventures were nothing but parodies. Because, he said, parody had stopped being what the followers of Tynianov thought, namely the signal of literary change, and had turned into the very center of modern life. It's not that I am inventing a theory or anything like that, Renzi told me. It's simply that I believe that parody has been displaced and that it now invades all gestures and actions. Where there used to be events, experiences, passions, now there are nothing but parodies. This is what I tried to tell Marcelo so many times in my letters: that parody has completely replaced history. And isn't parody the very negation of history? Ineluctable modality of the visible, as the Irishman disguised as Telemachus would say during the Trieste carnival, in the year 1921, said Renzi cryptically. Afterward he asked me if I had *really* met James Joyce. Marcelo told me that you met Joyce, it seemed so incredible, Renzi told me. I met him, I say, or at least I saw him a couple of times; he was extremely nearsighted and quite surly. A lousy chess player. He would, I suppose, have accepted your idea that everything is parody (because in fact, to insert a parenthesis, what was he but a parody of Shakespeare?) but he would have rejected your hypothesis that adventures no longer exist. I myself, I should confess, I confess to Renzi, I myself resist that hypothesis. Might that be because I am European? The Professor said of me that I was here to bring to a close the long line of Europeans acclimated to this country. I was the last of a line that began, according to him, with Pedro de Angelis and reached as far as my compatriot Witold Gombrowicz. Those Europeans, the Professor said, had managed to create the greatest inferiority complex that any national culture has ever suffered since the occupation of Spain by the Moors. Pedro de Angelis was the first one, the Professor would say, I tell Renzi. A cultured man, erudite, familiar with Vico and Hegel, preceptor of the children of Joaquín Murat, cultural attaché in the court of Saint Petersburg, contributor to the *Revue Encyclopédique,* friend of Michelet and of Destutt de Tracy, he landed in Buenos Aires and became Rosas's right hand man. In comparison to him Echeverría, Alberdi, Sarmiento all seemed like desperate copyists, dilettantes consumed by secondhand knowledge. I was, according to Maggi, the last link in that chain: a Polish intellectual who had studied philosophy in Cambridge with Wittgenstein and who ended up in Concordia, Entre Ríos, giving private lessons. In this sense, I tell him, my situation seemed to the Professor like the purest metaphor of the development and secret evolution of Eurocentrism as the cornerstone of Argentine culture since its inception. All of the contradictions in that tradition were incarnated in those European intellectuals who had lived in Argentina, and I was no more than the final example of its slow disintegration. I know, Renzi said, Marcelo told me some of all of that in his letters. A singular thesis, I tell him, but I wonder why I recalled all of this now? We were speaking of something else and then I. Ah yes, I say, what I really wanted was to disagree with your hypothesis about the lack of adventures; I was thinking that perhaps my disagreement had to do with my European origin, that's why I remembered de Angelis and all of that. In fact I thought, I told him, that Argentines, South Americans, whatever general term you prefer, have an excessively grandiose idea of what should be considered an adventure. Let me tell you a story, I tell him. Once I was in a Warsaw hospital. Motionless, unable to use my body, accompanied by a pathetic series of invalids. Tedium, monotony, introspection. A long white hall, a row of beds—it was like being in jail. There was a single window, at the end of the room. One of the patients, a bony, feverish guy, consumed by cancer, named Guy by his

French parents, had had the luck to be placed near that opening. From there, barely sitting up, he could look out, see the street. What a spectacle! A square, water, pigeons, people passing. Another world. He clung desperately to that place and told us what he saw. He was the lucky one. We detested him. We waited, to be frank, for him to die so as to take his place. We kept count. Finally he died. After complicated maneuvers and bribes I succeeded in being transferred to the bed at the end of the hall and was able to take his place. Well, I tell Renzi. Well. From the window all that could be seen was a gray wall and a bit of dirty sky. I too, of course, began telling them stories about the square and the pigeons and the traffic in the streets. Why do you laugh? It's funny, Renzi says. It's like a Polish version of Plato's cave. Why not, I tell him; it serves to prove that adventures can be found anywhere. Doesn't that seem like a beautiful practical lesson? A fable with a moral, he says to me. Exactly, I say.

Look at me, I say to him now. I came to this town more than thirty years ago and ever since I have been passing through. I am always passing through, I am what they call a migratory bird, only I always stay in the same place. I always stay in the same place *but* I am passing through, I say to him. That's how the two of us are, he and I—perhaps this will help you, I tell Renzi— rootless fellows, anachronistic people, the last survivors of a dying race.

Then I told him that the only means of survival was to kill off all illusions. To reflect, to kill off all illusions. So don't hesitate to reflect. The Professor, for instance, was a man who reflected on his principles. Better still, I tell him, he was a man of principle. A rare species these days. What do we have other than principles to sustain us in the middle of all this shit? That was one of the things he told me the night he spent at my house. He had faith in abstractions, I tell him, in what are commonly called abstractions. Abstract ideas helped him make practical decisions, I tell Renzi; they ceased being abstract ideas.

Then Renzi asked me why I told him that he had to reflect. Or at least, he said, to tell him what he should reflect on without illusions. About him, I tell him, about the Professor, about the adventurer. I would particularly like to be able to see him, Renzi tells me, so he would cease being an abstraction for me. See him? Why not? If he has told you to be here today, I tell him, it is because today is the day he has doubtless chosen to return. Let's wait for him, I tell him. If he wished to go away, it is also possible now that he may want to return, I tell him. We can wait all night for him. I am sure that today he will return. We have time, I tell him; the train doesn't leave for Buenos Aires until six in the morning. If he does not return you can still catch that train. We will stay together, I tell him, until the early morning, waiting for the Professor. Afterward we'll go to my house. There, in my house, if I am not mistaken, I have some notes that I took about the night I spent with the Professor, before he went away, some notes on what we talked about, I'll let you read them, if the Professor has not yet returned. In the meanwhile, I would like for us to stay here a bit longer at the club; we could even eat something. This is the place where I spend my life; in these rooms one can permit oneself the illusion of having a world of one's own, of having company, of time not passing.

At that table—see over there?—I tell Renzi, where they're waving at us, those are my friends. Those two are—besides the Professor—my best companions here. Tokray and Maier. We have drawn together, perhaps, because all three of us are foreigners. Expatriates. Driftwood that the tides of the European wars left on these shores. The oldest of the three, I don't know if you can see him, that man with glasses and a dark suit, is Anton Tokray. The natural son of a Russian noble, he suffered all of the misfortunes that the Revolution brought his family without receiving any of the benefits. When the Red Army occupied the huge patriarchal estate, he was eighteen years old and had been cloistered for two years in a monastery where a priestly vocation awaited him. In the time of the tsars the members of the religious elite were chosen from among the bastards of the nobility. But the Revolution broke out. The workers, peasants, and soldiers entered the monastery, put all the seminarians and monks—even, I suppose, Father Zosima—in a row against the wall and asked them whether they knew that the tsar no longer ruled the Russias. And who now ruled this land by the design and the mercy of God, our Lord? asked one of the monks, very possibly, as I have said, Father Zosima himself. The workers, peasants, and soldiers rule, said the workers, peasants, and soldiers. And as for God, they said, that gentleman has escaped from Russia with his whole heavenly court to go hide under the Pope's robe in the Vatican. For which reason Count Tokray, who had just recovered his title by his own decision, taking advantage of the changes brought on by history, saw his ecclesiastical career interrupted and had to cross to Finland disguised as a woman. From there, after infinite troubles, he was able to reach Paris; then, passing himself off as a Jewish peasant, he arrived in Argentina with one of the last contingents of immigrants sent by Baron Hirsch to the colonies in the foreign part of the pampas, and set himself up in Concordia, Entre Ríos, where he opened an academy devoted to the cultivation, by means of personal example, of the rituals, manners, and etiquette that should be used at table and in society if one wishes to be considered a gentleman or a lady of distinction.

At first the academy was successful, but later, as the Professor said, Peronism made Tokray's business go down the drain, due to its vulgar disregard for the observance and preservation of aristocratic virtues. The count had lived for so many years in exile that he ended up acquiring an air of dreamy indifference, and sometimes I think I see in him the image of my own future.

As for Rudolf von Maier, he was, almost certainly, a Nazi. Of course like all Nazis he entered the party against his will and one should never forget, besides, as he says, that all Germans sympathized at first with the Führer and his campaign against unemployment, inflation, and Bolshevism, plagues that were on the verge of destroying the nation. As for the concentration camps, he, like all Germans, knew nothing until the moment of the Nuremburg trials, which he followed, he says, with horrified attention from Buenos Aires in the pages of the *Argentinischen Tageblatt*. He didn't even take part in the war: his contribution to it consisted of putting in order the archives and the scientific library of a special section of the SS devoted to genetic research. That's where he gets the confused amalgam of biological theories and almost mystical confidence in scientific specialization that marks his conversation, as you will soon have the chance to discover; above all, I tell him, in his conversations with Pedro Arregui, the one sitting on the side of the table—see him over there? All of Maier's confused erudition is destined to instruct Arregui, who listens to him in fascination. They are made for each other. Arregui is the ideal listener and his confidence in the virtues of knowledge is infinite. They thus form the perfect pedagogical pair. They share the same room in a boardinghouse near here and survive thanks to Arregui's salary from his post at the city registry of real property. Maier teaches Arregui, instructs him, and I suppose that while the latter works he prepares the topics of his discourses. Maier is the one seated facing us. The one smiling at us now, see? He doesn't look at all like a German, as you can see, if there is such a thing as a German face. He is actually a curious Entre Ríos phenomenon of the universal species of self-taught walking encyclopedias. I don't know if you can hear him—if you sit like this, I tell Renzi, this way—I would like you to listen to him.

Phrenology, of course, one can hear Maier saying. One of the few almost exact sciences that can be applied to morality. Now it has been largely replaced by the Viennese superstition. Viennese? you can hear Arregui ask. Yes. From Vienna, Austria, where one night in 1897 a fellow dreamed of his uncle because Jews were not permitted to teach in the university. Phrenology, so, said Maier. From the Latin *frenum*, the bridle, to stop: *Halt, Caesar*, that is, control. *Logy*, from *logia*, in Latin: first meaning, secret society; second meaning, logic, or knowledge. The logical science of control. To control criminals, the maladjusted. They are classified according to the shape of their skulls. It is fundamental, says Maier, the *shape* of the skull. Evil has always respected geometric structures. For what other reason, for instance, does one speak of vicious circles? Eh? Vicious circle: as always happens with the established forms of language, there resides a nugget of ancient wisdom. That is why, by the way, says Maier, knowledge is always etymological. Why else would we be able to find in that phrase the secret link between geometry (the circle) and morality (vicious), the theoretical basis for phrenological science? we hear Maier say.

Bouvard and Pécuchet, says Renzi. They're like Bouvard and Pécuchet. Do you hear him now? I ask him.

Of course: the theory of relativity. The presence of the observer alters the structure of the phenomenon being observed. Thus the theory of relativity is, at its name indicates, the theory of relative action. Relative, from *relates:* to narrate. He who narrates, the narrator. *Narrator*, says Maier, that is to say: he who knows.

That duet between Maier and Arregui exemplifies in a condensed and exaggerated form the relation that fascinated the Professor: the European intellectual who, once installed in Argentina, comes to incarnate universal knowledge. He had examined a series of stages and typical pairs, with their tensions, debates, and transformations. De Angelis–Echeverría in the Rosas period. Paul Groussac–Miguel Cané in the 1880s. Soussens-

Lugones at the turn of the century. Hudson-Güiraldes in the twenties. Gombrowicz-Borges in the forties. The phenomenon continued, declining and becoming degraded as Eurocentrism lost its force, to conclude in an exemplary manner in the relation between Maier and Arregui. The last links in that long series, the Professor argued, were found in Entre Ríos. When the Professor was happy he used to say that even the relation between the two of us, him and me, formed part of the same structure. In those pairs the European intellectual was always, especially during the nineteenth century, the exemplary model, what the others would have wanted to be. At the same time many of these European intellectuals were no more than false copies, Platonic shadows of other models. Of course, for instance, Charles de Soussens, said Renzi, and for a moment he, Renzi, took charge of developing Maggi's theory as we devoting ourselves to reconstructing it in order to have the Professor there with us. A sort of copy, said Renzi, of Verlaine for domestic use, that's what Soussens was. He wrote poems in French in the bars and served as the local representation of what should be understood as a *poète maudit*. He perfectly incarnated the bohemian. He wandered drunk through the city, in the most utter poverty, telling anecdotes of his friend Paul Verlaine, while Lugones, the bureaucratic functionary, the corseted writer, delegated the prestige and the disadvantages of the passionate chaos of the Poet onto his European double residing in Buenos Aires. Lugones was of course a teetotaller, practiced fencing, wrote nonsense about philology, and translated Homer without knowing Greek, said Renzi. A truly ridiculous figure this Lugones, in fact: the very model of the National Poet. He wrote in such a way that now one reads him and one realizes that he is one of the greatest comic writers in Argentine literature. Involuntarily comic, you will say, but I think that's where his genius lies, said Renzi. That unrestrained ability to be comical without realizing it makes him the Buster Keaton of our culture. Did you ever read *The Gaucho*

War? Read it and you will find there such a refined, *natural* comic talent that compared to him even the jokes of Macedonio Fernández aren't funny. For instance this joke: "I don't understand how Lugones, being such a well-informed person, so well read, such a student of literature, has still not decided to write a book." The jokes of Macedonio Fernández, even this one, are totally lacking in wit compared with the texts of Lugones. A standup comic, that's what Lugones was, said Renzi. A humorist of the stature of Mark Twain. Even, Renzi begins to say but I interrupt him because I see Tokray approaching. Excuse me, I tell Renzi, the one who is approaching, the one coming in this direction, is Count Tokray.

Do I intrude? asks Count Tokray. Certainly not, Count, I tell him. How are you, Mr. Tardewski? asks the count. Very well, I reply. Won't you sit down? I wish to introduce you to Emilio Renzi, Marcelo Maggi's nephew. One minute, he says. I'll interrupt only for a minute, says Count Tokray as he makes himself comfortable in the chair. Young man, a pleasure to meet you. The count said that he would be going momentarily because he had never gotten accustomed to staying up late. In truth, he said, at times I think that I go to bed early because the first dreams are the most generous and I always have the hope of being able to dream of the house where I was born. Did you know, the count says to me, that I have been invited by the Russian consul in Paraná to attend a cocktail party in honor of God knows what dismal anniversary. Do you think I should go? Could it be a sinister prank? He said he had received an invitation, in fact an official card, inviting him to a cocktail party at the consulate. I confess, the count said, that I am tempted to attend, even though I fear it may be a joke or even a trap. And do you know why I am tempted, in spite of everything, to attend? Because for more than fifty years I haven't been anywhere where more than two living persons speak Russian. I hear the language of my ancestors in my dreams and sometimes I go to see Soviet films just to hear the dialogues, but on those occasions I always have the impression that I am watching a film made in Hollywood, say by Walt Disney, and then *dubbed* into Russian. I had the unpleasant sensation, said the count, that Russians today speak the language of Pushkin as if it were translated from English. None of you can imagine what the music of our native language was like. *Vesta fiave sogliadatay krasavitsa novosti jvat,* recited Count Tokray. Oh, words of my land, he said, unforgettable music. Another thing that made him doubt the true intentions behind that invitation, he said later, was that on the card they had written Mr. Anton Tokray. *Mr.* Anton Tokray, that seems to me a deliberate and gratuitous offense. I can assure you that had I the certainty that my title of count were recognized in Russia today, perhaps, I say perhaps, I would decide to go back. He had thought about it more than once, he said. More than once I have thought of going back. I have even thought, he said, what line of work could I follow? And I've had an idea. As a guide in a museum, the count thought that's the work he could do should he decide to return. I could teach the younger generations about the meaning and value of the old monuments that preserve the history of our ancient Russian fatherland. I have even thought, said the count, that I myself could be turned into a museum. Do any museums exist that consist only of a single person? That's something I've not been able to discover. I could be such a museum all by myself. It would suffice for me to be installed in a room in any of the old palaces, surrounded by the decoration and servants appropriate to those times, and I would be a living museum of the customs and manners of old Russia. They could come visit me to see how a Russian nobleman lived before the Revolution. It would be an instructive experience for young people; I could be visited by school groups, provincial delegations, even by foreign tourists. A museum with mannequins or wax figures is not the same, said the count, as a living museum. They could observe my manners, my breeding, my form of using the language, all those natural distinctions that the tides of history have not washed away. And I should add, said the count, that I would not feel uncomfortable: quite the contrary. I would not consider it an affront, nor a sign of open collaboration with the regime. It would instead be an example of my fidelity to the tsar and to the culture and customs of the period of splendor of the Russian nobility, conserved and preserved by me. The memory of that happy time would continue in me, that time when we all spoke French even from the cradle, when our governesses were French and we learned the alphabet in French, when we learned to pray and write in French. You have no doubt read something of all that in the books of Count Leo Tolstoy. But in this case it would be different: it is not the same thing to read about a period as to *see* that period, even in the restricted form of one of its last representatives. So that, said the count, were I designated a museum, don't believe for a minute that I would experience it as a form of collaboration with the regime, quite the contrary. On the one hand the best traditions of the ancient culture would be preserved in pure form, and on the other, the count said in a low voice, I am sure that it would be a way of taking up once more the program and duties of Restoration, defended so heroically but without success by the White Army. I mean that that museum would serve, I am convinced, to make Russian youth reflect on things, helping them compare the old way of life represented by me with their present life in those apartment blocks so *onereux et bizarres;* that would be enough to make the veils fall from their eyes. Couldn't that be a way of raising consciousness, leading at last to the defeat of the regime and to the Restoration? He said that several times in moments of melancholy and profound nostalgia he had begun composing a letter offering his services; if he had stopped, he said, it was because he understood that they would not allow the splendors of the unforgettable life of the Russian aristocracy to serve as an example for the younger generations raised in ignorance. Sometimes, he said, he imagined his return, the Nevsky Prospect, spring in Saint Petersburg, his life as an image and representation of the lost glories of the past; but little by little, said the count, he had had to tear that hope from his heart. He no longer had any hopes, he said; he had only the hope that God would have mercy on him from time to time and grant him the joy of dreaming of the house where he was born. I had torn out that hope and now suddenly this invitation arrives. An invitation, he said. What can one do in response to an official invitation? the count asked himself. What should a gentleman do, he asked, in response to an invitation? I vacillate, he said, before that apparent gesture of politeness. Because it may be politeness; I know that things have changed there, that they're no longer so fanatical, now that the technicians are in charge, those gray, realistic men. Even the fact, he said with a smile, that they are realistic already makes them more approachable. I also am a realist, said the count; a tsar, a king are no more than subtleties now. And they are realists; they have abandoned those pathetic utopias invented by the *sans culottes,* and are more and more concerned with efficiency and technique. *But,* nevertheless, I fear that that invitation may be a trap. Besides, what good would it do me to go? I would recover the unforgettable taste of caviar, but on the other hand would have, he said, to listen to my beautiful native language spoken as if it were translated from English. In any case, according to what they had told him, the Russian consul in Paraná was not an unpleasant person; he had observed him from above, one night, at the theater in Concepción del Uruguay, during a spectacle with the Bolshoi Ballet offered on the 9th of July for the diplomatic corps. The count had attended, he said, and from the top balcony, as his emotions were stirred by hearing the immortal music of our immortal Tchaikowsky, he had focused his opera glasses on the figure of the Russian consul. He looks like a distinguished man, somewhat *opaque mais distingué.* I believe he is an engineer, he said; they are all engineers there now, now that there are no more workers; it is a state of engineers, soldiers, and bureaucrats, and the consul belongs to the ranks of the engineers. I believe he is a musician, but above all an engineer. In fact the consul seemed like a person of good family to him. He was named Igor Suslow and if my memory serves me his mother was a cousin of the nephew of a sister of my paternal grandmother. Perhaps that is why he invited me, said the count; in a sense we are relatives, the engineer and I; but I shall not go, because international law guarantees the irrevocable nature of titles of nobility. *Mr.* Tokray? asked the count. *Nyet.* For me it's a question of honor. But, he said looking at the clock on the back wall of the room, I have entertained you much longer than necessary. He asked Renzi if he liked the city, if it didn't seem excessively tropical to him, and then, lowering his voice a bit, he told me of the passing of Malcolm Firmin. Did I know that he had died? he asked me. He had broken his neck in the bathtub; perhaps he had had too much to drink, he said, but what is certain is that he slipped and broke his head like an *oeuf* against the edge of the tub. He should have attended the funeral, he said, but the news arrived too late. He is a man, said the count, transported to the great beyond by alcohol, a bad reputation and misfortune. He died naked, he said, just as he was born. Naked. And in that we should see a sad image of our own dismal situation in this fragile *pont* of life. Speaking of that, said Count Tokray, imperceptibly lowering his voice still further, you wouldn't be able, my dear Tardewski, to lend me, if you could, some kopeks, I mean, some money. I would like at least to leave some flowers on that English tomb and I haven't received a certain sum of money I have been waiting for. Would it then be possible, asked the count, to arrange a small loan? a small amount for a short period of time so as to be able to go to the obscure grave where my friend lies? Is this enough? I ask him. Excellent. Most excellent. I am most grateful for your kindness, Mr. Tardewski. We will see each other here again, perhaps *demain?* Is that all right? I told him that that seemed excellent to me. Young man, said the count, standing up with difficulty, it has been a pleasure meeting you. Did you know, he said, that you are the very image of your uncle? *La même figure.* Isn't that so, Volodia? Isn't this young man identical to a picture of his uncle as a younger man? And by the way, he said, for some time the Professor has not been seen here at the club. He is on a trip, I said. On a trip? *Parfait.* He had heard it said that he was not in good health. But I will not keep you any longer, be well, have a good time, we shall meet again, said Count Tokray, who then began to draw off.

Do you see how he walks? I ask Renzi; his way of walking is like a confused quotation of the manners that the French governesses taught the young people of the Russian nobility, even the natural children of the nobility, as the most appropriate for a gentleman at the moment he must cross a public place. The body erect—see?—his feet barely sliding along the ground. A quotation, then, of what a Russian nobleman ought to think it is to draw off with dignity. A quotation improperly used, I tell Renzi, but not a parody. It has something pathetic about it, no doubt, I say, but it is not parodic. He is trying desperately to preserve his dignity but it is almost impossible for him to survive. Several of us keep him going, to be more precise, various Europeans who are living in exile in Entre Ríos: six of us. He asks each of us for a small sum each month, always under a different pretext. The pretext today has been, to his great relief, true. Firmin has died, yet another misfortune, and so the future looks even bleaker. Firmin was one of the six who gave him that small monthly allowance. I suppose that the fear that we will start dying off, one by one, before he dies himself is what keeps Count Tokray from sleeping.

Nevertheless it is not of Europeans like Count Tokray that the Professor built his theory, I tell Renzi. It was not a matter of immigrants either, nor even of travelers who write or have written about Argentina. It is instead a matter of those European intellectuals who, integrated into Argentine culture, exercised a particular function in it. That function could not be studied without taking into account the dominant pattern of Eurocentrism: for it was precisely its line of continuity and transformation that they in turn incarnated. The clearest example was, for the Professor, that of Groussac. He in fact saw Groussac as the most representative of those transplanted intellectuals, above all because he came into action at the precise moment when Eurocentrism became dominant. Groussac is the intellectual of 1880 par excellence, the Professor would say; but above all he is the European intellectual in Argentina par excellence. That is why he was able to fulfill that role as arbiter, judge, and true cultural dictator. This implacable critic, to whose authority everybody submitted, was irrefutable because he was European. He had what we might call an authenticated European perspective, and from that vantage point he judged the achievements of a culture that was trying to appear European. An authentic European amused himself at the expense of these dressed-up natives. He laughed at all of them; they seemed mere South American literati to him. And in turn he, Groussac, was nothing more than a pretentious little Frenchman who thanks to God had ended up at these shores of the River Plate, because without a doubt in Europe he would not have had any other fate than ending up in laborious anonymity, the victim of his meritorious mediocrity. What would have become of Groussac had he stayed in Paris? A journalist of the fifth rank; here, in contrast, he was the arbiter of cultural life. This character, not merely unpleasant but paradoxical, was actually a symptom: in him were expressed all the values of a culture dominated by Eurocentric superstition. But nonetheless Borges, Renzi says to me, laughs at him. At Groussac? I ask him, I don't think so. Of course it doesn't look like that, Renzi says. For on the one hand

Borges sings the praises that we all know, *says* things about Groussac. But the truth of Borges has to be found elsewhere: in his fictional texts. And "Pierre Menard, Author of *Don Quixote*," whatever else it might be, is certainly a cruel parody of Paul Groussac. I don't know if you are familiar, Renzi says to me, with a book by Groussac on the apocryphal *Don Quixote*. That book—written in Buenos Aires and in French—by this pedantic and fraudulent man of learning has a double objective: first, to announce that he has liquidated forever all of the arguments of all of the specialists who have ever written on this subject before he himself; second: to inform the world that he has been able to discover the identity of the real author of the apocryphal *Quixote*. Groussac's book is called (with a title that could be applied without difficulty to Borges's "Pierre Menard") *Une enigme littéraire,* and it is one of the most incredible gaffes in our intellectual history. After labyrinthine and toilsome demonstrations, in which he makes use of every imaginable kind of proof, among others an anagrammatical argument derived from one of Cervantes's sonnets, Groussac arrives at the inexorable conclusion that the true author of the false *Quixote* is a certain José Martí (a homonym of the Cuban hero altogether alien and even hostile to the spirit of the latter). Groussac's arguments and conclusion have, like his style, an air at once decisive and deceptive. It is true that among the conjectures about the author of the apocryphal *Quixote* there are all sorts of things, said Renzi, but none of them has the merit of Groussac's of being physically impossible. The candidate favored in *Une enigme littéraire* had died in December 1604, from which fact it becomes obvious that the supposed plagiarist and author of a sequel to Cervantes could not even have read the printed version of the first part of the real *Quixote*. How can one fail to see in this blunder of the Gallic man of learning, Renzi says to me, the seed, the basis, the invisible plot from which Borges wove the paradox of "Pierre Menard, Author of *Don Quixote*"? A Frenchman who writes in Spanish a sort of apocryphal *Quixote* that is, nevertheless, the real one, a pathetic and yet shrewd Pierre Menard, is nothing but Borges's transfiguration of the figure of this Paul Groussac, author of a book that demonstrates, with a deathless logic, that the author of the apocryphal *Quixote* is a man who died *before* the publication of the authentic *Quixote*. If the writer discovered by Groussac had been able to compose an apocryphal *Quixote* before reading the book of which his own is a mere sequel, why shouldn't Menard succeed in the great deed of writing a *Quixote* that is at once the same as and different from the original? It was Groussac, then, with his discovery of a posthumous author of the false *Quixote* who, for the first time, employed that technique of reading that Menard has done nothing but reproduce. Groussac was really the one who, to say it with the words most appropriate to the case, by means of a new technique enriched the halting and rudimentary art of reading: the technique of deliberate anachronism and of erroneous attribution.

Who is quoting Borges here in this faithless place? Marconi asked from a nearby table. In this remote province of the Argentine interior, who is quoting Jorge Luis Borges from memory? said Marconi, standing up. Let me shake your hand, he said, and came over. That technique, whose applications are infinite, prompts us to peruse the *Odyssey* as if it were later than the *Aeneid,* Marconi recited. That technique fills with surprises the quietest books. For literature is an art, Marconi kept on reciting, interrupting himself to ask—May I sit down?—for literature is an art that knows how to prophesy that time when it will grow mute, to lead mercilessly to its own dissolution and to court its own end. My name, he said, is Bartolomé Marconi. How are you, Volodia? Bartolomé for Father Bartolomé de las Casas and not for Mitre, a patrician who, as you well know, is a bad word here in the province of Entre Ríos. Bartolomé, then, said Marconi, by now seated, for that friar who in 1517 had such compassion for the Indians who were being worn out in the toilsome hells of the Antillean gold mines that he proposed to Emperor Charles V the importation of blacks so that they might be worn out in the toilsome hells of the Antillean gold mines. To that curious variation on a philanthropist, said Marconi, I owe my name. As for my surname, it is a curious local repetition of that of the inventor of the telephone. Of the telephone or the radio, Volodia? Of the radio, I think, I said. Young Renzi, I said after that, is a young writer, that is to say, I said, a young promise of the young literature of Argentina. Well, said Marconi, I am distraught and envious. In Buenos Aires, aleph of the native land, by some inconsiderate privilege of the port city, young writers are young even after having crossed the infernal wilderness of their 33rd birthday. What would become of Rimbaud or Keats in that city? They would classify them, I'm sure, in a subspecies of children's literature, never considered worthy of much prestige. To be blunt, said Marconi, I am dying of envy. What else can I do, resentful polygraph from the sticks, to join the cadre of the young (despite my already interminable 36 years) promises of the young literature of Argentina? I'll serve myself a bit of gin, said Marconi. Volodia? Renzi? Don't worry, Marconi, said Renzi, Argentine literature no longer exists. It no longer exists? said Marconi. Has it been dissolved? A lamentable loss. And since when have we been left without it, Renzi? asked Marconi. Can I address you with the familiar form? Let's make a first metaphorical approach to the subject, he said. Argentine literature is dead. Let us say, then, said Marconi, that Argentine literature is the Difunta Correa. Hey, said Renzi, that's not bad. She's a strap that got cut. And when? said Marconi. In 1942, said Renzi. In 1942—asked Marconi—just like that? With the death of Arlt, said Renzi. That's when modern literature came to an end in Argentina; everything after that is a dark wasteland. With him everything ended? asked Marconi. How's that? And what about Borges? Borges, said Renzi, is a nineteenth-century writer. The best Argentine writer of the nineteenth century.

That may be, said Marconi. Yes, he said, that's right. A sort of perfect realization of what a writer of the generation of 1880 should be, said Renzi. A member of the generation of 1880 who has read Paul Valéry, said Renzi. That on the one hand, said Renzi. And on the other his fiction can only be understood as a conscious attempt to complete nineteenth-century Argentine literature. To conclude and to integrate are the two basic traits that define literary writing in the nineteenth century. How's that? asked Marconi. Number one, Eurocentrism, said Renzi. That's easy, we were just talking about that with Tardewski; it starts with the first page of *Facundo*. The first page of *Facundo*: foundational text of Argentine literature. What does it consist of? asked Renzi. A phrase in French: that's how it starts. Which is as if to say that Argentine literature begins with a phrase written in French: *On ne tue point les idées* (memorized by all of us in school, already translated into Spanish). How does Sarmiento open his *Facundo?* By telling how in the first moments of his exile he writes a slogan in French. The political gesture is not in the content of the phrase, or not only in that content. It is, above all, in the fact of writing it in French. The barbarians arrive, look at those foreign words written by Sarmiento, fail to understand them: they have to get someone to come and translate them. And then? asked Renzi. It's clear, he said, that the line between civilization and savagery runs right there. The barbarians don't know how to read French; better still, they are barbarians precisely *because* they don't know how to read French. And Sarmiento makes a point of it: that is why he begins his book with that anecdote; it's perfectly clear. But it turns out that that phrase written by Sarmiento ("Ideas can't be killed," in the school version), and which for us is his own isn't his at all but a quotation. So Sarmiento writes a quotation in French, attributing it to Fourtol, although Groussac hastens to clarify, with his usual generosity, that Sarmiento is mistaken. The phrase is not by Fourtol but by Volney. So, Renzi says, Argentine literature begins with a phrase written in French, which is a false, mistaken quotation. Sarmiento misquotes. At the moment he wants to show off, to call attention to his familiarity with European culture, everything collapses, undermined by savagery and a lack of culture. And from that moment we could see the proliferation, in Sarmiento but also in those who follow him, including Groussac himself, as we were saying a little while ago with Tardewski, says Renzi, the proliferation of an ostentatious and fraudulent erudition, a forged bilingual encyclopedia. That is the first of the threads that constitutes the fiction of Borges: texts that are chains of forged, apocryphal, false, distorted quotations; an exasperating and parodic display of secondhand culture, constantly invaded by a pathetic pedantry: that's what Borges makes fun of. He—I mean Borges—exaggerates and carries to extremes, almost parodic extremes in fact, the line of cosmopolitan and fraudulent erudition that defines—even dominates—the greater part of the Argentine literature of the nineteenth century. But there's something else besides, says Renzi. Do you want some gin? asks Marconi. Sure, says Renzi. Volodia? With a bit more ice, I tell him. But there's something else, another line: what we could call Borges's populist nationalism. I mean, says Renzi, Borges's attempt to synthesize in his work another current, a current opposed to Eurocentrism, which is built upon the gauchesque tradition, taking as its model *Martín Fierro*. Borges proposes to bring to a close a tradition that in a way defines Argentine literature in the nineteenth century. What does Borges do? asks Renzi. He writes a sequel to *Martín Fierro*. Not only because he writes, in "The End," an ending for that poem. A cigarette? says Renzi. A bit later. Not only because he writes an ending for it, he says now, but also because he makes the gaucho, by now turned into a suburban thug, the hero of a series of stories that Borges intentionally sets in the decade from 1890 to 1900. But it's not only that, says Renzi, it's not only a thematic question. Borges does something different, something essential, to wit, he understands that the literary basis of the gauchesque tradition is the transcription of the voice, of popular speech. He does not write gauchesque works in educated language like Güiraldes. What Borges does, says Renzi, is to write the first work of Argentine literature after *Martín Fierro* that is written in the voice of a narrator who uses the inflexions, the rhythms and the lexicon of the spoken language: he writes "Streetcorner Man." So that, Renzi says, the first two stories that Borges writes, seemingly so different—"Streetcorner Man" and "Pierre Menard, Author of *Don Quixote*"—are the means by which Borges connects himself, maintains his ties, and yet completes the double tradition that splits Argentine literature in the nineteenth century. From that moment on his work is divided in two: on the one hand the stories about knife fighters, with the variations on them; on the other what we could call the erudite stories, where erudition, cultural display, is taken to the most extreme limits: the stories in which Borges parodies the superstitions of high culture and works with apocrypha, plagiarism, chains of false quotations, false encyclopedias and so forth, and in which erudition itself defines the *form* of the stories. It's not by chance that for Borges the best of his own texts is "The South," a story in which these two lines cross and are woven together. All of which is no more than a manner of saying, says Renzi, that Borges should be read, if you want to understand what he's about, from within the system of nineteenth-century Argentine literature, the fundamental lines of which—with its conflicts, dilemmas and contradictions—he comes to complete, to bring to an end. So that Borges is anachronistic, bringing things to an end, looking back at the nineteenth century. The one who opens things up, who initiates, is Roberto Arlt. Arlt begins over again: he is the only truly modern writer that Argentine literature has produced in the twentieth century. One of the definite virtues of Buenos Aires intellectuals, said Marconi, is their ability—never altogether envied by others—to say everything at once. Yes, said Renzi, theories are best expressed all at once, especially if one has had enough gin. So, said Marconi, now can I expect a rapid-fire theory about Roberto Arlt? Of course, said Renzi, I'll breathe a little and then at once will come up with a quick theory on the importance of Arlt in Argentine literature. In truth, said Marconi, this is starting to resemble a novel by Aldous Huxley. Huxley? said Renzi. I prefer the chapter in the Library, Scylla and Charybdis, in the Gaelic Telemachiad. Let's talk about Hamlet then, said Marconi. Wow, said Renzi, Concordia is full of erudite people. I'm just getting started, said Marconi. Shall we demonstrate by algebra that Hamlet's grandson is Shakespeare's father and that he himself is the ghost of his own father? Hey, Buck Mulligan? said Marconi. Old man, you have a memory that surpasses even that of José Hernández himself, said Renzi. A poet without a memory, said Marconi, is like a criminal who is overwhelmed and nearly undone by feelings of decency. A poet without a memory is an oxymoron. Because the Poet is the memory of the language. How then do you expect me to talk about Arlt? asked Marconi. Because, I say, begging pardon of all those present, what was Arlt other than the author of a column in *El Mundo?* That's exactly right, said Renzi—a chronicler of the world. After which you'll say, beyond a doubt, that he could be the chronicler of whatever the fuck he wanted but that he wrote badly. Exactly, said Marconi, here's where I tell you that Arlt wrote badly and in that way, I suppose, give you material for your quick run through theory. But apart from that, said Marconi, the truth is that he wrote like shit. Who? asked Renzi. Arlt? No, Joyce. Arlt, of course, Arlt, he said. The poor fellow deserves all possible honors, said Marconi, but the truth is that he wrote as if he wanted to make a mess of his life, to destroy his own prestige. His masochism comes from his readings of Dostoevsky, that taste for suffering in the manner of Alyosha Karamazov, though he turned it into a style: Arlt wrote to humble himself, said

Marconi, in the literal meaning of the expression. No doubt he has one undeniable merit: it would be impossible to write worse. In that respect he is unique and without rival. Have you finished, Morriconi? asked Renzi. Marconi, old man, said Marconi. My name is Marconi, don't pretend to be absentminded. Calm down, I said. Pacem in terris. There's nothing like Latin, said Marconi, to soothe hot tempers. So, he said then, we have agreed that Arlt wrote badly. Exactly, said Renzi, he wrote badly: but in the moral sense of the word. His is *bad* writing, perverse writing. Arlt's style is the Stavrogin of Argentine literature; he is the Pibe Cabeza of our literature, to use a local expression. His is a criminal style. He does what one is not supposed to do, what's wrong; he wrecks everything that for fifty years had been understood to be good writing in this pallid republic. A quotation from Borges, said Marconi: this pallid republic. Any primary school teacher, even my Aunt Margarita, said Renzi, can correct a page by Arlt, but nobody can write it. That's true, said Marconi, I'm sure that's so, nobody can write it except for Arlt himself. But I won't interrupt any more, I mean it when I say that I'm listening to you, he said. Some gin? Yes, said Renzi. Volodia? asked Marconi. Okay, I said. Arlt writes against the idea of a literary style, or rather, he writes against what they taught us should be understood as good writing, namely to write tidy precise prose without any gerunds—right?—and without repeated words. That's why the highest praise one can give Arlt is to say that at his best moments he is unreadable; at least when the critics say that he is unreadable they mean they cannot read him, using their system they cannot read him. Arlt's style, Renzi said, is the repressed side of Argentine literature. All of the critics (with two exceptions), all those who wrote on Arlt, from one end of the spectrum to the other, from Castelnuovo, let's say, to Murena, are in agreement about one thing: in saying that he wrote badly. That is one of the few moments of consensus in Argentine letters. When they reach this point the various factions lower their banners and agree with one another. A moving example of reconciliation, said Renzi, although it would not have made the late writer happy. They are right in that Arlt did not write from the same place they did, nor did he always follow the same rules. And in this regard Arlt is absolutely modern: he far surpasses those fools who accuse him. Because when does the idea of style appear in Argentine literature, asked Renzi, the idea of good writing as a means of distinguishing good works? It is a rather recent idea. It only appears when literature achieves autonomy and becomes independent of politics. The appearance of the idea of style is a key event: henceforth literature was to be judged according to specific values, of values, that is, said Renzi, that were specifically literary and not, as happened in the nineteenth century, according to the political and social values expressed in the work. Sarmiento or Hernández would never have thought of saying that they wrote *well*. The autonomy of literature, and the correlative notion of style as a value to which the writer must submit, is born in Argentina as a reaction to the impact of immigration. In this case it is a matter of the impact of immigration on language. For the dominant classes, immigration was to destroy many things—right?—it destroys our national identity, our traditional values and so forth and so on. In the sphere related to literature what they said was that immigration destroys and corrupts the national language. At that moment literature changes functions in Argentina; it comes to have a—shall we say—*specific* function. A function that, without ceasing to be ideological and social, can be performed only by literature as such, only by literature as a specific activity. Literature, they said everywhere and at every occasion imaginable, now has a sacred mission to perform: to preserve and defend the purity of the national language in the face of the mixture, intermingling and disintegration brought on by the immigrants. This comes to be the ideological function of literature at this point: to show what the model should be, the *proper usage* of the national language; the writer becomes the guardian of the purity of the language. At that moment, say around 1900, said Renzi, the dominant classes delegate to their writers the function of imposing a written model of what the true national language should be. The one who will incarnate this new function of the Argentine writer is Leopoldo Lugones. Lugones is the first Argentine writer who, unlike Sarmiento, Hernández, and company, performs a political function in society exclusively as a writer. He is the national poet, the guardian of the purity of the language. A while ago we—Tardewski and I—were speaking of the style of this man, so I won't insist on the point. But what must be said about him is the following: Lugones fulfills a decisive role in the definition of literary style in Argentina. Lugones's texts are an example of what it is to write well; he crystallizes and defines the paradigm of literary writing. For us, Borges said—as you must recall, Marconi—says Renzi, for us, Borges now says repentantly, writing well meant writing like Lugones. Lugones's style is constructed arduously and with the dictionary, Borges also said. It is a style dedicated to erasing any trace of the effect, or better still, of the confusion, that immigration produced in the national language. Because this good style consists of a fear of mixing. Arlt, of course, works in an absolutely opposite direction. From the first moment he works with what *remains*, what is sedimented in language, with leftovers, fragments, amalgams, that is to say, he works with what really is the national language. He does not understand language as a unity, as something coherent and smooth, but as an amalgam, a hodgepodge of slangs and expressions. For Arlt the national language is the place where different languages coexist and confront one another, with their various tones and registers. And this is the material from which he develops his style. This is the material that he transforms, that he has entered into the "poly-faceted machine," to quote him, of his writing. Arlt transforms rather than reproduces. In Arlt there is no copying of speech.

Arlt does not suffer from the illusion that abounds in the writers who surround Borges, like Bioy, Peyrou, the early Cortázar, who on the one hand wrote "well," with polish and "elegance," and on the other showed that they could transcribe and copy the picturesque speech of the "lower" classes. Arlt's style is a boiling mass, a contradictory surface, where there isn't any copying of speech or raw transcription of orality. So Arlt works with that atomized language, noting that the national language is not univocal, that it is only the dominant classes who, through the school system, impose a particular use of language as *the correct* usage; he perceives the national language as an amalgam. That's part of it, said Renzi. Another part is that Arlt gets away from the tradition of bilingualism; he is shut out of this, as he reads only in translation. All of our nineteenth-century literature extending as far as Borges springs paradoxically from a national writing riven by an absolute division between Spanish and the language of reading—which is always a foreign language, as in the Gallicisms that mark the works of Sarmiento, Cané, and Güiraldes; Arlt, however, does not suffer from this doubling of the language of literature (read in another language) and the language in which one writes. Arlt is a reader of translations and hence he receives foreign influences already sifted and transformed by the passage of the works from their original languages into Spanish. Arlt is the first, besides, who defends the reading of translations. Read what he says about Joyce in the preface to *The Flame Throwers* and you'll see what I mean. Where does he find his model of literary style? He finds it where he reads, that is to say, in the Spanish translations of Dostoevsky and Andreyev. He finds it in the *style* of the worst Spanish translators, in the cheap Tor editions. And that's the second body of material on which Arlt founds his style. Words like "jade" (for horse) and "lad": his texts are full of that, because he reworks what the Spanish translators establish as the clichés of translation and of diction, transforming them into the primary material of his writing. Arlt then comes from somewhere that is totally *other* than the space in which one can write "well" and find a "style" in Argentina. There is nothing like Arlt's style; there is nothing so transgressive as the style of Roberto Arlt. But there is something else, said Renzi, and I'll finish. That style of Arlt's, made of set phrases and mixtures, that alchemical style, so perverse and transgressive, is nothing but the verbal and stylistic transposition of the *theme* of his novels. That style of Arlt's is his fiction. And Arlt's fiction is his style: the one does not exist without the other. Arlt writes what counts: Arlt is his style, because Arlt's style is made, on the linguistic plane, of the same material of which the theme of his novels is made. That's why I laugh when those guys who are so condescending about him say: Arlt is a great writer *in spite of* his style; the guys who think that when a writer has *so much* to say, as they suppose Arlt had so much to say, then the sweeping force of his "inner world" makes him forget about form. Those are the people who think that the more "sincere" (to use a word they are fond of) a writer is, the more truths he has to express, the worse he writes; according to them it is precisely when a writer does not worry about form, lets himself get carried away, that he displays his natural force, the sweeping impulse and all the rest. Arlt has nothing to do with this. There are many writers who write badly in that sense, but not Arlt. Arlt's literature is a machine that always consumes the same fuel. But anyway, said Renzi, to explain what Arlt signifies in Argentine literature one would have to speak for a week. I am disappointed, Renzi, said Marconi. We got off to such a good start. Of course if one reads Arlt the way you read him one cannot read Borges. Or one can read him in a different way, said Renzi, read him, for instance, from Arlt. Better still, said Marconi, better to read Borges from Arlt, because if one reads Arlt from Borges there's nothing there. Aside from the fact that the very idea of imagining Borges reading a page of Arlt makes me very sad. I don't think the Old Man could avoid having a cataleptic fit were he to read more than two lines of what you are calling Arlt's style. I don't think, besides, that Borges has ever taken the trouble to read him, said Marconi. To read Arlt? asked Renzi. Don't be so sure. Don't be so sure, he said. Say, I'm sure you remember the story in *Dr. Brodie's Report* called "The Unworthy One." Reread it, take the time and you'll see. It is *The Furious Toy*. I mean, said Renzi, a transposition so typical of Borges, that is, in miniature, of the theme of *The Furious Toy*. A young man fascinated by the world of crime, for him incarnated in a delinquent who initiates him, whom he admires, and yet who, at the very moment the hero must abandon the so-called legal world and turn into a delinquent himself, he must betray. The thematic nucleus is the same in the two texts, said Renzi, and betrayal is the key to both. Now then, said Renzi, the policeman that the protagonist of the Borges story goes to see when he must betray his friend is named, in that story, *Alt*. You know better than I, beyond a doubt, the significance that names have in Borges's stories, so nobody will convince me that that surname, with the missing R (the first letter, I should point out, of another name, beginning with precisely the R that is missing here), is there by chance. It's as if Borges had baptized the gal in "The Aleph," Beatriz Viterbo, just for the fun of it, or as if Daneri in that story were not a contraction of Dante Alighieri. Never innocent, said Renzi; never so innocent as the Arlt the world proclaims as a naïve writer. So who is the unworthy one if not Roberto Arlt? The Great Unworthy One of Argentine literature. And what is that story but an act of homage by Borges to the only contemporary writer he feels is his equal? You know better than I, said Renzi. Get on with it, old man, said Marconi all of a sudden; enough of this business of claiming to know what I know. I am listening with attention and patience to what you say you know, but as for what I know let me speak for myself, said Marconi. What do you want now, for us to put up our dukes? said Renzi. Dukes, a copy of speech, said Marconi.

Let's say knuckles, he said. But no, I'm a peaceful sort; ever since folks from Entre Ríos killed López Jordan we have been totally pacified and our conflicts with Buenos Aires belong to the past. I simply don't like your pushy manner of giving your opinions about what I should know. And so, I said, what of the topic under discussion? Nothing, says Renzi, I think that in his fiction Borges renders homage and demonstrates his knowledge of Argentine literature (and not only Argentine, it should be said in parenthesis). If you wish to know what writers Borges values in Argentine letters, it's not a matter of listening or paying attention to what he *says*, because otherwise you'll get bogged down in praises of Mallea, Carmen Gándara, and similar masters. It's a matter of looking at what Borges's fiction is about, or better still, what Argentine writers he uses as themes in his stories. And Borges has written fictions about—Renzi enumerated—1. José Hernández ("Tadeo Isidoro Cruz," "The End," and another one in *Dreamtigers,* the title escapes me). 2. Sarmiento ("Dialogue of the Dead"). 3. Groussac ("Pierre Menard"). 4. Lugones (the text that opens *Dreamtigers*). 5. Roberto Arlt (the story I've been talking about). Those are the only ones that matter to Borges, the only names that matter in the history of Argentine literature. And so, Marconi? said Renzi. Don't you agree? Or are you still sulking? No, said Marconi, I am a man of momentary hatreds and passions. And do you agree? No, of course not, said Marconi. Too sophisticated for my taste. But anyway, he said, to keep on playing the role of courteous host, suppose that we agree to leave aside Borges as nineteenth-century writer and all of that; suppose then that we agree to leave aside Borges, which is more or less the same as leaving aside the river, if we should suddenly become so—can we call it Platonic?—as to decide to cross the Uruguay River on foot, as if there were no water in it. Leaving aside Borges, then, thanks to a modest philosophical operation worthy of Bishop Berkeley, referring in passing to someone mentioned by the guy we are leaving aside, setting Borges outside of the picture, said Marconi, as Berkeley did with sensible reality, and so? a rhetorical question destined to elicit a response from the young writer from Buenos Aires who is visiting us, and then? Then, says Renzi, we start from the assumption that Borges is a nineteenth-century writer, the end, conclusion, etc., etc. Arlt, for his part, died in 1942. Who, then, I ask now, what current writer might we consider to prove that Argentine literature has not died? There are many, said Marconi. For instance? asks Renzi. How should I know? Mujica Lainez, for example. *Who?* Mujica Lainez, said Marconi. He is a hybrid, Renzi said. Mujica Lainez is a crossbreed. In the sense that that term has in the Kafka story that is entitled precisely "A Crossbreed." A hybrid, said Renzi, that's what Mujica Lainez is. Of Hugo Wast and Enrique Larreta. That's Mujica Lainez. A half-witted cross of Hugo Wast with Enrique Larreta. He writes "sophisticated" best sellers for people like Nacha Regules to read. Besides which, and without wanting to be rancorous, to return to the matter of style, said Renzi, it's obvious that there is more style in a *single* page of Arlt than in all of Mujica Lainez. Have you finished? asked Marconi. I'm finished, said Renzi. Do you have any more of that kind of evidence? asked Marconi. Not for the moment, said Renzi. Well, said Marconi, I don't agree. I'm so sorry, said Renzi. Your kind of evidence, said Marconi, goes beyond anything that Thomas Aquinas ever dreamed of. Was it St. Thomas or St. Augustine, Volodia? Marconi asks me. The one with the evidence? I say to him. St. Thomas. Well, said Marconi, compared to Renzi, St. Thomas is just a rookie, at least as regards evidence. In any case, said Marconi, it's clear that even though you're something of a pedant you're a nice guy. How long are you staying? I don't know yet, said Renzi. He's waiting for the Professor, I say. The Professor? says Marconi. It seems to me that I saw him a little while ago in the square. He was coming from Salto, Uruguay, I think. Marcelo? asks Renzi. I'm fairly sure it was him, said Marconi. It's not what one could call evidence, just an impression in the dark. Because if you don't leave right away, he said, it would be great to organize something, who knows, a round table, a meeting, something at the library—right, Volodia?—a way of discussing all of this with people and stirring things up a bit. Maybe, said Renzi; if I stay that would be fine. Could it have been Marcelo? Renzi asks me. Maybe, I say. Now let's go to the hotel; if he arrived he must be there. I'm going, folks, said Marconi; I'm already very late. You're going? said Renzi. Don't you want to go with us to the hotel? No, says Marconi, it's getting late; I still have to go to the paper and write a note 36 lines long about Nabokov's latest novel. Do you work at a newspaper? asked Renzi. Well, calling it work is a manner of speaking, said Marconi. But apart from that what do you do? Me? asked Marconi. Nothing. I read Borges and write sonnets. Sonnets? asked Renzi. That's right, said Marconi, here in the provinces everything reaches us late. You see, here we still think that Arlt writes like shit. You're not the only ones, says Renzi, there are people who live in New York and Paris and other metropoli and yet they think that way too. So you write sonnets? says Renzi. Yes, said Marconi, I want to see if I can become the Enrique Banchs of the interior. You know what it is, he said: here we don't know how to use the code. Code? That's what you said, right? Don't kid me, said Renzi. I'm not kidding you, said Marconi, here we are like that, battle scarred but never spiteful. Hey, and in Buenos Aires do they keep screwing around with linguistics? Not so much, said Renzi. Now the fashion is for psychoanalysis. Don't you see, said Marconi, I need to go to Buenos Aires more often. Here I lose touch. In Concordia only now linguistics has become popular, and it seems that we are behind the times. Become popular? asked Renzi. Linguistics, said Marconi. If I tell you what Antuñano told me today, he tells me, Renzi is going to realize how receptive the interior is. Do you know why there are still gauchos around here? said Marconi. It's true, I did see one this morning when I got off the train, with his wide reddish brown breeches and broad-brimmed felt hat. I thought he was an undercover policeman. No, said Marconi, he was surely a gaucho. Just around here, in the neighborhood of Concordia, there are about two hundred and fifty. That's why the gauchesque tradition still survives here, said Marconi, but not without suffering—like everything else—the impact of linguistics. The gauchesque tradition? asked Renzi. The gauchesque and the gauchos themselves, said Marconi. At least if what Antuñano told me today is true. I will transcribe it for you, he said, that way you can take back to Buenos Aires the living folklore of the nation. *Hjelmslev among the Gauderios of Entre Ríos or an Exercise in Gaucho Semiotics,* announced Marconi, in a version by Antuñano, eyewitness and narrator of an event that occurred in La Colorada, a general store on his property, located between Ubajay and Derrida, about seventy kilometers from the provincial capital. One afternoon, Marconi said that Antuñano had told him, one afternoon various gauchos in the store were talking about topics having to do with writing and phonetics. Albarracín (who is from Santiago del Estero) does not know how to read or write, but supposes that Cabrera does not know that he is illiterate; he affirms that the word *trara* cannot be written. Cristanto Cabrera, who is also illiterate, argues that everything that can be spoken can be written down. I'll pay for a round for everyone, the one from Santiago tells him, if you write *trara.* I accept, answers Cabrera; he takes out his knife and with the point makes some squiggles on the dirt floor. Old Alvarez peers over, looks at the floor and pronounces: As clear as can be, *trara.* Wonderful, says Renzi. It's a wonderful story, he tells Marconi. Why don't you stop fooling around with sonnets and devote yourself to describing your town? Well, said Marconi, at the moment I am trying to write sonnets in the gaucho dialect. I really want to synthesize the language of Hilario Ascasubi and the sonnet form as it was handled by Stéphane Mallarmé. In that attempt, as you can see, I am following Borges. Better still, said Marconi, last night I dreamed a poem. Seriously. Some friends came over to eat at my house, they brought some incredible Chilean wine and we drank about six bottles; afterward I went to sleep and in the early morning I woke up with a poem in my head. I wrote it down exactly as I had dreamt it; here goes, he said:

> I am
> the tightrope walker
> who walks in the air
> barefoot
> on a string
> of barbed wire

Marconi recited the poem he had dreamt. It may not be a sonnet, but I dreamed it, no kidding. It's a sort of haiku, right? Too much narrative, he said, nothing too great but the fact is that I dreamed it. So what happened to Coleridge happened to me. What didn't come out in the dream was the title, he said. Call it "Portrait of the Artist," said Renzi. No, said Marconi, that's what it's about, but that title is too explicit. In a poem about the artist, the word artist should not appear and least of all in the title. Is that a rule or not? In literature, he said, the most important thing should never be named. An epigram, he said, that serves to bring to an end this long discussion or intellectual dialogue. I'm leaving, really, he said, it's gotten too late even for me to write about Nabokov, said Marconi, beginning to take his farewell.

An incredible fellow, said Renzi. A local character, I tell him, like everyone around here. That's what's good about living in a small town: we are all important characters. He went crazy with your theory, I tell Renzi. Tomorrow he'll repeat it all as if it were his idea. That wouldn't be so bad, said Renzi. Let's get going. Could Marcelo really be the fellow he saw? he asks me. Probably, I tell him. You don't sound very convinced, he tells me. Yes, why not? In any case we'll see now. Let's go out this way, I tell him. This club was one of Urquiza's summer houses. He liked mirrors, says Renzi. What a strange hallway. Is this the way out? he asks. No, it's better this way, I tell him, that way we come out on the boulevard. It's fairly cool, says Renzi. Shall we walk? Sure, I tell him, it's close; this way we go out right in the direction of the hotel, it's about ten blocks. On the way I'll show you the town. Although you were wandering around this afternoon. Everything is known around here, as you can well imagine, I tell him. Well, not everything, says Renzi. That's true, not everything. I like these towns by the river, says Renzi, they have such a melancholy air. And that building? asks Renzi. The jail, I tell him. Just now, I say, when I was listening to you speak with Marconi. I went a bit too far, says Renzi, all of a sudden I went sailing along, too much gin. No, I tell him, quite the contrary; but I listened to you talk and remembered your uncle. You are very much alike in what matters, I tell him. Everyone tells me that, today, says Renzi. I learned from him, he says, in a way that is hard to explain. We wrote to each other for almost a year and only now do I realize that it was as if he were trying to explain something to me. Marcelo has a sort of innate tendency toward teaching, he tells me. He is a very entertaining sort, right? said Renzi. The most unbelievable part is that I do not know him; personally, that is. I never spoke to him, never saw him. He came to my house when I had just been born but then stopped coming and later on I heard people talking about him but never saw him. Now I am here and we will see him, but we're not completely sure that we're going to meet up with him either. The more I think about it, he says, the more incredible it becomes. He always spoke to me about you, I tell him, and at times he read me parts of your letters. He got tremendous pleasure out of those discussions you had, I tell him. Emilio, he told me, I remember, one night, Emilio thinks that all that exists in the world is literature; when he gets over it, and I hope to be there to witness that moment, the Professor told me, I tell Renzi, only then will he be able to climb out from under all the family shit. I don't understand, Renzi tells me. Neither do I, I reply, but that is what he said.

Later Renzi told me again how incredible it seemed to him that I had met Joyce. Well, he was hardly what you could call an acquaintance, I say to him. I saw him a couple of times in Zurich. He spoke little or not at all; he came to a bar where there were chess matches and sat there reading an Irish paper that the owner received; he sat there in a corner and started reading it with a magnifying glass, the paper almost glued to his face, scanning the pages with just one eye, his left eye. He would spend hours like that, drinking beer and reading the newspaper from beginning to end, even the ads, the obituaries, everything; every so often he would laugh to himself, with the strangest little laugh, a sort of whisper more than a laugh. Once he asked me how to say "butterfly" in Polish; I think that was the only time he spoke to me directly. Another time I heard him exchange a few words with a fellow, a Frenchman who had told him that *Ulysses* is actually quite a trivial book. Yes, Joyce said. It is a bit trivial and also a bit quadrivial. Seriously? says Renzi. Brilliant. The one who visited him at home was a friend of mine, Arno Schmidt, a very shrewd critic who later died in the war. One afternoon he dared to ask him if he could visit him. For what purpose? Joyce asked him. Well, said Arno, I very much admire your books, Mr. Joyce, and I would like, well, I would like to talk to you. Come to my house tomorrow at five, Joyce told him. Arno spent the night preparing a sort of questionnaire, noting down what he wanted to ask; he was very nervous, as if he had to take an exam. Let's cross the street now, I tell Renzi. Joyce himself opened the door; the house was a mess, it was almost without furniture, Nora was frying a kidney in the kitchen and Lucia was looking at her teeth in a mirror; they went down a very long hallway and then Joyce threw himself into a chair. It was hellish. Arno began repeating that he very much admired his work, that the technique of the epiphanies was the first advance in short story technique since Chehov, that sort of thing, and then at some point he said that he thought that Stephen Dedalus was a character of the stature of Hamlet. Of the stature of whom? Joyce interrupted him. What do you mean by that? Hamlet was probably short and fat, he tells him, just as all Englishmen were short and fat in the sixteenth century, Joyce told him. Stephen however was five nine, Joyce told him. No, said Arno, I mean a character of the level of Hamlet; he was a sort of modern Hamlet. That's true, says Renzi. He is a sort of Jesuit Hamlet. And it's also true, Renzi tells me, that there is like a continuity: the young esthete—right?—who does nothing but live in a kind of dream world and who instead of writing spends his time expounding his theories, says Renzi. I see like a line, he says, let's say: Hamlet—Stephen Dedalus—Quentin Compson. Quentin Compson, Renzi explains, the Faulkner character. Well, I tell him, Arno said all of this and I suppose some other things besides and Joyce didn't say a word. He looked at him and from time to time he rubbed his face with his soft hand, like this. This is the boulevard, I tell him, now we pass by the square and we'll reach the hotel. And then? Renzi asked. Then Arno began to ask him more direct questions, I mean questions that required answers. For example: Do you like Swift? What do you think of Sterne? Have you read Freud? That sort of thing, and Joyce answered yes or no and other than that kept quiet. I remember an exchange, I think it is one of the few exchanges they had in the whole conversation. What do you think of Gertrude Stein, Mr. Joyce? Arno asks him. Who? says Joyce. Gertrude Stein, the American writer, do you know her work? Arno asks, and Joyce sat completely still for an endless moment until he finally says:

Who would think of naming anyone Gertrude? he said. In Ireland that's a name we give to cows, Joyce tells him, and then he sat completely mute for the next fifteen minutes, at which point the interview ended. He didn't care at all about the world, says Renzi, Joyce didn't. He didn't care at all about the world or his surroundings. And when you get right down to it he was right. Do you like his work? I ask. The work of Joyce? I don't think there's another writer in this century that can be named in the same breath, he tells me. Well, I say, don't you think he's a little too—how should I put it?—a little too realistic? Realistic? says Renzi. Realistic? Without a doubt. But what is realism? he said. A representation based on an interpretation of reality, that is realism, said Renzi. In essence, he said later, Joyce set himself a single problem: How to narrate real events. What events? I ask. Real events, Renzi tells me. Oh, I say, I understood moral events. Well, I say, over there is the hotel. And how do you say "butterfly" in Polish? Renzi asks me, but before I forget, where can I buy some cigarettes? Here, I tell him, at this bar. Or I can give you some, I say. No, I'd rather buy some, he says.

I'm here killing time with old Troy, just around the corner, says a fellow who is standing at the bar. I'm standing there peaceful as can be, González here will bear me out; there I am, along with old Troy and Gonzalito, the three of us; Troy says to me, old Troy goes and says to me, look Cholo, he said, look who's coming. Let's say I'm standing here, as if this were the corner, this glass is me, here is old Troy, right Gonzalito? Right, says Gonzalito. Look, Cholo, says Troy to me, look who's coming, said the guy who was standing at the bar. Cigarettes, said Renzi. I almost fall flat on my ass, I look over toward the garage and see Goñi there, coming over, dressed like a prince. Gonzalito, isn't that so? Right, says Gonzalito. I always say that in this world the sobs and the crazy people are loose, says the guy standing at the bar. I always say it, he says, but when I see Goñi I almost fall flat on my ass. Cholo, said Troy to me, don't do anything stupid, he says, don't be a fool. But do you see him or not, I say to him, that madman, do you see him or not, I say. I see him, he tells me. The Sad Guy, free as a bird, you see him; but, I say, I say to Troy, is everything upside down and backward? Take it easy, Cholo, Troy says to me. But no, old man, I say to him, what's this about taking it easy and all that shit, it can't be, look, look, I say. I'm looking, Troy says to me. Do you see him? all decked out? Something's wrong, I say to Troy, there's something here that's gone fucking wrong. Or have you guys forgotten that Sad Guy Goñi killed his five brothers one after another? He killed all five of them one after another with an upholsterer's needle; it turned out that he finished them off one by one, all five of them, while they were lying there bleeding, with a blow of the needle, bam, the Sad Guy, like someone making an incision, here, on the neck, right here, bam, on the trachea, here—see?— on the gullet, touch your throat there, González, see how there's like a little hole? says the guy standing at the bar. A pack of Colorado Shorts, says Renzi. See how there's like a little hole? says the guy. Right, says González. You make an incision there and so long, if I've seen you before I don't remember, your life is over in a moment. And that degenerate, that runt Goñi, dressed from head to toe in white, his little eyes here over his nose, dressed like a prince, I see him, I can't believe it. Look, but look here, I say to Troy. Calm down, Cholo, the old man says to me. Keep it cool, he says to me when he sees that my blood pressure is rising. But how? He finished them all off at once, bam, with an upholsterer's needle while they were just lying there asleep, all of his brothers—but I say, what sort of a country are we living in?— one after another, in the trachea, God only knows how screwed up the guy was but thanks to that the youngest brother survived, did you know that the youngest one survived, González? asked the guy. No, says González. Think how far gone he must have been that he sent the youngest one to the bus terminal to buy him a ticket to Baradero. He said to him, he says: Go and buy me a ticket to Baradero. One way, he tells him. To Baradero, think about it. And you know why? Because he thought that Baradero was outside of the range of the federal police and that he could stay there until the danger passed. And then what happens? says the guy standing at the counter. Little Goñi, the youngest brother, goes running out, runs straight to the police, comes out with it, because they can tell right away that something screwy has happened, the boy, they can tell he's no retard, I tell you, he was seven or eight years old at that point, now he works as a trucker, drives the route Santa Fe—Resistencia, Chaco—Santa Fe, right, Gonzalito? says the guy. Right, says Gonzalito. He sees the expression of joy or something like that on the face of the Goñi boy, and right away he sees that something weird is going to happen, but when he goes back to the trenches with all the policemen it was too late. Bam, the trachea, all dead at once. The five Goñi brothers lying in the patio, all in a line, in the patio, the five of them, dead as can be, says the guy. Colorado Shorts? asks the bartender. Yes, says Renzi, one pack. A spectacle beyond all others, said the guy, only comparable to the San Quentin massacre; all five of them lying under the grape arbor, listen carefully to what I'm going to tell you, okay? each of the brothers with a little red hole in the gullet, as if they were wearing tiepins, let's say, tiepins adorned with rubies. With what? asked a guy who was sitting at a table near the door. Rubies, speaking in metaphorical terms, says the guy who is standing at the counter. A red spot on the neck, right next to this little depression, in the trachea, that's where he stuck the needle in. What a spectacle, everything's all fucked up, says the guy. His own brothers, naked, the five lying there, in the patio, naked, the five of them, because he caught them all asleep, and Goñi sitting there on a bench, with a coat and hat on, waiting for the boy to bring him the ticket to Baradero. Do you realize the enormity of it all? And what happens but today, there we are at the corner, right Gonzalito? Look, Troy says to me, and that degenerate comes walking up, walking calm as can be, all dressed up, says the guy. Here you are, says the bartender. Thanks, says Renzi. Something happened to me, I saw yellow, I swear to you by the light that shines on me, everything was yellow yellow yellow. I say to Gonzalito: Hey Gonzalito, I say, and now what do we do? Isn't that so, Gonzalito? Right, says Gonzalito. Shall we go? I say to Renzi. But look at that asshole, I say to him, did I say to you or did I not say to you that in this country if you are an SOB, but a royal SOB, nothing short of a world-class SOB, I say to him, sooner or later you end up living like a prince. That's what you said, says Troy to me. He's going to come right by here now, says the guy who's standing at the bar. Right here at this place, and what are we all going to do? I ask Troy. Yes, let's go, Renzi told me. The guy seems rather indignant, he says to me. Very, I say. Quite the match for Marconi, Renzi says to me. Careful when crossing, I tell him, the boulevard has two-way traffic. And so? Renzi says to me, how do you say "butterfly" in Polish? *Alaika*, I tell him. You say *alaika*. This is the hotel, I say to him. This is where the Professor lives.

2.

The hotel looks to have been built about 1900. It has a facade of black marble with great windows opening onto the square. This way, Tardewski says to me. First we have to go by the front desk. Do you know if Professor Maggi has returned? asks Tardewski. The receptionist says that he just started on his shift, but perhaps someone has come back, he says, because the key is not on the keyboard. Let's go up, then, says Tardewski. It's very possible that if he returned we will find him asleep here, he says; perhaps he doesn't even know that you have arrived. We knock on the door of a room on the fourth floor; because no one answers and the door is unlocked, we enter. The room is empty. It would be funny, Tardewski says to me, if he were looking for us at the club. He says that the best thing is to call on the phone and ask if he is there. The room is of generous size; from the big windows there is a good view of the river, there in the background, by the willows. There is a desk against the wall. A bed. A wardrobe. An armchair. Some books on a shelf. I go over and look at the titles while Tardewski calls the club on the phone and leaves word that if the Professor shows up there they should tell him that we are at his place. In a row on the shelf I read the titles: Irazusta's *Life of Juan Manuel de Rosas through his Correspondence*. Ignacio Weiss's *European Background of Pedro de Angelis*. Robert Lacour's *Everyday Life in the United States (1830–1860)*. Mayer's *Alberdi and His Times*. José Carlos Chiaromonte's *Nationalism and Liberalism*. Jacques Duprey's *Alexandre Dumas, Rosas and Montevideo*. Tulio Halperín's *Revolution and War*. After that I go up to the desk, which is clean, by which I mean that there is nothing on it except for an empty tin of Mazawattee tea, used to hold pencils, a red felt-tip marker, a ruler, an eraser, a metal clasp; on one side of the table there is a note pad with the following written on it—"Call Angela (Monday)"—and after that something written in pencil and then crossed out with the red marker. I could only make out clearly the word "seminar" and after that another one, almost illegible, that might be "project" or "process" or perhaps "protector." At the center of the sheet there are various triangles, circles, and other geometric figures drawn in pencil, and an account, or at least a series of numbers, lined up in a column, along the left side of the paper:

6750

12800

17300

8970

22500

I open one of the drawers in the desk. Actually the Professor always worked at the library, Tardewski tells me. At the library or in the provincial archives. In the drawer there are various newspaper clippings, especially news from *La Prensa* and the *Buenos Aires Herald* of about five weeks ago, held together by paper clips, and a box of liver pills (Novo-Prohepat) and various rolls of aspirin and a bus ticket from Paraná to Santa Fe, on the Condor line, from last month. We should go, Tardewski says to me, let's go to my house. I open the other drawer: there is a framed photograph. It is a picture of Marcelo as a young man, sitting in a sidewalk café on the Ramblas in Mar del Plata, beside a woman who must be Coca. Whatever you want, I tell Tardewski. I left word at the club that we would be at my house and we can leave a note in case he shows up here, he says. There's just one picture in the room, on the left wall. Actually it's not a picture, just the cover of a magazine, cut out and pasted onto a piece of white cardboard, showing a huge crowd at a scene that, I am almost sure, must be the funeral of Hipólito Yrigoyen. I go up to the wardrobe; in the mirror I can see Tardewski sitting at the desk, with a pencil from the box of Mazawattee tea; he has ripped the first sheet from the notepad and has started writing. I can't see what he has done with the first sheet from the notepad. Perhaps he has tossed it somewhere, though the floor is clean. The wardrobe is also empty, except for a white summer suit on a hanger and some very worn-out sandals on one of the lower shelves. Well, says Tardewski, we can go. "Professor Maggi," Tardewski has written. "Your nephew Emilio and I have been waiting for you. It's 12:30 at night. We will be at my house until it's time for the morning train to Buenos Aires. We'll be waiting for you. Volodia." Let's leave the note here, he cannot fail to see it, he says.

We go downstairs and leave word at the front desk also that if Professor Maggi returns, no matter how late it may be, that they should let him know that we are waiting for him at Tardewski's house. The night receptionist looks at us with an expression of surprise and then nods, but does not write anything down. He only says: that's fine, sir, and repeats to us that his shift ends at six in the morning. He seemed not to have understood very well, I tell Tardewski. Half-asleep, the poor fellow, says Tardewski.

We cross the square again and follow the boulevard along the river. Tardewski talks to me about the hydroelectric project at Salto Grande; he says that a lot of people who live along the river are being moved out. All that part over there, he says, pointing at a corner of the river, is going to be wiped away by the reservoir. In any case for me nature no longer exists, he tells me now, and begins to expound to me his theory on the artificial character of what we call nature, though in fact Marcelo has already told me about that in one of his letters.

When I arrived here, in 1945, he is telling me, all of this was a wasteland. He had been living for several years in Buenos Aires, he said, after arriving from Europe; he was working at the Polish Bank and then they transferred him to the Concordia branch, which had just been inaugurated. As we approached his house he told me a little about his life. He had been born in Warsaw, but at 23, he said, he went to England to work on a doctorate in philosophy at Cambridge, under the direction of Wittgenstein. The war found him in Warsaw, he said, where he had gone to spend his summer vacation. I managed to escape in the midst of the total collapse of the Polish army, and after crossing half of Europe, we embarked in Marseilles in the last ship that crossed the ocean before the submarine war interrupted the traffic. In his youth, he said, he had never imagined that he would spend forty years of his life in this corner of the world. At times, he said, he started thinking about what his life would have been like had he stayed in Europe or had he returned after the end of the war. Perhaps he would have died in a concentration camp, or perhaps, he said, or perhaps he would have continued in London without having the idea of going to spend the summer in Warsaw in August 1939, no less, and had he survived the bombing raids, perhaps, in that case, he said, I might have finished my doctorate and now I would be a professor of philosophy at some

British or North American university. More than once, he said, he had reflected on his life, on the role that chance had played in his destiny. We were talking about that as we walked along the river, the length of the boulevard, and I could see, in the distance, the twinkling lights of the Uruguayan shore. In one sense, Tardewski told me, you might say that I am a failure. And yet, when I think of my youth, I am sure that in fact that was what I was looking for. At that time, while I studied at Cambridge, he said, I drank a lot. Let's say, he said, that I drank more than I do now. I got drunk at least twice a week, and when I got home all plastered I would read Pascal's *Pensées,* the book I always read when I got drunk. He said that in a conscious and clandestine way he contrasted his drunken readings of Pascal with the luminous teaching of Wittgenstein. He saw in that fragmentary book, composed of drafts and ideas jotted down before they had been thought out completely, the greatest monument that intelligence had constructed in honor of its own failure.

In his personal case, he said that he saw with clarity that his fascination with failure was something that went all the way back to his youth, to his years in Warsaw, prior, of course, to his drunken readings of Pascal's *Pensées* in Cambridge. He identified with what are usually called failures, he said. But what, he asked, is a failure? Perhaps a man with less than all the talents imaginable, but talented, more talented than many successful men. He has those gifts, he said, but he does not make use of them. He wastes them. So, he said, in essence he wastes his life. He was fascinated by all of those failures who wander around, especially on the fringes of the intellectual world, always with projects and books they mean to write, he said. There are many, he said, all over the place, but some of them are very interesting people, especially when they get older and know themselves well. I would search them out, he said, when I was young, as one seeks out the wise. There was a fellow, for instance, that I used to see often. In Poland. This man had made a career of being a student at the university, without ever being able to make up his mind to take the exams that he needed to finish his degree. In fact he had left the university just before getting a degree in mathematics and had then left his fiancée waiting for him at the altar on their wedding day. He saw no particular merit in finishing anything. One night, Tardewski tells me, we were together and they introduce to us a woman that I like, that I like a lot. When he observes this he says to me: Ah, but how is it possible? haven't you noticed her right ear? Her right ear? I answered him: You're crazy, I don't care. But then, take note, he told me, Tardewski. Take note. Look. At last I managed to look at what she had behind her ear. She had a horrible wart, or a wart anyway. Everything ended. A wart. Do you see? The guy was a devil. His function was to sabotage everyone else's enthusiasm. He had a deep knowledge of human beings. Tardewski said that in his youth he had been very interested in people like that, in people, he said, that always saw more than they needed to. That's what was at issue, he said, at bottom: a particular way of seeing. There was a Russian term, you must know it, he tells me, as I understand you are interested in the formalists: the term, in any case, is *ostranenie*. Yes, I tell him, it interests me, of course; I think that's where Brecht got the idea of distancing. I never thought of that, Tardewski tells me. Brecht knew a lot about the theory of the Russian formalists and the whole experience of the Russian avant-garde in the twenties, I tell him, through Sergei Tretiakov, a really notable guy; he was the one who invented the theory of *literatura fakta*, which has since circulated so widely, that literature should work with raw documents, with textual montage, with direct testimony, with the techniques of reporting. Fiction, said Tretiakov, I say to Tardewski, is the opiate of the people. He was a great friend of Brecht's and it was through him that Brecht surely found out about the concept of *ostranenie*. Interesting, said Tardewski. But returning to what I was saying, that form of looking that I would call *ostranenie:* to be always outside, at some distance, in some other place, and thus to be able to see reality beyond the veil of custom and habit. Paradoxically the tourist's vision is like that, but so too, ultimately, is the philosopher's vision. I mean, he said, that philosophy is definitely nothing other than that. It is constituted in that way, at least since Socrates. "What is this?" Right? Socrates' question. A failure, not all of them, a certain class of failures, sees everything, continually, with that sort of vision. That aberrant lucidity, of course, makes them sink deeper into failure. I was very interested in people like that, in my youth. They had a devilish enchantment for me. I was convinced that those individuals were the ones who exercised, he said, the true function of knowing, which is always destructive. But here we are at my house, Tardewski says now, going up to open the front gate.

The house was low and white, of a single story, and made me think, I didn't know why, of an aviary. We crossed a very well kept garden and Tardewski took a moment before he was able to open the front door. Come in please, he said. We can sit here, he said, and pointed to some armchairs arranged face to face in the middle of an almost empty room. I have a bit of white wine, I think, in the ice box.

Tardewski left the room and I was left alone. Apart from the armchairs and a low octagonal coffee table, painted black, there was no other furniture in the room, except for a sort of chest with several drawers and a double door. On the wall facing me, held up with thumbtacks, there was an enlarged photograph of someone who looked vaguely familiar to me, but whose face I was not able to identify.

I live alone here, said Tardewski, as we arrange the glasses and the bottle of wine. A woman comes every day and takes care of the house. She is named Elvira; she has been with me for some years, and yet I know absolutely nothing of her life. Only that her name is Elvira and that she lives on the outskirts. The Professor was very fond of her, said Tardewski. He corrected himself at once: he had really meant to say that the Professor is very fond of her. Some times, he said, it suffices for someone to be away for a few hours for us to speak of him as if he were dead. The opposite of what happens in dreams.

Afterward he said that while he was in the kitchen he had thought about my conversation with Marconi. Right away, he said, he had remembered a conversation that he, Tardewski, had had with Marconi some time ago. In that conversation Marconi had told him of an extraordinary event having to do with a woman. That chat they had had some time ago at the club, he said, had begun with certain comments by Marconi on women.

Marconi was, he said, as he had already told me, a sort of local character. The local character of the Poet. His poems, perhaps not those he dreams, but certainly the few that he writes or at least the few that he publishes, I will confess to you, he said, are not at all bad. They are of a cultivated difficulty, of an almost maniacal obscurity. That time, as I was telling you, Tardewski says to me as he serves me some wine, we were talking with Marconi about a certain peculiarity of women, or rather, of a certain peculiarity in the relations that women established with him, with Marconi. I attract the very young ones, the adolescents of fifteen or sixteen, or the old ones, but the very very old ones, Marconi was telling me, Tardewski tells me. He receives a lot of correspondence at the newspaper where he works and where from time to time he publishes his sonnets. I receive, Marconi told me, at least two or three letters a week, written to me by the most varied women. Some of those letters are remarkable; they are of all sorts, Marconi told me, Tardewski tells me, as you might imagine: girls who are attracted by poetry and who write silly sentimental letters; ladies who write me in secret to confess that they have always been interested in literature but that marriage, children, and the duties of domestic life have drawn them away from what they understand to be their true vocations. Many of them write to me to tell me that sort of thing. But there is another kind of letter that is really remarkable, for instance, obscene letters, Marconi told me. I usually receive letters of a terrifying obscenity from women who write to me at the paper without identifying themselves. Almost never am I the object of those letters; it's not that they are thinking of me as they write. I am simply the recipient. They tell me of adventures with their present lovers or recall their past sexual exploits. Some are letters with fantasies of a fascinating perversity, accompanied, at times, by atrocious drawings, anatomical descriptions to make precise the character of their fantasies or of their erotic experiences. Isn't it remarkable? Marconi told me that night in the club, Tardewski recounts. Isn't it remarkable that they choose me, the poet, as the recipient of those letters? In general they do not expect any reply; they simply sit down and write, he told me, Tardewski says. Marconi finally said that he received a great deal of correspondence and that sometimes the same woman would write to him for months. For reasons of principle, he said, I never answer, and never include in my sonnets the slightest allusion, no matter how obscure or oblique it may be, to the content of the correspondence I receive. And yet, Tardewski said that Marconi had told him, some of those letters are so extraordinary that I can say, he told me, Tardewski says, that in them I find not only the primary material, but also the deepest inspiration for all of my poetry. For some time, Marconi told me, I began receiving exceptional letters from a woman. This was not a case of pornographic letters or of letters so silly that one might, as sometimes happens with me, consider them exceptional. The letters I started receiving were exceptional in another sense. In every sense they were exceptional, I would say, Tardewski said that Marconi had told him. They were letters of such literary quality that if it were not for an occasional comic word, I would say, Marconi told me, they seemed written by a writer of a talent that was absolutely out of the ordinary. For one thing, they were written in a slightly archaic Spanish, almost like Quevedo, I would say; they were written in a Spanish so pure and crystalline that on reading them, what I had written seemed unbearably coarse and unexpectedly clumsy. The very idea of comparing those letters with my own writing left me completely paralyzed. Besides, in those letters the woman did not write about herself, but instead told strange stories, tales that had the texture and the impersonal density of parables. At the end of the letter, the woman added a sentence that was, in truth, I thought, said Marconi, the only part of what she had written that was directed to me personally. At the end of the letter, the woman always wrote: "Yours." After that, she would sign with her full name, which I will not reveal, Tardewski said that Marconi had told him that night at the club, and beneath her name she put her post office box and a telephone number. The ending of the letters, then, was always the same, but the letters were always different and always perfect, said Marconi, the closest thing to literary perfection that I had seen in years and years. After three months I finally decided to answer her, Marconi said, Tardewski said. I answered. I told her that I had no intention of seeing her and that for that reason the telephone number was useless; I told her that I did not intend to answer her either and that I had only written to her that one time to tell her that her letters seemed like a senseless waste of energy because what she wrote, those stupid parables, were nothing but the worst kind of literature. Yours truly: Bartolomé Marconi. Two weeks passed without her writing me, Marconi said, Tardewski said; then she resumed. Her letters had not changed; I mean that she did not condescend to discuss my opinions and that besides she kept on writing me the same strange and extraordinarily beautiful stories as ever, in that hypnotic Spanish that was hers alone, that had the purity of a crystal and the flexible elegance of the cats in the Baudelaire sonnet. One afternoon, Marconi said, Tardewski said, I was listening to music. I like Beethoven's quartets very much, and he added, Tardewski said, Marconi added that of course that was nothing original on his part. I like those Beethoven quartets very much, Marconi said, Tardewski said, and they put me in a strange frame of mind. Every time I listen to the Beethoven quartets, Marconi repeated, by now rather drunkenly, Tardewski tells me, I think: I would give ten years of my life to be able to write something that sounded, as one read it, like those Beethoven quartets. Have you read *Doctor Faustus?* Marconi asked me, Tardewski says. No, I answered, I don't like Mann; I prefer Kafka. I have, however, Tardewski tells me he answered Marconi that night, at the club when Marconi asked him if he had read Mann's *Doctor Faustus,* I have read Adorno's essays on music so I understand you perfectly. I understand perfectly, I told him, Tardewski tells me, and so? So, Marconi answered, that afternoon I was listening to the Beethoven quartets and I thought: that's how one must write, damn it, and I was ready to sign a pact with a devil then and there. That is to say, Marconi said, that I was in a very peculiar state of mind and then I said to myself: I have to see that woman. I call her on the phone, Marconi said. I tell her: I have to see you at once. Can you come to my house? I live more than ten miles from Concordia but I can take a cab, Marconi said the woman answered, said Tardewski. Come right away, Marconi tells her. Yes, the woman said. I changed my clothes, put on a suit and tie, Marconi said. I was in such a strange state of mind that I had to see *that* woman and no one else in the world, for her to say: you are the greatest, the best, there is no other poet like you. The moments of weakness that one has, said Marconi. Moments of weakness in every sense of the word. I paced back and forth across the room, waiting. An hour later the bell rang. I open it and as soon as I do so, Tardewski says that Marconi told him that night at the club, I start laughing or coughing like an idiot. I had a glass of something in my hand, a glass of gin or geneva or whiskey, some alcoholic drink I was drinking with ice; when I coughed the glass trembled and the ice made a noise that I could not but listen to as I thought: this is the noise that ice makes as it bangs against the walls of a glass. She was an incredibly ugly woman, of a fascinating, almost perverse, ugliness. I put the glass down on a table. I invited her in. We sat down. She stayed for four hours. I will never be able to forget her. It was totally extraordinary. She told me everything that she had not told in her letters, I mean, she spoke to me of her life. Situations, moments in her life, her adolescence; she was a monster but had a very refined, subtle intelligence, and that strange and very beautiful way of handling Spanish, a bit archaic or Latinized. The woman lived with her sister in a house on the outskirts and made a living embroidering tablecloths. She had started writing because she liked the sonnets that Marconi wrote, he said, although she noted in them an excessive desire to surprise by means of technical skill. As for her, she had always had a passion for literature, but she felt incapable of devoting herself seriously to writing because, the woman said, Marconi said, Tardewski says: What can writers base their works on other than their own lives? What, other than their own lives, she said. And her life, she said, was every bit as abominable as her body, and that was why it was impossible for her to devote herself to literature, because for her to write it would be necessary to forget the very thing that should be the theme of her work. She had written those letters, she said, because sometimes at night she couldn't stand it any more. Sometimes, at night, she couldn't stand it any more, and writing those letters made her feel better, allowed her to forget herself and her life for a while. But he, Marconi, had been right when he told her that they were lousy as literature. She had half expected it, she said; she knew that they were poor as literature because literature can only be based on the story of a life. One writes, said the woman, and the words are one's body: since I want to erase my body in what I write I will never be able to construct anything other than empty words, bloodless, hollow words, made of air. That, but expressed in a much more beautiful and enigmatic way, was what the woman told him, Marconi said, Tardewski tells me. And then I, said Marconi, who knew perfectly well that the woman was completely mistaken in her absurd theory about literature being made of one's own life, who knew besides that the woman was totally mistaken because I had read what she was capable of writing, then I, Tardewski told me that Marconi had told him that night at the club, I told her that she was right, that she had not been born for literature, that her letters were, despite her effort to forget herself as she wrote them, as formless as her body. I advised her, Marconi said, Tardewski tells me, that she put all of her energy into the embroidering of tablecloths or some other impersonal art like that. I told her what of course my whole fucking life I had believed, I told her that she was right, that literature was always autobiographical, and that she ought to forget once and for all about that temptation. Do you see, Tardewski? Marconi asked me. With a coldness that surprised even me, I convinced her that it was senseless for her to suspect that she might have even the slightest possibility of devoting herself to literature. And I did it in a state of strange exaltation, helped no doubt by the atmosphere that the Beethoven quartets had created in me, feeling at once at my very core a sordid kind of fear, Marconi said, says Tardewski. The sordid fear that the woman might not believe me. Because if she should not be convinced, I thought, and that woman, that monster, should decide to publish anything that she writes, I am the one who will have to abandon writing forever. If that woman kept on writing, nobody, at present or at any moment in the future, would ever remember that a poet had ever existed by the name of Bartolomé Marconi. That's what I was thinking, and I was carried along by my very baseness, Tardewski tells me that Marconi told him. And the woman thanked me for having been sincere, although she had, she said, always known that in her heart, and had even told herself all of that in practically the same words that he had used now. One can only write on one's own body, the woman told me, Tardewski tells me that Marconi had told him. One can only write on one's own body, to record the books on the flesh of one's body, but my body, she said, is so abominable and I hate it more than anyone has ever hated anything in this world. Nobody can know, the woman said, what sort of hatred I have for my body. Nobody, she said, can know what I know, to know what it is to feel disgust at oneself. How could she then, she said, write about her life? And for that reason, once again, I am condemned, the woman said; because then what I write cannot be anything more than stories woven on the poor fabric of forgetfulness. False stories that have no flesh, because literature cannot have any substance other than one's own lived experience. False, fraudulent, artificial stories, in which sincerity and truth are like the hollow rings of wood on which I embroider my tablecloths. Frayed fantasies that you, sir, said the woman, have had the courage and the concern to define for what they are. That is what the woman said, in a different way and with better words, and then she got up with difficulty and I accompanied her to the door, Tardewski tells me that Marconi told him that night at the club. I walked behind her and watched her walk: she moved with a pathetic swaying motion, as if crossing the air cost her the same effort that it could cost one of us to walk in a river, with the water up to the level of the groin. I followed her to the door; we said goodbye; and I have never heard anything about that woman again, Tardewski said that Marconi had told him, that night, at the club.

After that Tardewski spoke once again of that destructive quality, of that strange lucidity that one acquires when one has succeeded in failing sufficiently. Because another of the virtues of failure, he said, is that it teaches us that nobody ever leaves the slightest trace in the world. Everything that we have lived is erased, and that, perhaps, he said, is what that woman had understood in Marconi's tale.

Would you like some more wine? Tardewski said then, and a bit later he began to take up the story of his life again. If I have spoken to you about all of that, he said, it's because I am of course also a failure. I mean a failure in the fullest sense of the word, that is, he said, someone who has wasted his life, who has thrown away the chances he had. I was, he said, what is usually called a brilliant young man, a promise, someone before whom all possibilities are open.

I have, he said, been *marked* by Wittgenstein. I should tell you that he was not what is usually termed a charitable man, but I would not hesitate to call him a genius, or the closest thing to a genius that one can imagine. For one thing, Tardewski says, he is the only philosopher in history who has elaborated two totally different philosophical systems in one lifetime, each of which dominated at least one generation and produced two currents of thought, each with its commentators and disciples totally opposed to each other. To try to get to know Wittgenstein, Bertrand Russell wrote, who for a semester had him among his students because Wittgenstein, after reading the *Principia Mathematica*, abandoned his career as an engineer and went to Cambridge and signed up in one of Russell's seminars. To try to get to know him, Russell said, was the most exciting intellectual adventure of my life. Wittgenstein was a man of genius, if such a thing exists, but in his life he was extremely unhappy and he lived tormented until his death. Tormented by his ideas, not by anything else; tormented because he wanted to think clearly and because he had enormous difficulties in writing. In fact he published only one book in his lifetime, the *Tratatus Logico-Philosophicus*, in 1922, which he finished, besides, when he was 29. Few works in the history of philosophy had the effects that that sixty-page book had. Wittgenstein was convinced, and that was why he wrote in the preface, with a kind of outrageous humility, that his book finally resolved in all essential respects the problems that philosophers had addressed since Parmenides. That being the case, he indicated, there was no reason to keep on doing philosophy. He therefore bid it farewell, to devote himself, he said, Tardewski tells me, to other activities, among them algebra. Nonetheless, shortly thereafter, two or three years later, he began to have the sinking feeling that the *Tractatus* was a fraud. A tragic situation, if such exist, said Tardewski. Tragic, above all, because he was the only one who realized where the error was in his book. So he returned to Cambridge to say so and began to do philosophy again or, as he said, if not to do philosophy then at least to teach philosophy. While his book made his influence ever greater, while his ideas were decisively influencing the Viennese Circle and in general all of the later developments of logical positivism, Wittgenstein felt more and more empty and dissatisfied. He viewed his own philosophy, he once said in class, the way Husserl had said that psychoanalysis should be viewed: as a sickness that confuses itself with its cure. That was what Husserl said about psychoanalysis, Wittgenstein said that time in class, and that is what I think of my own philosophy, expounded in the *Tractatus*. That is what Ludwig Wittgenstein would say about himself and about his ideas to his students at Cambridge in 1936, Tardewski tells me, which should at the very least be considered an example of what some people call intellectual courage and fidelity to the truth. He was the most like what I imagine Socrates must have been like, only he was much more ruthless. More ruthless and more gloomy than Socrates, or at least than what Plato has made us believe Socrates was like. He of course had enormous prestige and international success, but he was desperate because it infuriated him to think that he might not reach the truth. He was that sort of person, and he spent all the rest of the years of his life, until his death in 1951, in a state of exasperating emptiness, arduously erecting another philosophical system on the ruins of the philosophy that he himself had taken it on himself to destroy. Only after his death did his *Philosophical Investigations* appear, an impressive unfinished book, put together from the scattered notes he wrote during the years he rejected everything he had affirmed before, and in it he founded, as I was telling you, Tardewski says, a new philosophical system destined to influence all of modern philosophy in English. "What we cannot speak about we must pass over in silence," he wrote in the famous last sentence of the *Tractatus*, famous if we measure fame by the criterion of the number of times a sentence has been quoted.

Anyway, said Tardewski, during all of those long years in Cambridge, while he felt defeated by himself and by his own intelligence, in those years, which were the ones when I was one of his students, I would not say that Wittgenstein was a man who would reveal himself as generous or friendly. He was instead a bitter, cruel man, pedantic, cynical; a ruthless man who used his wonderful intelligence against others, with the same contempt he used it, above all, against himself and against his own ideas and convictions. And yet I cannot deny that he had a special fondness for me, that he was generous and offered me all of the possibilities that a man in his position can offer, opening the doors of a brilliant academic career to one of his favorite students. He let me know, without ever saying it, that he was offering me all of the possibilities so that my career might attain the greatest triumphs that someone can aspire to who has as his objective in life triumphing in the academic world. And now, I have thought it over many times, I now know that it was a sort of expectation, extremely elusive and subtle and not at all explicit, that he had in me, which was what led me, quite literally, I should say, to Warsaw, that summer of 1939, at the moment when all of us, even the most abstract students of philosophy at Cambridge, had the certainty that war was going to break out at the very moment and in the very place where it did indeed break out. It could be said, said Tardewski, that that apparently un-thinking act or, if you like, that random act by which I found myself trapped by the entry into Warsaw of the Nazi troops was the first conscious decision (although I could not know it at the time) that would lead me to the place where I am: living in Concordia, in the province of Entre Ríos, devoted to giving private lessons in philosophy, which means that I earn my living preparing secondary school students for an exam in philosophy or logic or however one calls the subject that Argentine young people study in a manual written by a fellow of an almost brilliant ignorance named, I think, Federico García Morente, Federico or Manolo García Morente, whom I call Spanish Ass the Second.

And all of this, for what? you will ask, Tardewski says, per-haps because of that fascination I felt in my youth for the world of the failures who circulate in intellectual worlds. He said that in his heart he felt proud to have been capable of taking the most secret illusions of his youth to their final consequences. Few men, he said, can say the same for themselves: that they have been faithful to the illusions of their youth. Many give up, he said, so the fact that I haven't given up, that I have been capable of going onward until finding myself here in Concordia, Entre Ríos, is one of my reasons to be proud, although not a soul, as the Professor would say, will ever notice.

All of this, he said, had cost him a great effort that at times seemed interminable to him. He had needed strength and an iron will. A force of will, for instance, in 1939, not to return to London but instead to find his way toward Marseilles, and there take the first ship (which also turned out to be the last one) leaving for the Americas.

And what was most remarkable, he said, was that when he embarked, he hadn't the slightest idea that the destination of that voyage was a country called Argentina. A country, he said, of which I had to take his word that he was absolutely and totally

ignorant, so much so that he did not hesitate to term his ignorance about the characteristics and the reality of a country called
Argentina, he did not hesitate, he said, to term it an *erudite*
ignorance. I knew *nothing* about Argentina, Tardewski said
emphatically, not only did I come close to not knowing that a
country of that name existed, but in addition I did not know that
that journey would take me to Argentina. I had run up the
gangplank of that ship in such a hurry, to occupy what was no
doubt the last spot available, in the middle, he said, of a series of
people who were desperately escaping from the war, without
knowing precisely, he, Tardewski, said Tardewski, where it was
going. I believe that I thought it was going to the United States;
that would have been logical, he said, given that I spoke English
well but not a word of Spanish, but at a certain moment in the
crossing I found out that we were headed for a place called
Argentina.

In any case, he said, it had not been easy to achieve the
fantastic failure of which he had dreamt in his youth. For a time,
he said, even in the midst of the general desperate situation, the
opportunities for success kept on presenting themselves to him,
and more than once, he said, the help of chance was needed for a
young man as brilliant as he was said to be to reach the very
pinnacle of failure that he had discovered, late but with absolute
conviction, as the only true form of a life that could be considered philosophical in the fullest sense.

For instance, he said, when I arrived in Buenos Aires and I
presented myself at the Polish consulate and told them that for
four years I had been the recipient of a fellowship from the
Polish government and that I had been working on my doctoral
thesis at Cambridge under the direction of Ludwig Wittgenstein (a thesis, by the way, said Tardewski, the topic of which was
"Heidegger in the pre-Socratics," which I have lost completely,
because of course I left the papers at my boardinghouse in
Cambridge, where they were destroyed, along with everything

else in my room, by a V2; that thesis, he said, of which he retained nothing except the memory of the title, from which one could infer that it was an attempt to prove, not so much the influence, for example, of Parmenides or Hippias, he said, on Heidegger, but the influence that a reading of *Being and Time* might have on our conception of the pre-Socratics, something a bit like "Kafka and His Precursors," to use an example familiar to you). The friendly and rather desperate functionaries at the Polish embassy in Buenos Aires took care of him. They found me lodging, promised, he said, to see to it that the fellowship was still paid to me, as if I were in Cambridge, for six months, while the situation in Europe cleared up, and immediately put me in touch with what we could call the philosophical circles in Buenos Aires.

These last, he said, actually consisted of a group of professors of philosophy linked to the University of Buenos Aires, although the assortment of people who surrounded these *soi disant* philosophers, said Tardewski, was varied and one could find among them all the various species and subspecies of humanistic thought. In general the fellows were fascinated by Orientalism, and there was one in particular who was a sort of bureaucrat of Zen Buddhism, named, I think, Victorio Fatoni or Valentín Fratone, something like that. But these guys, Tardewski said, referring to the philosophical circles that he began frequenting upon his arrival in Buenos Aires at the end of 1939, these guys, he said, were not only enthusiastic about Zen Buddhism: at the same time, he said, they admired and praised as the two greatest philosophers of our age (this, by the way, I mean, the expression "of our age" enchanted them and they repeated it every little while) two personages, two creatures, whom I would categorize, for the moment, as indescribable.

One of these two great philosophers of our time was, said Tardewski, the one I will call the King of the Spanish Asses, or Ass the First, José Ortiga y Gasset (I'm no good at plays on words, Tardewski said by the way; I used to be, when I could play with my mother tongue). Would you like some more wine? Tardewski asks me, it's been so long since I told of my adventures, he says, that I am getting carried away, as you can see, but you can stop me or go to sleep whenever you like; this good man devoted himself, as I was saying, to writing philosophy in a sort of crazy Germanic form of Spanish. He was what they call a Spanish lecturer, right? The foremost radio lecturer of Spain, whom all those I met when I arrived, in those circles in Buenos Aires, considered a True Master of the Thought of Our Time, a true Ace (Ass?). But besides that, I discover as soon as I disembark, with the deep reflective voice of Wittgenstein still echoing in my ears, says Tardewski, there was another Philosopher, another Thinker, also admired by all, I discover. One who was, shall we say, of the same stature as the other one: so that this Ass shared the unconditional admiration showered on the other Ass. This one, a German Ass, that is to say a proper German who was actually Swiss, I believe: none other than Count Keyserling. So that when I opened the door of the academic circles of Argentine philosophy I met up with this mixture of bureaucratic Orientalism, Spanish radio broadcasting and a count: this was the trinity on which one carried out High Speculation. It was all really what one might call a philosophical thing—right?—in truth a truly *philosophical* Thing. These circles were also frequented by various very elegant young ladies and a series of very polite and very quiet gentlemen.

Tardewski said that he did not want to be unfair. There were at that moment, he said, other philosophers in Argentina, and at least two of them were excellent, first rate. For one thing, he said, there was Rodolfo Mondolfo, who had gone into exile, fleeing from Mussolini; I had used his edition of the fragments of Heraclitus in Cambridge, but didn't have the slightest idea that he was in Argentina. And there was also Carlos Astrada, no doubt the only true philosopher that this country had produced in all of its history, who at that point was a disciple of Heidegger; he was the only one in the whole Latin world whom Heidegger considered a true disciple. People of whose existence I only learned much later, and with whom I maintained for some years a correspondence, he said, as infrequent as it was warm. (By the way, he said, somewhere around here I must have a very amusing letter from Astrada, written at the time he had broken with the school of Heidegger, at the very moment that the admirers, henchmen, and reciters of Heidegger had begun to multiply like rabbits; in this letter Astrada, apart from discussing the ever more obvious turning toward mysticism of the German philosopher, laughed at the popularity of Heidegger and the proliferation of his disciples. He recalled an anecdote about an Argentine philosopher who after having made his ritual pilgrimage to Freiburg had taken a devotional photograph of Heidegger's house, but by mistake had taken a picture of the house next door. The photograph of the wrong house was exhibited, if not with discretion then at least with respect, on one of the walls of his office at the university, with a little sign underneath on which this Argentine philosopher had written: "This is where the truth of Being lives today." Which demonstrated, to the merriment of Astrada, the philosophical exactness of the photographic error: because beyond a doubt the residence of Being is located *next door* to Heidegger's house, for which reason its walls do not allow poor Martin to see anything more than the dark ineffable essence of language, Astrada told me in that letter, Tardewski said, bringing to a close the imaginary parenthesis that he had opened when he began the digression.)

Well, he said, so I, a young Pole, a student at Cambridge, a disciple of Wittgenstein's (perhaps, they suspected, a fake one), began to frequent that circle of thinkers who carried out their activities in the official academic institutions and spread their wisdom in pathetic publications. I, the Pole, felt rather disoriented, a bit lost and discouraged. Nevertheless, Tardewski said, he had been able once again in his life to pursue the course indicated to him by the deepest and purest ideals of his youth.

I spoke with those Argentine eminences and began to hint, with a certain shy reserve, in French, to hint that that duo, Ortiga and Gasset, seemed to me, let it be said with all respect, I tell them, Tardewski says, the fullest example of the identity of contraries proposed by Hegel as one of the laws of his logic, although in this case the identity functioned in an absolute way and the contraries were absolutely spectacular, because this Spanish philosopher, despite the imaginary duplication that his surname suggested, was none other, I said to them, shyly, in my suave French, was none other than being One, that is, I said: an ass. This seemed excessive to them, fruit of the excesses of youth and of the unfortunate situation that my native land was caught in, crushed by a combination of German philosophy, Nazi tanks, and the Falangist volunteers of the Blue Division. They were confident that with the passing of time, which soothes and placates everything, and with my slow but inevitable assimilation to Argentine cultural traditions, I would eventually be tamed. It was about then, continued Tardewski, that I, like St. Anthony, had to resist another of the temptations by which life offered me prospects of success. Because they hinted that if I could only learn to be a bit more respectful of their masters and a little less irreverent with the (philosophical) authorities, and if I could obtain any document whatsoever that would confirm my relations and studies with Wittgenstein, that I might obtain what all young philosophers should never fail to desire as the prize for their metaphysical reflections, namely a university job. Temptations. Offers. As they say in French, la *securité académique*. At that moment, at the age of 29, I was fairly ignorant, that much I know, but even so I knew more philosophy than all of them combined, and I was constantly proving it to them, without even wanting to, with a pedantry that was involuntary, at least at the beginning. Besides, I shone like a sun and my brilliance consisted of the fact, second nature to me, that I could pass, in philosophical conversations or other kinds of conversations, from Greek to German to French, to German again, to Greek to English to Latin, and then back to French, something that in this country, as Professor Maggi would say, impresses even the best and the brightest.

So that had I been a bit more respectful, had I reined in my youthful excesses and taken advantage of the six months that the generosity of the Polish consul had given me by extending my grant, had I concentrated on quickly perfecting my Spanish, so as to be able to face students, I might have let myself be tempted. That's what Mondolfo did, with infinitely greater merits than I had at that moment, but at the same time without my perverse vocation for seeing failure as the truest realization of the life of a philosopher. I could have been accepted, been polite, let myself be tempted. In that case today I would be, I, Vladimir Tardewski, shall we say a full time professor (in the event, he said, of knowing how to cloister myself in the crystalline precincts of pure philosophical exegesis, without ever looking out to see what was happening in the world) of modern or contemporary or ancient or medieval philosophy or some other sorry shit like that, instead of being here, in Concordia, Entre Ríos, devoted to preparing your secondary school students to pass their March exams in the field of logic. Instead of being here, I mean, said Tardewski, transformed into a parodic version (to use a word that you are so fond of) of a *Privatdozent,* such a prestigious tradition in the history of European philosophy since Kant. But I rejected, as you can well imagine, that temptation: instead of being respectful I let myself get carried away more and more in the direction of frankness, an unpardonable crime among academics. I began to express with ever greater clarity what I really thought. I, the Pole, well treated by these gentlemen, let myself be dragged along by the blunt expression of my own thoughts.

Then, Tardewski recounted, at a select gathering of selected thinkers and people of culture, in whose hands, you could say, my future lay, I began to argue with one of these masters of Argentine thought, whose name I prefer not to recall. I began arguing, Tardewski said, always in French, having had a bit too much to drink. Or rather not to discuss or argue but to insult all of the imbeciles who could pretend or hint or even claim to glimpse the remotest possibility that an idiot of the caliber of the *soi disant* Count Keyserling might be considered someone in full possession of his senses; someone, any sensible person, not even a philosopher necessarily, for that profession supposedly implies the ability to think, to have ideas, someone, any sensible person that you should care to name, upon reading two pages of that ill-starred Count West-West, who claims to inhabit the castle of philosophy; I will go so far as to say, I said at that select gathering, that just upon seeing his face or even just a photograph, that person would realize instantly that anyone who considered that count a philosopher or a person of ideas was none other, the person who thought like that, none other I told them than an imbecile. General consternation, widespread amazement. Everyone looked at me dumbfounded. Disciple of whom? asked someone who was sitting on a stool. Of Wittgenstein, whispered someone else who was sitting on another stool. *Mon vieux, oh la la,* said the first one. Perhaps they believed that I had gone mad. Anyway, the sentence or paragraph I quoted above caused general consternation among those present. They all then were even more scandalized when I said that that Count Montecristo of philosophy (who had already been invited on numerous occasions to visit Argentine as Guest of Honor, distinguished guest, I discovered later at the Polish embassy, and in whose honor a president of the republic—Ortiz maybe?—let's say Ortiz, had once gone to meet him at the North Harbor with a military guard and band as if the one arriving were Thales of

Miletus himself. Because first of all this count not only visited the country, he was toasted and honored and spoiled, but also, with a slight flutter of his noble eyes, he began at once, as soon as he had disembarked, as soon as he had finished shaking the presidential right hand of Roberto M. Ortiz, right there, this count, there in the Northern Harbor, after taking a quick glance around, began to shoot off a rapid-fire but at the same time slow and carefully meditated metaphysical X-ray of Argentine Being, an explanation that was immediately jotted down in notebooks and pads brought there for that very purpose by the attentive thinkers who formed the reception committee who, some months later, according to what I heard, celebrated, paraphrased, and commented on the count's reflections and were thus able, with such invaluable help from abroad, to work through a national philosophical interpretation, one all their own, I mean, said Tardewski, made in Argentina, a metaphysical interpretation of Argentina and of its National Being that included the pampa as the There of the *Dasein* and the gaucho as the representative in and of himself of the invisible Argentine, that is, the rustic pampas resident as a sort of equestrian version of the Kantian *noumeno,* said Tardewski closing the parenthesis opened so long ago), when I said that Count Keyserling, that count, was a speaking puppet who couldn't even sit down on the ventriloquist's knees, they, then, those present at that gathering, were alarmed and looked at me with a certain *scorn;* with well-mannered disdainful conceit I was looked down upon from that moment by the Argentine philosophical circles. They looked on me as a nasty little Pole who was ill sounding, dissonant, insane, unhealthy, sickly, feeble, infirm, battered, maimed, resentful, harmful, noxious, pernicious, knavish, mean, annoying, dull, difficult, disagreeable, *a failure.* That's how they looked on me, how they saw me: as I really was, Tardewski said.

So that, I said, when I left that salon I had broken forever with that sector or caste of the Argentine intelligentsia that could have assured me a decorous entrance into the decorative national university world.

What was I to do then? asked Tardewski. My possibilities of triumphing in the Argentine academic circles were finished, *kaput*. But I still had *one* chance left, in reality the last one, that held out any possibility of success. And to achieve failure at this point, he said, certain events had to connect with one another once more in my life. But what time is it? Tardewski asks me. Two thirty, I tell him. Are you sleepy? he says. No, I reply, not at all. Your uncle, Tardewski told me, must be arriving at any moment. Yes, I add, he must be arriving any moment. Continue, I told him: and then?

Then, Tardewski continued recounting, I was walking around Buenos Aires by myself, in those months of the summer of 1940, alone, in exile, knowing only a few words of Spanish and thus without the slightest possibility of speaking to anyone. And as the war in Europe progressed, as the Nazi troops were flattening European culture, I felt myself being flattened, as if I were its representative. I was living among ruins, among the remains of myself; that was when I grasped at what was my last chance. I grasped at precisely the thing that had brought me where I was: during that summer of 1940, I walked along Three Sergeants Street and meditated on Hitler and the devastation of European culture, although what I was really doing was meditating on Hitler and Kafka.

For two years before, said Tardewski, he had made a discovery that could be considered, viewing it objectively, a quite extraordinary discovery. I grasped at that discovery; I expected all sorts of things from it, he said, as I had still not convinced myself that I should instead expect everything from failure.

I was wandering around the city and thinking about my discovery, he said. He realized with clarity that there he had the chance to become famous and thus, he said, to permit me to avenge myself and prove my abilities to the scornful members of the Argentine academic circles. Because I want you to know, Tardewski told me, that intellectual pride, the hope of being able to prove what one is really worth (or what one thinks one is worth) is the hardest thing to give up. Intellectual pride, you know, is the last thing one loses, even after turning into a shadow of oneself. I did not think of that only for that reason but also because some results of that discovery were the only material I had for reading and reflection during those months of the summer of 1940 in Buenos Aires. I had a six-volume set of the first edition of Kafka's *Complete Works* and a notebook with my jottings and annotations: that was all I had managed to rescue from my disaster in Europe. In truth, he said, those notes and the works of Kafka had been saved from the disaster because that was all that he had taken with him to work on in Warsaw during the vacation that was interrupted by the war. The work, he said, consisted of the first results of that extraordinary discovery he had made by chance at the British Library one afternoon in 1938.

When I made that find I plunged into a sort of feverish activity that made me divert my attention, in every sense, from my thesis and my studies. I had not known that that discovery had already started to undermine my philosophical convictions, as I will explain to you in a moment; it had simply happened that by chance I had encountered something so extraordinary that, you might say, I could not afford to give it up. My thesis could be put off for a couple of weeks. It turned out to be more than a couple of weeks: that discovery brought me here, where I am now.

1938: those were hard years; you had not been born yet but can probably imagine. Munich. The Sudetenland. German expansion. In the middle of that situation I was searching for information about Kafka, *certain* information about Kafka. I knew his texts well. In 1936, to complement a course on natural and formal language, Wittgenstein had invited the Czech critic

Oskar Vazick to give a seminar on Kafka in Cambridge. The concise and almost artificial use that Kafka made of German was of special interest to Wittgenstein, who saw in it the confirmation of some of the hypotheses that he would later develop in his *Philosophical Investigations*. Kafka handled German as if it were a dead language; his bilingual status, his belonging to a German-speaking minority in the midst of a mostly Slavic population, his displaced and somewhat alien situation with respect to the language, served, or so Vazick (a member of the recently created Prague Circle) expounded and analyzed, as a practical example of one of the theoretical problems discussed by Wittgenstein. I remember that at the beginning of the first of his four lectures Vazick said: I want to speak to you about a writer who is barely known and who will no doubt one day be seen, together with Proust and Joyce, as part of the decisive trinity of the literature of the twentieth century. All of us, Tardewski said, knew of Proust and Joyce, but Kafka? Who was this fellow with such a cacophonous name? At that time the first three volumes of the *Complete Works* had just been published and the majority of students in the seminar plunged, of course, into the reading of the author of the *Metamorphosis*. Even today, said Tardewski, I remember the impression that he produced on me, and I don't think any other writer has ever produced or could ever produce the same effect. Or so at least I hope.

So it was not a better knowledge of the texts of Kafka that I was seeking then at the end of 1938 and the beginning of 1939, but something else. Certain facts about his life that would serve to document and confirm a discovery about whose truth I had no doubts. I needed what universities call a greater certainty in the documentary proof. I really needed to confirm some facts about Kafka's life. I intended to interview Oskar Braum, Janouch, and of course, if possible, Max Brod. I decided to travel first to Prague, but the German invasion erased that possibility. For a time I thought that I would never find a way of establishing what I needed through talking to someone who had known Kafka in 1909 and 1910. Then some rumors reached me that Oskar Braum had moved from Prague to Warsaw and was living there. That was why I decided to spend my summer vacation in Warsaw in 1939. The shock of Kafka and the Nazi troops marked my life once again. When I had been in Poland only ten days, and without my being able to locate Oskar Braum (who was blind to boot), the war broke out. So that was why the only let's say intellectual material I had in my suitcase when I disembarked in Buenos Aires were some notes, the partial result of my research, and the six volumes of Kafka's *Works*. That was all I had to save myself when I broke with the philosophical circles of Buenos Aires.

So I wandered around the city and shut myself into my room at the Three Sergeants Hotel to work on what I considered (quite rightly, as you shall see) a *great* discovery. During those months of the summer of 1940, while Hitler was leveling Europe, I decided to write an article so as to claim for myself the intellectual *property* of the idea I had about the relations between Nazism and the works of Franz Kafka. I wrote it in English and had it translated at a place on Talcahuano Street by a girl, I remember, who knew neither Polish nor English, but who knew Spanish so well that she produced what I think was an excellent translation. The cultural attaché of the Polish embassy managed to get it printed in *La Prensa* on Sunday, February 21, 1940. Poland at that point constituted the very symbol of the holocaust brought about by the Nazis, and that aided in the publication of an essay that, by the way, went totally unremarked. As I worked on the article I did not feel quite so bad, but after turning it in I began to take the measure of my real situation and the emptiness that surrounded me. The night it was published, I mean the night before, I felt so desperate that I decided to wait until dawn so as to buy the newspaper as soon as it appeared. It was very hot that night and I walked around the city at random, and ended up sitting at a bar on Avenida de Mayo waiting for the newspaper to arrive. I was desperate and at the same time full of hopes, anxious like any young writer who is waiting to see the newspaper where something he has written has been published. As you can see, I still had a lot to learn. Nevertheless I was on the verge of the fundamental experience that would permit me to understand my life in a single moment, to understand what I was really seeking and in what direction I really needed to go.

Though I didn't know it yet, less than two hours remained before I discovered all of that. In the meantime, it must have been about three in the morning, I was sitting at a table at the Tortoni, drinking coffee and smoking, thinking, I believe, about the following paradox: in a little while I would be able to see something of mine published, the first really personal writing I had published in my life, because everything else that appeared on my curriculum vitae was no more than commentaries and summaries of others' ideas, melancholy exercises of philosophical pseudo-erudition (of the sort that my thesis would have been had I finished it, to tell the truth) published in specialized journals. This was different: it was *my own* idea, the product of a personal discovery, something original that I had thought out without help. The paradox (the first paradox, in reality) was that I would not be able to read the text I published because I did not know how to read Spanish. Which could not fail to be, I thought, Tardewski tells me, a metaphor of my situation. Finally, the minutes and hours passed, the newspaper arrived, I bought a copy, and there, next to the catastrophic headlines about the advance of the Nazi troops, I could see, in the middle of the paper, in a supplement printed by rotogravure on sepia paper, *my* article, an article I couldn't read but that was mine, entitled, I think, "The Cross between Hitler and Kafka: a Working Hypothesis" by Vladimir Tardowski. A new metaphor? The other metaphor? No, there was still one more. I walked along

Avenida de Mayo toward the river, with the newspaper under my arm, and when I got to the hotel, went up to my room and went in, I found myself facing a reproduction in miniature, but real nonetheless, of Europe flattened by war. During my absence, that morning, thieves (or perhaps just one thief) had come in and had taken *everything* I had. Everything, including my notebook and my edition of the *Works* of Kafka, to say nothing, of course, of my money, clothing, and suitcase. They had even taken a photograph of my parents that I had on the night table. They were thorough thieves, shall we say.

Now, Tardewski says, I had really touched bottom. Not only was I in an unknown country, but all of my earthly possessions had been reduced to what I had on (some summer trousers, a shirt, a pair of shoes without socks, underwear, a belt, a handkerchief), not counting, of course, a copy of *La Prensa* of Sunday, February 21st, with an article by Vladimir Tardowski in the cultural section. In my pocket I had the equivalent, in Argentine pesos, of eleven dollars. I sat down on the bed while the dawn came on, I remember, and started thinking. I had reached the point of absolute dispossession to which a man can aspire: I had *nothing.* Compared to me, any Kafka character, Gregor Samsa for instance, could be considered a satisfied man. I was dispossessed, in the most perfect state of dispossession that could be imagined, sitting on a bed, in a room, in a hotel, in a city, in an unknown country, plunged into the most absolute lack. Well then, what has brought me to this point? That was one of my lines of thinking. What had brought me to this point? What things had connected to one another? I went back to the afternoon in November 1938 at the British Library, and then returned, by way of Warsaw, the war, Marseilles, the ship, Buenos Aires, etc., to that room in a hotel on Three Sergeants Street, on one of whose twin beds I was sitting (it was Sunday afternoon). The other line of thinking was pointed, shall we say, toward the future. What was I to do? A dangerous question. For the present to *think:* the only means known to me of not going crazy. To reflect. To follow one direction of logical and coherent thought. Looking back, to the British Library but also further back, for example, to my youth, with my friend the former mathematician and the beautiful young lady who had the horrible wart behind one of her beautiful ears. All of my life passed before me, as they say happens to those who are going to die. On the one hand I saw my whole life march by: scenes of my past life. On the other, I tried to imagine scenes of my future life. I looked at my room in ruins in the Three Sergeants Hotel, just as the Poles were looking at the ruins of their country. On all sides: remains, desolation. To make things worse, when I looked out the window it had started to rain. A real summer downpour.

And then? A grave situation: I am sitting on the bed, like Descartes in his armchair facing his philosophical fireplace in Holland. I think therefore I am. Fine, but I didn't have a cent. All of my other losses had a tragic sense, a—shall we say— symbolic quality: my native language, my country, my friends. But money? Without money, what was I to do, not just to think but more urgently to exist? I started thinking about that, or rather, I started thinking (second line of reflection) on *how* to do something to exist.

That Sunday I reached several conclusions that for the moment, Tardewski told me, I'll skip over, to focus on the sequence of events. It rained all of Sunday, all of Sunday night and into the next morning. The next day, that is, Monday, I presented myself once again at the Polish embassy. The storm had made the temperature fall so suddenly that I, dressed in a thin cotton shirt, trembled like a character in Dostoevsky, my teeth chattered with cold (that is what they really do, Tardewski explained to me, even though it seems improbable: the teeth make a sort of little noise like this—see?), I was frozen, gray. In any case I betook myself to the patient building of the Polish embassy in Buenos Aires; I explained my new situation; they listened to me with an ever more disapproving air. Hadn't I gone a bit too far? Hadn't I gone too far with my personal problems? Hadn't they helped me gain entrance to the distinguished philosophical circles of Buenos Aires? Hadn't they even managed to get an article, a rather wild article at that, published in *La Prensa? What* was it that I *really* wanted? A coat, I told them, a sweater: wouldn't one of you have, for instance, some sort of pullover? My teeth chattered. They looked at me with their disapproving Polish eyes. In any case they were, once more, kind to me. They did not fail to understand that I had turned into the most authentic Representative of the unfortunate situation of the Polish Fatherland. I was in a sense the ambassador of that misfortune; I wore the Polish cross on my back.

Generously they lent me a sweater, a bit too small for me but in any case a sweater, and they gave me the final two payments on my six-month grant in advance. With that money I was able to buy clothing, a suit and so forth. A week later, on March 1, 1940, I started working as a supernumerary second assistant in the Polish Bank of Buenos Aires. A world worthy of Kafka. A pittance of a salary, something around a hundred dollars a month, barely enough to live on. I had a supreme lack of talent for everything that had to do with banking and finance (I was a philosopher), so I understood nothing of all of those papers. They had given me a post in the section of European accounts due to my fluency in all of the Indo-European languages *except* Spanish. Now then, these were times of war, so there were no transactions of any sort and the European accounts section was dead as could be. The hours passed, absurd, exasperating, sterile. I bought a Spanish-English dictionary and a grammar book and devoted myself to learning Spanish. Also I got a notebook and began writing down sentences and passages from the books I was reading. I decided to write nothing that I had thought myself, nothing of my own, no ideas of my own. I had no ideas, besides; I was a sort of Polish zombie. At that point I started keeping a sort of diary of my life made up of other people's words. In the dead hours at the bank I read and noted down other people's ideas in a notebook that I had to hide in a drawer when the assistant subdirector came by, as he didn't like seeing me doing nothing but on the other hand had no work to give me to do. The first thing I did, I remember, was to copy the quotations that appeared in my article in *La Prensa*. Even now, as you can see, I maintained a sense, even if a ruined sense, of the feeling for intellectual property. I copied them into Spanish, which I did not understand, so that it was like copying hieroglyphics; I drew the letters, one by one, without understanding what I was writing, finding my place by the commas, an international sign. Wasn't that a good image of the situation of the Kafkaesque writer? Copying a text of one's own but unable to read it. Finally, to continue with Kafka, said Tardewski, some weeks later, at a used bookstore on Corrientes Street, I was able to buy back one of the volumes of my edition of the *Gesammelte Schriften* of Kafka, no doubt sold by the same person who had stolen it from me. It was the sixth volume (*Tagebücher und Briefe*). What had become of the other five volumes? Tardewski asked himself. Surely Borges bought them, I tell him. Yes, for sure, he says to me.

So I read and took notes and learned Spanish and let the time pass. I was in that situation for almost five years. Meanwhile, I continued reading with ever greater skill the newspaper accounts of the resistible rise and irresistible fall of Adolf Hitler and his hordes. Finally, in 1945, a branch of the Polish Bank opened in Concordia and they sent me here, in reality to get rid of someone as useless as I was.

I arrived in this beautiful city in Entre Ríos, Tardewski continued, in January 1945. Three months later I resigned from the bank, devoted myself to giving private lessons in languages and to playing chess for money at the Social Club. There every game is played for money, but when they saw how good I was they stopped betting and offered me a chess column in the newspaper. A column I am very proud of and that I still keep.

In Concordia I assimilated very quickly. Nobody knew anything about me. I was what I was, a failure. Along the way I had lost that natural pedantry that I had had since my time at Cambridge, that almost involuntary expression of disdain and ennui that people who are confident of the superiority of their refined intelligence and of the success that awaits them in the future exude, like an aura. I no longer was, or at least no longer believed, even to the slightest extent, that I was the brilliant young man that I had been, so it was easy for me to make friends. As far as they were concerned I was an exile who played chess very well and who (like all Europeans) knew various languages.

At the same time I had turned into a solitary person, the prototype of the loner, without a career, without any social bonds, an individual without a past and without illusions.

One night at the club, almost without realizing it, I discussed some philosophical problems with Maier and my fame as a polyglot chess player was supplemented by that of an amateur philosopher (which is what I am). That increased my professional possibilities. I stopped teaching languages and began preparing secondary school students—for as you know there is a fresh crop of such students every year, and they take examinations more frequently than the inhabitants of Entre Ríos go abroad. So I was able to improve my life in many ways.

I improved it, he said, in more than one sense because thanks to my local fame as a philosopher I was able to get on close terms with Professor Maggi. The Professor had arrived at the end of the fifties and I knew him, because here everyone knows everyone else; one night he came up to me and said that he would like to talk to me about Vico and Hegel; he explained that he needed to know about them because someone named Pedro de Angelis had been an expert on Vico and well acquainted with Hegel and that Enrique Ossorio, a sort of confused and unfortunate hero whose life he was interested in reconstructing, had taken courses with de Angelis, and that Ossorio's writings contained some philosophical references that he would like to discuss with me. That's how we started spending time together.

The Professor, said Tardewski, instantly understood my situation; he understood that what inspired a vague pity in the others had been constructed by me, arduously but also with the help of chance, throughout the entire course of my life. He understood at once and was the only one capable of being ironic about what everyone else thought was a tragedy. Not because he was like me: he had nothing of the failure about him. At least in the sense in which I am using the term. He was a man who devoted himself squarely to whatever he had before him; he never thought in terms of individual success or failure. Once he read me a sentence by Emmanuel Le Roy Ladurie, the French historian; it must be somewhere over there, Tardewski said, getting up and going over to a chest that stood at the end of the room. He took a black notebook with a rubber cover out of a drawer and came back across the room as he leafed through it. Then he put on a pair of wire-rimmed round glasses and began reading. The ability to think about the achievements of one's personal life in historical terms, Tardewski reads the sentence from Ladurie noted down in his quotation notebook, was as natural among the people who participated in the French Revolution as it is natural for our contemporaries when they reach the age of forty to meditate on their lives as examples of the frustrated hopes of their youth. Marcelo said that that sentence condensed for him, he said, as he took off his glasses and put the notebook back in the drawer, what he called, without a trace of irony, historical vision. He laughed at me and said that my theory of the failed man as the modern incarnation of the philosopher was nothing but a rationalization. A man always fails by himself, said Maggi, Tardewski says. The only thing that matters, he said, is to ask oneself what use is this individual failure, or what benefits can be had from it. Of course you cannot understand a question posed in terms of historical usefulness, he said. You know little about history, the Professor would say to me, Tardewski tells me; excuse me for saying it. You have let yourself get carried away by your personal utopia. That lucidity you seek in solitude, in failure, in the cutting off of any social bond, is a false private version of the utopia of Robinson Crusoe. There is no lucidity there, the Professor would say; there is no way of being lucid other than thinking in terms of history. For the Professor it was obvious that only history makes possible that *ostranenie* of which we were speaking earlier. How could we bear the present, the horror of the present, the Professor said to me the last night we talked, if we didn't know that it was no more than a historical present? I mean, he told me that night, that it is only because we see what it will become and how it will change that we can stand the present. That was always what we could call his line of thinking. We were antagonists and yet united. I, the skeptic, the man who lives outside of history; he, the man of principles, who thinks only in terms of history. The unity of opposites.

That was why, Tardewski said, he had chosen Maggi to tell him what he had understood that Sunday in his room in the hotel on Three Sergeants Street. Dispossessed and alone in the midst of that disaster, I told the Professor, I suddenly saw the meaning of what had happened to me. Sitting on the bed, while it rained outside, I started thinking, I tell the Professor. Everything appeared to me with extreme clarity. What had brought me to this place? I found myself in a state of absolute dispossession, in exile, with my country erased from the map, without money, without my native language, without a future, without friends, without clothes to put on the next day, and well—for what? To understand I had only to turn my head a little to see what I had next to me (a copy of *La Prensa*). That was it, I told the Professor. Because in that newspaper there was an article written by me that I couldn't read, written by a Pole named Tard*o*wski, in which I had wanted to set down a thesis, record the discovery as they say one records a deed. In that paper I preserved one of my last pieces of ballast, that is, the old ballast of my academic life. Because I had really written that article to establish that I was the first to have had that idea or to have made the discovery that I had made. That is to say that in the hypothetical case that someone else were to have the same idea, I would be able to show that I had had it first, by which means the other's idea would be transformed into my idea, that is, an idea of mine later repeated by the other. The theft, as you have realized, happened somewhere else. To defend myself from some future thief, etc. What had I done in that article? I let people know that I planned to write a book based on that personal discovery. I noted down the central hypothesis; I indicated that the events in Europe and my forced exile prevented me, for the moment, from finishing my research, completing the documentary material, and so forth, *but* that in any case the idea was there and was mine. It was ridiculous, once you thought about it. To publish an article translated from English in *La Prensa* and thereby to assure myself of my holding the intellectual property of a yet unwritten book—and to receive in reply a real robbery. Wasn't that a lesson? I had acted like a ridiculous academic. An academic without an academy; a university student without a university; a Pole without Poland; a writer without a language. *But* it was difficult to cast out the instinct of property. There are few ideas in the universities (there are few ideas anywhere—Wittgenstein had two in his whole life) but everybody thinks that *what they are thinking* is an idea. Few ideas, extremely few original hypotheses, fine gold: theft is the ghost that stalks European universities (and not just European ones). Now then, to say it all at once: that idea, that discovery that had cost me (in every sense) so much—was it mine? It wasn't mine because I had found it by chance, thanks to the accidental crossing of two events or facts. Everything really depended on an error in the catalog of the British Library. You and I, Tardewski, the Professor would say to me, cross paths, in a figurative sense, at the British Library. You are coming from the British Library and I am going to the British Library. I understood perfectly what he was trying to tell me, Tardewski says to me. I was coming from there, from reading, by accident, something that pulled me away from philosophy and from Cambridge and carried me to Warsaw and then to Marseilles and then to a room at the Three Sergeants Hotel and then here, to Concordia, Entre Ríos. The Professor for his part was ever more interested in the philosopher who had spent years working in a room in the British Library. He was on his way there. I was coming from there. A metaphorical crossing of paths. To understand better, perhaps it would be helpful if I explained, Tardewski said, what it meant to say that I was coming from the British Library, or in what sense I was coming from there, or, if you prefer, what it was I discovered that afternoon in 1938.

I had gone the same as every other day to the library to study some books I needed to use for my thesis. I had gone to consult a volume of the writings of the Greek sophist Hippias and, when I requested the book, due to an error in the classification of the entries, instead of the volume by the Greek philosopher they delivered an annotated edition of Adolf Hitler's *Mein Kampf.* I must confess, Tardewski continued, that I had never read that book; it would never have occurred to me, in any case, to read it, had it not been for the error that upset and amazed the reference librarian there at the British Library and that also amazed and upset me, but for a period of many years.

That confusion in the order of a catalog, which occurred in 1938, was what made it possible, among other things, for you and me to be here conversing; at least it made it possible for me to come to Concordia, to get acquainted with Professor Maggi and so forth. But let's not get ahead of ourselves, he said. There's still a little wine left, he says to me. Do you want some? Fine, I tell him.

Tardewski said that it had never occurred to him to read Hitler's book and that beyond a doubt he would never have come across that edition, annotated by a German historian of firm antifascist convictions, had it not been for that chance. He said that that afternoon he had thought: since chance (perhaps for the first time in history, as the trembling reference librarian asserted) had found its way into the cards that began with HI in the British Library, since chance, he said, or some hidden Nazi, which in this case would be the same thing, had confused the cards in that way, he, Tardewski, who was superstitious besides (like a good logical positivist), believed he perceived in that event what in fact had really happened, that is, he said, a call, a sign from fate. Even if I did not see it with clarity, I obeyed all the same, using the argument that I could put aside for one afternoon the reading of the Greek Sophists and take a rest from the arduous development of my thesis. In any case, said Tardewski, I spent that afternoon and part of that evening at the British Library reading the strange and delirious autobiographical monologue that Hitler had written, or rather had dictated, in Landsberg Castle, in 1924, while he suffered (as they say) a sentence of six months of obliging prison. The first thing I thought, what I understood right away, was that *Mein Kampf* was a sort of perfect complement or apocryphal sequel to the *Discourse on Method.* It was a *Discourse on Method* written not so much (or not exclusively) by a madman and a megalomaniac (for Descartes was also a bit of a madman and a megalomaniac) but by an individual who uses reason, supports his ideas, erects an ironclad system of ideas, on a hypothesis that is the perfect (and logical) inversion of the starting point of René Descartes. That is, said Tardewski, the hypothesis that doubt does not exist, must not exist, has no right to exist, and that doubt is nothing but a sign of weakness in thought and not the necessary condition for rigorous thought. What relations existed, or better still, what line of continuity could be established (this was my first thought that afternoon) between the *Discourse on Method* and *Mein Kampf*? The two were monologues of an individual who was more or less mad, who is prepared to negate all prior truths and to prove in a manner that was at once commanding and inflexible in what place and from what position one could (and should) erect a system that would be at once absolutely coherent and philosophically irrefutable. The two books, I thought, Tardewski said, were a single book, the two parts of a single book written far enough apart in time so that historical developments would make it possible for their ideas to be complementary. Could that book (I thought as the library grew dark) be considered something like the final movement in the evolution of rationalist subjectivism as inaugurated by Descartes? I think it can, I thought that afternoon, and I still think so now, said Tardewski. I am therefore opposed, of course, as you will have noted immediately, to the thesis argued by Georg Lukács in his book, *The Destruction of Reason,* for whom *Mein Kampf* and nazism are nothing more than the culmination of the irrationalist tendency in German philosophy that begins with Nietzsche and Schopenhauer. For me, in contrast, Tardewski says, *Mein Kampf* is bourgeois reason taken to its most extreme and coherent limits. I would even say, said Tardewski to me, that bourgeois reason concludes in a triumphal way in *Mein Kampf.* That book is the realization of bourgeois philosophy. It is philosophy as a critical practice; not philosophy (by the way) as it was understood by that other German philosopher who spent his days in a reading room at the British Library reading the careful reports written by honest British factory inspectors at the time of the Industrial Revolution, but instead that *other* philosophy as critical practice, the philosophy I was studying at Cambridge.

Tardewski said then that if philosophy had always sought a path toward its becoming real, was it so surprising that Heidegger should have seen the Führer as the very concretion of German reason? I'm not making a moral judgment, said Tardewski; for me it's a matter of a logical judgment. If European reason is realized in this book (I said to myself as I read it), what is surprising about the fact that the greatest living philosopher, that is to say, the one who is considered the greatest philosophical intelligence in the West, should have understood that right away? Then the Austrian corporal and the philosopher of Freiburg (with Being living in the house next door, as Astrada said) are nothing but the direct and legitimate descendants of that French philosopher who went to Holland and there sat down in front of the fire to found the certainties of modern reason. A philosopher sitting before a fireplace, said Tardewski, isn't that the basic situation? (Socrates, in contrast, as you know, he told me in parentheses, wandered around the streets and the squares.) Isn't the tragedy of the modern world condensed in that? It's totally logical, he said, for a philosopher to get up from his armchair, after having convinced himself that he is the sole proprietor of the truth and that there is no room for doubt, and for him to take one of those burning logs and devote himself to setting fire with his reason to the entire world. It happened four hundred years later but it was logical, it was an inevitable consequence. If at the very least I had stayed *sitting down.* But you know how difficult it is to remain seated for very long, said Tardewski, and he got up and began pacing back and forth across the room.

So there's this fellow sitting there in Holland, said Tardewski as he paced back and forth, there in Amsterdam, I think, writing his monologue. He stopped. Did you know, he asked me, beginning to walk once more, that Valéry says that the *Discourse on Method* is the first modern novel? It is the first modern novel, says Valéry, Tardewski tells me, because it is a monologue that instead of narrating the story of a passion tells the story of an idea. Not bad, huh? In essence, looked at that way, one could say that Descartes wrote a detective novel: How can the investigator, without moving from his armchair before the fire, without leaving his room, using only his reason, eliminate all the false leads, destroy his doubts one by one, until he finally succeeds in discovering who is the criminal, that is, the *cogito*. Because the *cogito* is the murderer, of that I have not the slightest doubt, said Tardewski, and he stopped once again and stood facing me. Not bad, huh? Valéry's idea. No, I reply, it's not bad. Around the same time, I tell him, Brecht said that there was nothing more beautiful than a theorem. Gödel's theorem, said Brecht, I tell Tardewski, is more beautiful than the most beautiful of Baudelaire's sonnets. Tardewski began roaming around the room once again. "Fervent lovers and austere scholars," he recited, "love equally, in their ripe season, powerful and gentle cats." The sonnets of Charles Baudelaire, he said, are not so bad either.

Well, he said then, if the *Discourse on Method* is the first modern novel in this sense, then *Mein Kampf* is its parody, as you would say, said Tardewski, sitting down once more. That German monologue closes off the system inaugurated by the French monologue. Hitler's tale shows how the forms of discourse that begin with Descartes have been canonized and how they have aged. That's why it could be seen as a parody.

In sum, he said then, and leaving Valéry aside, the *Discourse on Method* is to *Mein Kampf* as *Madame Bovary* is to *Finnegans Wake*. We pass from romantic dreams to infernal wakes. *Madame Bovary c'est moi* (that is to say, I am the romantic dreams of reason, that French lady); the Jews are the twins Shem and Shaun (that is to say, the luminous discourse of reason has been fragmented in the broken murmurs of the nocturnal victims).

In that wake nobody awakes, all have died, said Tardewski. And Anna Livia Plurabelle? I ask him. Anna Livia Plurabelle is Eva Braun. Better still: she is Madame Bovary reincarnated as Eva Braun (both of whom killed themselves with arsenic, besides). Or isn't *metempsychosis* the word that Molly does not understand, the meaning of which she asks Bloom, the wandering Jew? It could also be said, added Tardewski, that Eva Braun is Anna Livia Plurabelle on drugs. But it was not his intention, said Tardewski, to propose the hypothesis that *Mein Kampf* be read as a novel.

That was not what I was thinking about that darkening afternoon in 1938 in the British Library, Tardewski says now, standing up again and leaning against the wall, beneath a photographic reproduction of the face of a man that seems vaguely familiar and yet whom I cannot identify. I thought, as I read *Mein Kampf,* that in that book was found, as I have said, the practical criticism and culmination of European rationalism. That verification meant the beginning of the end of philosophy for me. I understood it, he said, much later, but that afternoon, he said, philosophy, as they teach it at Cambridge, was finished for me. I prefer, he said, being a failure to being an accomplice. You do remember Maier? I didn't do anything, he says when remorse forces him to justify himself. I didn't kill anyone, I didn't do anything but spend the whole Hitler period closed off in a library, classifying biology books. I was also in a library—where else could I have been when I spent half my life shut in a library?—but chance helped me and I began—slowly but inevitably—to understand. This is the philosophy, I thought, this is what we have come to, this is what the *cogito* is like, this is what the infernal egg hatched by Descartes by the fireplace, in his house in Holland, has developed into. The sleep of *that kind* of reason produces monsters. At bottom, you should know, I am a rationalist, I believe in reason, don't imagine that I've joined today's fashion and started preaching the virtues of the irrational. But *that kind* of reason carried us straight to *Mein Kampf.* That's why Heidegger, I thought, could say in July 1933, in his famous *Völkischer Beobachter,* in Freiburg: "Neither postulates nor ideas are the rules of Being. Only the person of the Führer is the present and future of Germany and also its Law." He had read and understood *Mein Kampf,* I thought. "From now on it does not matter to them whether something is the truth, only whether or not it is in accord with the direction of the national socialist movement." The year 1933. Heidegger *in* Hitler. And I was writing a thesis on Heidegger *in* the pre-Socratics? Hadn't it been some sort of philosophical revelation, a metaphysical exchange, that when I asked for the book of an old and wise Sophist philosopher I had received Hitler's *Mein Kampf?* That's exactly what Heidegger had done. To exchange, without requiring any help from chance, Parmenides (or Hippias, it came to the same thing) for Hitler. There was nothing monstrous there, I mean, it's not a moral error but a logical decision. That fellow Heidegger had read *Mein Kampf* and later, sitting in front of his fireplace, perhaps at his neighbor's house in Freiburg, he had started to *think. Being and Time:* one has to give being time enough to be incarnated in the Führer, that's all, I thought that afternoon, sitting in the reading room at the British Library. So philosophy had begun to come to an end for me. The order of the HI catalog cards in the library. You see, a simple change of cards sufficed. Hi, hi, I screamed. Hi, hi, like an animal that's being forced to leave its lair. Hi, hi, I screamed, in terror.

I was beginning to prepare, without knowing it, for the journey that would take me to Concordia, to this house, to this pleasant conversation with you. What would have happened if I had received, as expected, the volume of the writings of Hippias? If the perverse interpolation hadn't happened? A senseless question, said Tardewski, but easy to answer. I would have advanced, with that luminous happiness that pure philosophical abstraction can produce in a person, in my reading of the fragments that have been preserved of Hippias the Sophist, and at the end of the afternoon I would have put my papers in order and returned to my scholarly abode in Cambridge with the same blind confidence in my own future that I had had at noon that day when I climbed the stairs of the British Museum. I would have gone on working on my thesis and no doubt would not have decided to spend my vacation in Warsaw in August 1939, searching for certain facts about Kafka, and so would not have ended up in this corner of the Argentine interior, and so forth.

But I am not interested in reflecting, he said, on the laws of chance with you here today. All of us are fascinated to think of the lives we might have lived and all of us have our Oedipal crossroads (in the Greek and not the Viennese sense of the word), our crucial moments. We are all fascinated, he said, to think about that, and some pay dearly for that fascination. For example, he said, that kind of thinking cost a friend of mine his life. Tardewski's friend, because he had stopped to look at the window of a shoe store, arrived twenty minutes late at the station and saw that his train was leaving. He missed that train, arrived late at a date with his fiancée, who was waiting for him at the other end of the line, she was offended, considered the delay a flagrant example of a lack of love, refused to listen to reason, broke off her engagement with my friend and married an officer in the Polish army, causing such profound pain in my friend that for days it was literally impossible for him to get out of bed and he spent hours and hours lying, thinking of the military couplings of his beloved with the cavalry officer. He smoked, thinking of frequent and terrifying erotic scenes in which his ex-fiancée gave herself over, with cynical and licentious joy, to all of the equestrian fancies of the officer; lying in his bed he saw the last wagon of the departing train, thinking of the delay caused, in the last instance, by the window of a shoe store where, by the way, there were women's shoes and boots on display; he thought about all of that, smoking, until finally one morning he fell asleep with a lighted cigarette and died passionately burning in the flames of his bed, burned only figuratively by the fire of passion.

It avails nothing to think about chance, especially if the person thinking is someone like me, said Tardewski, convinced that everything is determined and that chance is nothing other than the name we give to the arrangement of the cards in the HI series in the catalog of the reading room of the British Library. It was not, then, he said, a matter of the laws of chance, but of something much more secret. Be that as it may, instead of returning to my room as I would have done had I received the book that I had really gone to consult, I stayed until midnight fascinated by Hitler's book and above all by the discovery I made that day as I read *Mein Kampf.* Not the discovery linked to the disjointed philosophical reflections I just expounded, but another one. Another discovery. Or better still, *the* discovery, the story of which I will try to tell you concisely now, said Tardewski, trying to avoid digressions. You, Tardewski, the Professor would always say to me, are like General Lucio Mansilla, you have the same digressive zeal that he did. And who is that General Mansilla? I would ask him. A nineteenth-century gentleman with a gift for words comparable to yours, the Professor would answer. A dandy of whom it might be said that he made a single great digression of his entire life. So I will try to avoid digressions, said Tardewski, and will limit myself to the story of the discovery that helped change my destiny.

I received Hitler's *Mein Kampf* in an excellent and very rigorous critical edition, with introduction and notes by a German historian, Joachim Kluge, who at that moment was living in exile in Denmark and was a friend, by the way, of Walter Benjamin. *That* edition, precisely, was what made me what I am, said Tardewski. That edition and the reading the previous Sunday of the *Times Literary Supplement.*

Apart from his reflections on the philosophy implicit in *Mein*

Kampf, he had also been interested, as is logical, in the ins and outs of the strange, not to say extraordinary, life of Hitler. And especially in one period of his life, the least historical we might say, or at least the least public; I mean, he said, I was especially interested in his early years and particularly in the commentaries and notes in which Doctor Kluge analyzed and amplified the story that Hitler gave of that period of his life.

Between 1905 and 1910, that is, starting when he was eighteen, Hitler's existence is at once incredible and pathetic. What Hitler really wants in that period is to become someone in the world of art, to be an artist, a painter. He practices a sort of nomadic bohemian existence in the bars and other establishments frequented by writers and intellectuals, by that whole gang of failures we were speaking of a while ago. It is his mother who supports him while he pursues the typical existence of the solitary dreamer who expects to do great things in his life. In reality Hitler wanted to be a great painter. Now then, said Tardewski, Hitler's intention to become a great painter was impossible from the outset. That colorless and spiteful young man had more chances of becoming, let's say, a dictator, a sort of petty Caesar who subjugates half of Europe, than of becoming a painter, not even a great but an average one. But he wanted to be a great painter. What did Adolf Hitler understand by a great painter? It's rather difficult to know; perhaps he fancied, above all, enjoying the success that a painter supposedly has after his work is recognized and admired. Hitler, no doubt, wanted to have the posthumous fame of the great painters, but right from the beginning. In any case, Hitler as a painter was terrible. Worse than terrible, kitsch. He copied and illustrated postcards and sold them in the bars, so just imagine. Intent, however, on having a career and improving himself, he tries to enter the Art Academy, but is rejected twice. First in 1907 and then in 1908. He cannot pass the entrance exams. What would have happened had he succeeded in being admitted? A question we leave aside because we have already discarded all variants on the possible. In any case the adventures of Hitler as a painter, his entrance into the Academy, his first exhibition, his move to Paris and so forth, could serve someone to write an excellent picaresque version of science fiction. Something in the line of Philip Dick but comical. Did you ever read Philip Dick? Tardewski asks me. I answer that I have.

Well, says Tardewski, we'll leave aside what would have happened if Hitler had triumphed as a painter; here we are only interested in real events. What matters is that in those years, let's say between 1905 and 1910, Hitler acquires or absorbs, in a more or less spontaneous fashion, the typical anticapitalist ideology of the marginal artist who feels rejected by materialist and vulgar bourgeois society. Besides, Hitler pursues at the same time what we could call his *education*, his apprenticeship in the German sense of the word, so we now enter into his intellectual *Bildungsroman*.

Kluge's detailed research permitted one to have an idea of the type of texts that constituted Hitler's ideological grounding and that propelled him into politics. One of the main ones he emphasized was a magazine, an enormously popular sort of *feuilleton* that took its title from the sonorous name of the Germanic goddess of spring, *Ostara*. (Kafka makes two references to this magazine in his Diary, an important matter when we approach the center of the story that I am trying to tell you, Tardewski said, closing another of his imaginary parentheses.) That magazine, a collection of which I consulted a few days later, at the British Library, preached a racist mythological history, as eccentric as it was bloodthirsty, put together by a former friar named Adolf Lanz (1874–1954). That *other* Adolf takes the name Adolf Lanz von Liebenfels and attempts to found an Order of Men composed of Aryans, blondes with blue eyes and so forth. The Castle of the Order, Tardewski continued, was found in Werfenstein, in lower Austria, and was bought with economic aid lent by German industrialists interested in the ideas of von Liebenfels. That primitive alliance of a messianic Adolf with powerful German industrialists looks like a parody before the fact of what would be the sinister conspiracy between Hitler and his gang of maniacs and the refined circles of the upper reaches of the German industrial bourgeoisie, the Krupps and the Gerlachs, who would bring him to power in 1933. In 1907, at the Castle of the Order in Werfenstein, the former friar raises a flag with a swastika as the symbol of his movement. The system of this extravagant premature founder of a heroic Aryan mythology is laid out in his work *Theozzologie,* 415 pages published in 1904. As can be seen from the title, it was a sort of theological zoology that, in an inflexible baroque prose that tries unsuccessfully to imitate the rhythms that the German Bible acquires in Luther's translation, puts forward an abstruse mystical hodgepodge, animated by a genetically based racism sublimated into a religion. Hitler read and reread this work, entire paragraphs of which he transcribed in *Mein Kampf.* Also, in 1908, Hitler writes to Lanz and asks him for various issues of *Ostara* because he wishes to complete his collection.

We see then, Tardewski says, that in those wandering years, years of disordered readings and a bohemian artistic life, Hitler's vision of the world begins to take shape. But first allow me to read you something. He gets up and crosses the room toward the chest at the opposite end. He opens the drawer and takes out the black notebook. Well, here, says Tardewski after putting his glasses on, here, he says and sits down again, Hitler himself points out, look at this, he says and begins to read. During this time, Tardewski read, then he looked at me, this is what Hitler says in *Mein Kampf.* During this time I worked out an image of the world and a *Weltanschauung* that would finally convert itself into the granite foundation of my work. Apart from what I had already accumulated in those years, Tardewski read, and then he looked at me again, he's referring, he said, to the years between

1905 or 1906 and 1910. Apart from what I had already accumulated in those years I had little to learn. And to change, nothing, Tardewski read what Adolf Hitler had written in *Mein Kampf*. And to change, nothing, he said, that's worth thinking about, said Tardewski, taking off his glasses. We could say then that, without ceasing to dream of his future as a great artist and without ceasing to live as a bohemian, toward the end of 1908 and at the beginning of 1909, Hitler had a concept of the world that was almost complete, albeit complete in a raw and facile way. That is the first point I would like you to remember, said Tardewski.

Second point. Central question. A dark and mysterious episode in the life of Hitler that was like a magnet for me, that afternoon in 1938.

Hitler disappears from Vienna for almost a year between October 1909 and August 1910. He disappears, no one knows what happened. His official biographers alter the chronology and Hitler himself modifies the dates in *Mein Kampf* to erase that void.

Kluge, a patient and very wise investigator, discovers around 1935 the secret of that disappearance so carefully hidden by Hitler. He discovers, above all, the *motive* for that disappearance. Allow me to read you something again, says Tardewski as he adjusts his glasses. It's Kluge this time, he says. The reasons for his hidden, abrupt disappearance were unclear for a long time. The truth, as is demonstrated by the documents that I reprint in Appendix III of this edition, Tardewski read from his notebook of quotations what the antifascist historian Joachim Kluge had written in his critical edition of *Mein Kampf* of Adolf Hitler, published in London in 1936 by the German exile publishing house German Liberty, is the following. Hitler avoided enlisting in the army, which he was required to do between 1909 and 1910. His disappearance was a flight from military service. The search by the Austrian authorities led to his provisional detention and then to his transfer to Salzburg in September 1910, Tardewski read, then looked up. That was one of the objectives of Kluge's investigation, he said as he took off his glasses. A fact that was really parodic, once again: the exalted defender of Prussian militarism, the sinister builder of an abominable militarized society, had been a deserter. The highest crime a German could aspire to, according to the Nazi laws. But this paradox was not the most important thing, at least for me.

The fundamental issue was something else; what turned for me into a discovery and a decisive event was the reading of a marginal annotation, a brief footnote, the result of the extreme mania for exactitude and detail on the part of the German historian whose edition of *Mein Kampf* I was examining that afternoon. Kluge indicated that Hitler had passed those months in hiding in Prague. In that footnote he added, in passing, to demonstrate how detailed his research had been, that one of the places frequented almost every day by Hitler was the Arcos Café, on Meiselgasse in Prague, a meeting place for a certain sector of the German-speaking Czech intelligentsia, the "Arconauts," as Karl Kraus called the artists, writers and bohemians who gathered in that bar.

When I read that little footnote I made an instant connection, the only thing that philosophers and scientists alike tend to experience, or at least describe, with some frequency, and which they term a *discovery:* the unexpected association of two isolated facts, of two ideas that, when they combine, produce something new. In my case it had to do with an altogether random connection between two texts read in close succession.

The afternoon in 1938 that I spent at the British Museum was a Monday. The day before, Sunday, in the *Times Literary Supplement,* I had read an excellent and extensive review in which two works were commented on at the same time: the publication of volume VI (*Tagebücher und Briefen,* Prague, 1937) of Kafka's *Gesammelte Schriften* and Max Brod's biography (*Franz Kafka.*

Eine Biographie. Erinnerungen und Dokumente, Prague 1937), which completed and rounded out, as a supplemental volume, the first integral edition of those *Complete Works.* Among the quotations and texts by Kafka or Brod that were transcribed in that review there was a reference I barely noticed that Sunday but that came on like a light the next day, as I was reading Kluge's footnote. It was this, Tardewski said, opening his notebook once more. Max Brod encouraged the always indecisive Kafka to join the intellectual gatherings at the Arcos Café, Tardewski read, and prevented Kafka until at least 1911 from isolating himself from the world that surrounded him. That was what the author of the review in the *Times* wrote, Tardewski said, and then he included a fragment of a letter by Kafka in January 1910, quoted by Brod in his biography. I am happy because I am finally learning something, Tardewski read what Kafka had written, so this week I will keep on taking my place at the Arcos. I would happily spend the whole night there, since at seven in the afternoon the best people have arrived, but I fear that if I immerse myself too deeply in the murmur of those conversations I would find it impossible to work the next day. And I shouldn't waste any time. It's better to stay at the café only until midnight and then to read Kügelgen: both good occupations for a small heart, enabling me to fall asleep when I am tired. A warm greeting. Franz.

January 1910. Café Arcos, says Tardewski, Meiselgasse, Prague. What we could call a discovery was produced, borne along by the purest chance.

For the weeks following I worked on gathering the data that might broaden and confirm this hunch. And I found, with an ease that surprised me, a series of irrefutable proofs about a fact that was so extraordinary. I even found the proofs in much less time than I had expected and in a succession that made me think that discoveries are always within anyone's reach but that one usually passes by treasures that shine in the light of day without anyone seeing anything. Because even a researcher, let's say a Kafka specialist, might not have found, even had he looked, what I, in a totally chance fashion, found and was able to discover. The facts and evidence were so clear that it seems impossible that nobody has never noticed. For instance, there are two letters of Kafka's that refer to an Austrian exile who frequents the Arcos. In one, written on November 24, 1909, to his friend Rainer Jauss, Kafka speaks of a strange little man who claims to be a painter and who has fled Vienna for some obscure reason. His name is Adolf, says Kafka, Tardewski tells me, leafing through the pages of the notebook. His name is Adolf, and he speaks German with a strange accent, though the stories he tells are even stranger. Strange at least for someone who claims to be a painter, for painters are mute, says Kafka, said Tardewski when he finished reading the first of Kafka's letters in which there is a reference to an Austrian exile named Adolf. The second is a letter to Max Brod, written a few days later—to be more precise, Tardewski says now, on December 9, 1909—in which Kafka speaks of a manuscript, very possibly one of the rough drafts of "Wedding Preparations in the Country," that he had taken the day before to Brod's house to read aloud. Yesterday, Tardewski reads, then he clarifies, it's the end of the letter. Yesterday when we were discussing the manuscript I was still under the effects of my conversation with Adolf, about whom I had not spoken to you up to that point. He had said certain things and I thought about them and it's very possible that due to the memory of those words I may have expressed myself awkwardly, in a way that is only strange when one is keeping a secret, Tardewski read. From Kafka to Brod, he said, December 9, 1909.

Adolf, Tardewski says now. How is it possible, I thought, that nobody has discovered it before? But that's how things are, he tells me. Nobody knows how to read, nobody reads. Because to read, Tardewski said, one must know how to associate. The first, note this carefully, the *first* entry in Kafka's diary is May 12, 1910. There he writes, says Tardewski: the spectators are standing still when the train passes them, Tardewski reads the first sentence of the first entry in Kafka's diary, written on May 12, 1910. Then, says Tardewski, there's a space. After that one reads, he says, and reads aloud: His seriousness kills me. With his head stuck in the neck of his shirt, the rigid hair combed onto his skull, the muscles of his jaw tense, in his place . . . ellipsis, read Tardewski. Right after that, on the next line, Kafka writes this: Discussion A. I didn't mean that, he tells me, Tardewski reads. You know me by now, Doctor. I am a completely harmless man. I had to relieve my feelings. What I said were just words. I interrupt him. That is precisely what is so dangerous. Words prepare the way; they are precursors of acts to come, the sparks of future fires. I had no intention of saying that, A. replies to me. That's what you say, I answer, trying to smile. But do you know what aspect things really have? It could be that we are sitting on a barrel of gunpowder that turns your desire into reality.

How could it be that nobody understood? Tardewski had asked himself. Or do we only read what we have already read, over and over again, to look at words for what we know is in them, not allowing any surprise to change their meaning? That is what I asked myself, as I became more and more certain of that discovery.

Now observe this, he tells me: one of Hitler's friends in his youth, that is to say, one of the friends in the period when Hitler was nothing but a hunger artist who supported himself with illusions and dreams of grandeur, while he read the magazine *Ostara*, the musician August Kubizek, writes in his *Adolf Hitler mein Jugendfreund* (Gatez, 1933), Tardewski quoted, referring to the years that interest us, 1909 and 1910: Adolf knew how to plan what he intended to do with the future of the world so wonderfully well, he knew how to explain in such a fascinating way his plans and projects, Tardewski read from his notebook of quotations, that one could have listened to him forever, such was the charm and seduction of his words and the excessive yet at the same time meticulous and tidy character of his descriptions of what the world would receive from him in the future.

To whom can Kafka be referring if not to that propagandist of delirium, to that insignificant prophet of the sorrows of the world, when he writes the following in the fourth draft of *Description of a Struggle:* Tell me everything from beginning to end, read Tardewski. I won't listen to anything less, I warn you. But I am burning to hear the whole thing from you. Because what you are planning is so atrocious that only when I hear it can I conceal my terror.

In those months, in Prague, there was this man who had nothing more than words and plans, a man who has been defined as such, said Tardewski. Already in 1909 the traits that would characterize the fanatic and the dictator were present: a delirious egocentrism, mixed with a hysterical degree of compassion for himself. Besides this, Hitler already clearly exhibited, Tardewski read, a wild obsession with the future, an incessant flood of words in which he would construct his projects, as grandiose as they were unscrupulous. That was what Joachim Kluge wrote, said Tardewski, about Hitler's youth in his notes to the critical edition of *Mein Kampf.* As for Kafka, he said, we could say a great deal about the Kafka of those years. Brod has told of the impression he produced. An extraordinary strength radiated from him, Tardewski reads now, that I have never again seen in anyone. He never spoke an insignificant word; what sprang from him was the precise expression of an all-encompassing irony, of a pained humor in the face of the absurdities of the world. That is how Max Brod describes that Kafka, defining him, above all, as one who was able to listen. Kafka, Tardewski reads, was capable of listening for hours. In the world he behaved above all as a reserved listener who spoke in monosyllables. He truly behaved, Tardewski read from his notebook of quotations, as one who listens, as one who knows how to hear. And that is the best way of defining him, said Tardewski. The man who knows how to hear, for beneath the incessant whispering of the victims are the words that announce another kind of truth. Let us listen for a moment, said Tardewski, to the voice of that Kafka.

I have such an urgent need to encounter someone who will at least touch me with their friendship that yesterday I took a tart to my hotel. She was too old to keep on being melancholy; she is only troubled, she says, although it does not surprise her, that one is not as affectionate with tarts as with one's beloved. I have not consoled her but she hasn't console me either.

Kafka, the solitary one, says Tardewski, sitting at a table in the Arcos Café in Prague, February 1910, facing Adolf, the painter, a false and almost dreamlike Tittorelli. With his style, which we now know well, the insignificant and louse-bitten Austrian petty bourgeois living a semiclandestine life in Prague because he is a draft dodger, that failed artist who earns a living painting postcards, speaking to someone who is not yet Franz Kafka but is on the way to becoming him, tells of his nasal, extravagant dreams, in which one can half-glimpse his transformation into the Führer, the Chief, the absolute Master of millions of people, servants, slaves, insects, all in subjection to his will, says Tardewski.

The word *Ungeziefer*, said Tardewski, which the Nazis would use to designate prisoners in the concentration camps, is the same word that Kafka uses to describe what Gregor Samsa has turned into one morning, when he wakes up.

The atrocious utopia of a world converted into an immense penal colony: that's what Adolf, the insignificant, grotesque draft dodger talks about to Franz Kafka, the one who knows how to listen, at the tables of the Arcos Café, in Prague, at the end of 1909. And Kafka believes him. He thinks it is *possible* that the impossible and atrocious projects of that ridiculous hungry little man may come to pass and that the world may be transformed into what the words were constructing: the Castle of the Order of the Twisted Cross, the machine of evil that engraves its message on the flesh of its victims. Couldn't he hear the abominable voice of history?

The genius of Kafka resides in his having understood that if those words could be spoken then they could be realized. *Ostara*, Germanic goddess of spring. Tell me everything from beginning to end. Because what you are planning is so atrocious that only when I hear it can I hide my terror. The words prepare the way; they are precursors of acts to come, the sparks of future fires. And wasn't he already sitting on the barrel of gunpowder that turned his desire into reality?

He knows how to listen; he is the one who knows how to listen.

I thought of Kafka today, Tardewski says now, when Marconi recited to us that sort of poem that he says he dreamed of. I thought to tell you, when you were discussing the title, says Tardewski, that the title should be: "Kafka."

> I am
> the tightrope walker
> who walks in the air
> barefoot
> on a string
> of barbed wire

Kafka, or the artist who does tightrope walking on the barbed wire of the concentration camps.

You read *The Trial*, Tardewski says to me. Kafka could see in precise detail how horror was constructed. That novel presents in a hallucinatory way the classic model of the State converted into an instrument of terror. It describes the anonymous machinery of a world where all can be accused and found guilty, the sinister insecurity that totalitarianism insinuates into the life of human beings, the faceless boredom of the murderers, the furtive sadism. After Kafka wrote that book, there has been knocking on countless doors at night, and the name of those who dragged off to die *like dogs,* just like Joseph K., is legion.

Kafka, in his fiction, realizes, even before Hitler himself, what Hitler told him he would do. His texts are the anticipation of what he glimpsed as only too possible in the perverse words of that Adolf, half-clown, half-prophet, who announced, in a sort of lethargic somnolence, a future of symmetrical evil. A future that Hitler himself saw as impossible; a Gothic dream in which he, the louse-bitten and failed artist, would be transformed into the Führer. Not even Hitler himself, I am sure, thought that all of that was possible in 1909. But Kafka did. Kafka, Renzi, said Tardewski, knew how to listen. He was attentive to the sickly murmurs of history.

Franz Kafka dies on June 3, 1924. In those same days, in a castle in the Black Forest, Hitler walks back and forth in a room with high ceilings and stained-glass windows in the walls. He walks back and forth and dictates to his assistants the final chapters of *Mein Kampf.* June 1924. He, the Führer, paces and dictates *Mein Kampf.* Kafka is dying in the sanatorium at Kierling. Tuberculosis has claimed his larynx so he is no longer able to talk. He makes signs. Smiles. Tries to smile. He writes notes on a pad for Max Brod, for Oskar Braum, for Felix Winbach, the lifelong friends who are there, together with Dora Dymant. I think I have begun at the most opportune moment the study of the noises emitted by animals: those are the things he writes, because he can no longer speak. June 1924. He paces, the Führer, surrounded by his assistants, and dictates: The first objective will be the creation of a Great German Empire, whose dominions, he dictates, paces back and forth, whose dominions should extend from North Cape to the Alps and from the Atlantic to the Black Sea, period, he dictates surrounded by his assistants. Kafka agonizes in the sanatorium at Kierling, near Kloster-neuburg. He cannot speak. He makes signs. Smiles. Lying on his back in the bed, he writes on a pad that he holds, with difficulty, very close to his face. Can he hear? The Führer paces. A Great German Empire, comma, he paces, dictates, surrounded by his assistants, from one end to the other, comma, furrowed by a powerful network of highways, beside which German military colonies will be established, period, the Führer dictates *Mein Kampf.* In the sanatorium Kafka is dying; he studies the noises emitted by animals. Hi, hi, the shriek emitted by terrified rats in their lairs. Hi, hi, they shriek. To study at the most opportune moment the noises emitted by animals. The Führer paces around the room, surrounded by his assistants. In the sanatorium Kafka is dying; unable to speak, he writes. Can he hear? June 1924. The Führer is dictating *Mein Kampf.* Europe to the east of the Danube will be in the future, colon, in part, comma, an enormous field of military maneuvers, comma, and in part a place where the Reich's slaves settle, comma, he paces, back and forth, surrounded by his assistants, slaves who will be selected throughout the whole world according to racial criteria, comma, being used and mixed, he paces, back and forth, in accord with a preestablished plan, comma, that will be detailed at the appropriate moment, period, he dictates as he wanders through the rooms of the Castle. And the Surveyor? He is dying. He cannot speak any longer; in order to make himself understood to his friends, to his beloved Dora Dymant, he can *only* write. He has been left without a voice. He dictates: all of the East will be an enormous colony, comma, a sort of pasture land for the non-Aryan slaves, Hitler dictates *Mein Kampf,* Tardewski says, while Kafka, whose larynx has been taken from him by tuberculosis and who no longer has a voice, only writes to his most beloved friends and to his beloved Dora Dymant. He, the Führer, wanders back and forth, slowly: a pasture land for the non-Aryan slaves, comma, surrounded by his assistants. Little notes written in pencil on the map, arduous handwriting. I remember an oriental book: it was only about death. A dying person lies in bed, Kafka writes, and with the independence that the proximity of death gives him, says: I am always speaking of death and never finish dying. Can he hear? The non-Aryan slaves, comma, with a direct land link to the German lands that will become their central axis, period, and once more he paces, surrounded by his assistants, from one end to the other. I am always speaking of death, he writes, and never finish dying. But now, to be exact, I am singing my last aria. Some last longer, some not so long. The difference is always a matter of a few words, says the dying man, Kafka writes as he lies in bed. The 180 million Russians, comma, however, comma, must be plunged little by little into utter degradation, colon, the Führer wanders back and forth. He is completely right, he writes; the dying man is always right, Kafka writes. No one has the right to smile at the hero when he lies wounded to death, singing an aria. We lie here and sing, for years; all of our lives we do nothing but sing the final aria, always, Kafka writes to his friends at the Kierling sanatorium. June 1924. Plunge them little by little into utter degradation, colon, prevent them from procreating, comma, punish them if they speak until they forget the use of language, comma, he dictates as he wanders about the rooms of the Castle. The disease has deprived him of his larynx. Can he hear? He *writes* his last words. No one has the right, he writes, these are his last words, no one has the right, the pad held in his hands almost next to his face as he lies on his back, no one has the right to smile at the hero when he lies dying, singing an aria. He paces. Until they forget the use of language, comma, deprive them of any opportunity for learning so as to squelch all signs of intelligence and all possibilities of rebellion, comma, in a word, comma, turn them into brutes, the Führer dictates, says Tardewski. Who can laugh at the aria that the dying person sings?

He tries to smile. Makes gestures. He wanders back and forth. The most they can learn will be the signals necessary so that their leaders with a capital letter Leaders, he dictates, can methodically organize their day's labor. June 1924. Kafka agonizes in the sanatorium where he will die at the stroke of midnight. In the Castle, can the dying man's last aria be heard? Naturally, comma, they should learn, he stops, his assistants immediately stop also and surround him. Better, he says, cross out the previous sentence and he begins pacing around again, his hands behind his back. Naturally, comma, we should teach them, comma, using the necessary severity, comma, to understand the German language so as to assure in that way their obedience to our orders with a capital letter Orders, period, wandering through the rooms of the Castle the Führer dictates *Mein Kampf.* Midnight of the third, the fourth of June 1924. The dying man, can he still hear him? I am studying the noises emitted by animals. Has he heard him? Hi, hi, shrieks the *Ungeziefer* in its lair, hi, hi, it shrieks in terror in the middle of the night, while far away can be heard the paces of someone who is pacing back and forth, walking around, in the Castle, from one side to the other, surrounded by his assistants. Hi, hi, the *Ungeziefer* shrieks in its lair, while far away can be heard the extraordinarily beautiful, almost imperceptible, final aria that the dying man is singing.

June 3, 1924, says Tardewski.

Kafka is Dante, says Tardewski now, his scribbles, as he called his writings, unpublished, fragmentary, unfinished, are our *Divine Comedy.* Brecht said, with reason, says Tardewski, that if one had to name the author who came closest to having with our time the sort of relation that Homer, Dante, or Shakespeare had with theirs, Kafka is the first writer one would think of. That is why I, said Tardewski, don't share your enthusiasm for James Joyce. How can you compare them? he said. Joyce, as that woman who embroidered tablecloths said about Marconi's poems, he is too—how to say it?—too much of a toilsome virtuoso. A juggler, he said. Someone who performs word plays the ways others use their hands. Kafka, on the other hand, is the tightrope walker who walks in the air, without a net, and risks his life while trying to keep his balance, moving one foot and then very slowly the other foot, across the tense wire of language. Joyce was a clever man, there's no doubt of that; Kafka, however, was not clever, he was clumsy and soon turned into an expert in his own clumsiness. Joyce carries a banner that says: I am the one who overcomes all obstacles, while Kafka writes on a pad and then hides the sentence in a pocket of his buttoned jacket: I am the only one who is overcome by every obstacle. Kafka has said, Tardewski says: I face the impossibility of not writing, of writing in German, of writing in another language, to which a fourth impossibility could almost be added: that of writing. That fourth impossibility was, for him, the supreme temptation. For him who had known how to say: Anything I write. For instance the sentence—He looked out the window—when written by me is already perfect. What sort of perfection did it have? asks Tardewski. On the one hand, Kafka's ideal as regards formal and stylistic perfection was so rigorous that he did not tolerate anything less. But at the same time he knew better than anyone that truly great writers are those who constantly face the almost absolute impossibility of writing.

What we cannot speak about we must pass over in silence, Wittgenstein said. How to speak of the unspeakable? That is the question that Kafka's work tries over and over again to answer. Or better still, he said, his work is the only one that in a refined and subtle manner dares to speak of the unspeakable, of that which cannot be named. What would we say is the unspeakable today? The world of Auschwitz. That world is beyond language, it is a frontier filled with the barbed wire of language. Barbed wire: the tightrope walker walks, barefoot, alone up there, and tries to see if it is possible to say anything about what is on the other side.

To speak of the unspeakable is to put in danger the survival of language as the bearer of human truth. A mortal risk. In the Castle a man dictates, paces, and dictates, surrounded by his assistants. Words saturated by lies and horror, said Tardewski, cannot easily be used to sum up life. Wittgenstein glimpsed with all clarity that the only work that could approach his own in its suicidal restoration of silence was the incomparable fragmentary work of Franz Kafka. Joyce? He tried to wake up from the nightmare of history so as to perform a pretty juggling act with words. Kafka, however, woke up every day to *enter* that nightmare and tried to write about it.

3.

As you have understood, Tardewski says now, if we have talked so long, if we have talked this entire night, it was so as not to speak, or rather, so as not to say anything about him, about the Professor. We have talked and talked because about him there is nothing that can be said.

He will not come tonight, said Tardewski. Perhaps the Professor will not arrive tonight; you, therefore, will for a time perhaps not see him. That has no importance, he said. All that matters, he said, is what a man decides to do with his life.

I admired him, you know, he said later. It was impossible to know him and not to admire him. He attracted in others what was the best in them.

As for me, Tardewski says now, you will perhaps have noticed, I am a man entirely composed of quotations. That is why in order to say something about him I have once again to open this notebook. And what I am going to read you, he said, could perhaps be an example, the best example, of what the Professor was for me. A synthesis, perhaps, of why I respected him. A summary, if you like, of what the whole long conversation we had, he and I, meant for me, the last night we spent together, the same as you and I now, here, in my house, in this very place.

Nine days before his death, Tardewski reads, Immanuel Kant was visited by his doctor. Old, sick, and almost blind, he got up out of his chair and stood up, trembling from weakness and muttering unintelligible words. At last I, who have been his loyal friend, realized that he would not sit down until the visitor did so. That's what he did, and Kant, Tardewski read, permitted me to help him sit down; then, after having recovered some of his strength, he said: "The sense of Humanity has still not left me." We are deeply moved because we understand that for the philosopher the old word *Humanität* had a very deep meaning, one which the circumstances of the moment served to accentuate: a man's proud and tragic consciousness of the persistence of the principles of justice and truth that had guided his life, in opposition to his total submission to illness, pain, and everything that the word mortality implies. The moral man, I remembered that Kant had written thirty years earlier, Tardewski read, knows that the most valuable of his possessions is not life but the preservation of his own dignity. And he knew how to live in accord with his principles to the end.

I should not want to have to express myself only with quotations, said Tardewski. The Professor is someone of whom one can say that he has never abandoned the sense of the word *Humanität* in the purest sense of that old German word.

And a man who is capable of living according to that principle is someone who merits, even from me, the cynic, the Sophist, all of my respect.

For that reason he was a moral man, said Tardewski, and for that reason he was the antithesis of me. If I have said what I have it is to show you to what an extent the Professor and I were worthy antagonists for each other. I, the unbeliever, a man who only uses thought to be able to survive; he, the man of principles, capable of being faithful all of his life to the rigor of his ideas. I, the exile; he, a man who was born and will die in his own country. I don't think that anything else could be added to make you see that I am not the most appropriate person to say anything about what the Professor decided to do with his life. I cannot say anything, except read and remember the words of others. And yet you see that he has trusted me.

That is why, beyond a doubt, the Professor has sent you to see me. Because I am the one who can't say anything about him.

That is why, I think, said Tardewski, the Professor has left me the only thing he needed to give up to be completely free. Once he gave up everything he really had, now, wherever he is, he, the Professor, now he has nothing to fear.

That is why, said Tardewski, he left these papers for me to give to you. If he hasn't come it's because it's no longer really necessary. More important, he said, was leaving you those papers, deciding to give them up and choosing you as the one who would receive them.

Tardewski says this and we sit together in silence. Then he gets up. He goes to the chest there at the end, off to one side of the room, against the wall. He opens a drawer. He takes out some folders. And he comes back here to give them to me. He says that these papers are now mine. They're yours, Tardewski says.

In a sense, he said later, this book was the Professor's autobiography. This was the way he had of writing about himself. That is why I think that in these papers you will find everything you need to know about him, everything I cannot tell you. I am sure you will find there the clue to his absence. The reason why he has not come tonight. There is the secret, if there is a secret. What he wanted to leave you, what he wanted you to travel here to receive, is the only thing that really matters, the only thing that can explain it all.

There are three folders, with documents and notes and pages written in a firm, clear hand.

Tardewski has gone over to the window. He looks out at the weak light that is turning the night air gray. He is facing away from me. He looks out and says that it has begun to dawn, that soon it will be day.

It's dawning, he says. Soon it will be day.

I open one of the folders.

To the one who finds my body

I am Enrique Ossorio, born and died an Argentine, who all of my life have wished for a single honor: the honor of being called a patriot, always ready to give everything for the Freedom of my country. My temporary residence is the following: 12, Eagle Lane, here in Copiapó, Republic of Chile. At that place you will find the Argentine citizen Mr. Juan Bautista Alberdi, who is my dearest friend; I have written him a letter explaining this decision of mine; the letter can be found in the left drawer of my desk. He will know what to do with what I leave behind, because for him I am like a brother.

NOTES

•

Translator's note: To avoid interrupting the flow of the text, endnote numbers have been eliminated. Instead, the following notes are keyed to page number and keyword. To the extent possible, I have referred the reader to English-language bibliography. A useful general reference work on Argentine history is Ione S. Wright and Lisa M. Nekhom's *Historical Dictionary of Argentina* (Metuchen: Scarecrow Press, 1978). I am grateful to Cristina Iglesia and Tulio Halperín Donghi for help with these notes.

13: Yrigoyen and Alvear Hipólito Yrigoyen (1852–1933) was a leading Argentine politician in the Radical party, president of Argentina for two terms, 1916–22 and 1928–30 (the second interrupted by a military coup). Marcelo T. de Alvear (1868–1942) was president from 1922 to 1928 in the period between Yrigoyen's presidencies, and their association became progressively more difficult toward the end of the decade. Both belonged to the same party, the Unión Cívica Radical, but to different tendencies within the party. Yrigoyen's phrase after being overthrown in a military coup led by General Uriburu was "Hay que rodear a Marcelo" (It's important to support Marcelo [Alvear]), although Alvear had not supported him in the period immediately prior to the coup. On the military coup against Yrigoyen, see Potash, *The Army and Politics in Argentina 1928–1945: Yrigoyen to Perón* (Stanford: Stanford University Press, 1969), 42–54.

14: Prolixity of the Real This is the last line of a Borges poem "La noche que en el Sur lo velaron." The English version by Robert Fitzgerald, "Deathwatch on the Southside," in *Selected Poems 1923–1967,* ends "the daily round of the real," which leaves out the sense of tedium and wordiness of "prolijidad."

14: Popham Sir Home Riggs Popham (1762–1820) was the British admiral involved in the first British occupation of Buenos Aires, from June to September, 1806. Popham was returning from Capetown, and the expedition to Buenos Aires took place without orders from the British government; he was tried and ultimately exonerated for having acted without orders. For a brief account, see David Rock, *Argentina 1516–1982* (Berkeley and Los Angeles: University of California Press, 1985), 71–73.

15: Radical The Unión Cívica Radical (Radical Civic Union) was founded by Leandro Alem in 1891, and was transformed into a mass movement by Hipólito Yrigoyen. Other Radical presidents include Marcelo T. de Alvear, Arturo Frondizi, Arturo Illia, and Raúl Alfonsín. The populist flavor of the Radical party was later largely taken over by Peronism, which became the great rival movement to Radicalism.

15: Sabbatini Amadeo Sabattini was a Radical governor of the province of Córdoba, then leader of a faction of the Radical party in the 1940s and 50s that was initially closer to Perón than the other factions of Radicalism. See César Tcach's *Sabattinismo y peronismo* (Buenos Aires: Editorial Sudamericana, 1991), and scattered references in Robert Potash's *The Army and Politics in Argentina* (Stanford: Stanford University Press, 1969 and 1980), especially in the second volume.

15: Rawson General Arturo Rawson (1885–1952) was one of the leaders of the coup of 1943 against President Ramón Castillo, which led eventually to the presidency of General Ramírez and then to the rise of Juan Domingo Perón. For a detailed account of the coup, see Potash, *The Army and Politics in Argentina,* 1: 182–200.

17: Macedonio Fernández Macedonio Fernández (1874–1952) was a writer much celebrated by Borges and others for his ingenuity. Most of his works are fragmentary and have only been published posthumously. Two book-length studies of his work in English are Naomi Lindstrom's *Macedonio Fernández* (Lincoln: Society for Spanish and Spanish American Studies, 1981) and Jo Anne Engelbert's *Macedonio Fernández and the Spanish American New Novel* (New York: New York University Press, 1978).

18: Cabral, Arlt Sergeant Juan Bautista Cabral (d. 1813) was a hero in a battle against the Spanish in the province of Corrientes who gave up his horse to General San Martín and lost his life. His dying words in Guaraní were: "I die happy. We have vanquished." Roberto Arlt (1900–1942), an Argentine novelist about whom much will be said later in the novel, often used narrators from the lower classes, the idea here being that Argentine history is told by the subordinate who sacrifices himself instead of by the victorious general.

18: Lavalle Juan Lavalle (1797–1841) was an Argentine general who fought with San Martín in the independence wars and later became a leader of the Unitarian forces against Juan Manuel de Rosas. For a discussion of his part in the political struggles of the early Rosas period, see José Luis Romero's *A History of Argentine Political Thought* (Stanford: Stanford University Press, 1963), 115–17 and 130–34.

18: Rosas Juan Manuel de Rosas (1793–1877) dominated Argentine political life from 1829 to 1852, serving as governor of the province of Buenos Aires. For an excellent account of his career, see John Lynch's *Argentine Dictator: Juan Manuel de Rosas 1829–1852* (Oxford: Oxford University Press, 1981). Lynch synthesizes his ideas on Rosas and the entire period of Argentine history from 1810 to 1870 in an article in the third volume of *The Cambridge History of Latin America*, ed. Leslie Bethell (Cambridge: Cambridge University Press, 1985), 615–76.

18: Hernández José Hernández (1834–86) was an Argentine writer and politician, best known for his gaucho epic *Martín Fierro* (1872 and 1879). At the end of his life he was a senator in the provincial senate of the province of Buenos Aires, and it is said that his dying words (quoted here) refer to the province, not the capital city.

20: Ataliva Roca Ataliva Roca was one of President Julio Argentino Roca's brothers, reputed to be the manager for the shady family businesses. The reference here is to the speculation in the lands opened up by Roca's 1879 campaign against the Indians, the so-called "Conquest of the Desert."

20: May 25th Argentine independence day, commemorating the declaration on May 25, 1810, by the Cabildo of Buenos Aires, of independence from Napoleon's puppet monarch of Spain.

20: Roca, Pellegrini Julio Argentino Roca (1843–1914) was the Argentine general who led the "Conquest of the Desert" against the pampas Indians in 1879; he was elected president for two terms, from 1880 to 1886 and from 1898 to 1904. The Argentine historian Félix Luna has recently written his fictional autobiography, *Soy Roca* (Buenos Aires: Editorial Sudamericana, 1991). Carlos Pellegrini (1846–1906), initially Roca's vice president, was president from 1890 to 1892; they became the bitterest of enemies.

21: Uriburu   José Félix Uriburu (1868–1933) was the general who led the coup against Hipólito Yrigoyen in 1930; he was president in 1930–31. See Potash, *The Army and Politics in Argentina*, 1: 55–78.

23: Sommariva   Luis H. Sommariva's multi-volume *Historia de las intervenciones federales en las provincias* [History of the Federal Interventions in the Provinces] was first published from 1929 to 1931. Under the constitution of 1853, the executive branch of the federal government may "intervene" a provincial government, replacing it temporarily.

23: Alem   Leandro Alem (1842–96) was the leader of the revolution of 1890 against the government of Juárez Celman and the founder in 1891 of the Unión Cívica Radical; he died by suicide. See Rock, *Argentina 1516–1982*, 183–85.

23: Balbín   Ricardo Balbín (1904–?) was a leader of the Radical Party for several decades from the 1940s on, and was a principal adversary of Perón. See Rock, *Argentina 1516–1982*, 303, 337, and numerous references in Potash's second volume, *The Army and Politics in Argentina 1945–1962: Perón to Frondizi* (Stanford: Stanford University Press, 1980).

23: Captain Gandhi   This was the nickname for Fernández Alvariño, a schoolteacher who was put in charge of the commission that looked into the alleged suicide of Juan Duarte, Evita Perón's brother. The commission botched its job, so it was never determined whether Duarte was murdered or committed suicide. Fernández Alvariño's nickname referred to his belief in nonviolence.

23: Consultative Board   The Junta Consultiva Nacional or National Consultative Board was a twenty-man civilian group of non-Peronist politicians who were to serve as advisers to the military leaders of the "Liberating Revolution" led by Generals Lonardi and Aramburu against Perón in 1955. See Potash, *The Army and Politics in Argentina*, 2: 226.

23: Fugitive Tyrant   This was how the anti-Peronist newspaper *La Prensa* referred to Perón after he was overthrown in September 1955.

25: Literary Society   The Salón Literario or Literary Society of Buenos Aires was organized in 1822 by Rivadavia, and became the focus of activity by the liberal intelligentsia in the following years of civil war between Unitarians (the party of the Buenos Aires liberals) and Federals. See Nicolas Shumway, *The Invention of Argentina* (Berkeley and Los Angeles: University of California Press, 1991), 87–97.

25: Alberdi   Juan Bautista Alberdi (1810–84) was one of the leading figures in the generation of 1837, and one of Argentina's greatest political theorists. His major work was *Bases y puntos de partida para la organización política de la República Argentina* (Bases and Points of Departure for the Political Organization of the Argentine Republic), published in 1852, which influenced the new constitution of 1853. See Shumway, *The Invention of Argentina,* 168–87, for a discussion of his differences with Sarmiento.

25: López   Vicente Fidel López (1815–1903) was another leading member of the generation of 1837, author of numerous historical novels (such as *La novia del hereje* [The Heretic's Fiancée] about Sir Francis Drake's expedition to Lima in 1578–79). His other works include several histories of Argentina. He was the son of the author of the Argentine national anthem.

25: Frías   Félix Frías (1816–81) was secretary of General Lavalle, and carried the latter's remains with him to Bolivia. After years in exile, he returned to Argentina to found a newspaper in 1855, and embarked on a political career that culminated in his being named by President Sarmiento as ambassador to Chile in 1869.

25: Tejedor   Carlos Tejedor (1817–1903) was the author of Argentina's first penal code. He was governor of the province of Buenos Aires during the conflicts of 1880; after his defeat in a series of battles with the forces of Julio Argentino Roca, Buenos Aires lost its autonomy, being designated as federal capital.

25: Angelis   Shumway, *The Invention of Argentina,* calls Pedro de Angelis (1789–1860) "an Italian literato imported by Rivadavia who became Rosas's in-house intellectual; a servile flatterer of whoever happened to be in power, de Angelis left a remarkable (if probably insincere) defense of Rosas's dictatorship, compelling refutations of Unitarian arguments against Rosas, and an admirable body of serious writings on Argentine culture, language, and geography" (215).

25: Maza   Manuel Vicente Maza (1779–1839) was elected governor of the province of Buenos Aires in 1834; after conspiring against Rosas, he was assassinated in his legislative office in 1839 at the height of the Mazorca's terror.

26 Sarmiento   Domingo Faustino Sarmiento (1811–88) was one of the foremost intellectuals in Argentina in the nineteenth century. His works include *Facundo* (1845) and *Campaña en el Ejército Grande* (1852). He was president of Argentina from 1868 to 1874.

26: Echeverría Esteban Echeverría (1805–51) was one of the leading figures in the generation of 1837, author of a poem on a white woman captive to the Indians ("La cautiva," 1837), an allegorical short story on a slaughterhouse in Buenos Aires during Rosas's Terror ("El matadero," 1840; published 1871), and numerous political writings.

26: Gutiérrez Juan María Gutiérrez (1809–78) was another figure of the generation of 1837, heavily influenced by Echeverría. He was the author of poetry, fiction, and works of criticism, and became rector of the University of Buenos Aires in 1861.

26: Urquiza Justo José de Urquiza (1801–70) was governor of Entre Ríos, leader of the united forces against Rosas in 1852, and president of the Argentine Confederation from 1854 to 1860.

27: Caseros The definitive battle between the followers of Rosas and the army led by Urquiza took place near Buenos Aires on February 3, 1852. Rosas was then exiled to Southampton, England, where he died in 1877. Sarmiento's history of the campaign against Rosas (*Campaña en el Ejército Grande*, 1852) is one of his greatest works.

28: Mitre Bartolomé Mitre (1821–1906) was one of Argentina's leading public figures for decades, president of the republic from 1862 to 1868, unsuccessful leader of the allied forces in the early stages of the war against Paraguay, and one of Argentina's greatest historians, author of major biographical studies of San Martín, Belgrano, and others.

31: Truco This is an Argentine game requiring great verbal skill as well as a lucky hand of cards.

41: Sáenz Peña Law The Sáenz Peña Law establishing universal male suffrage (with various limitations) was enacted by the Argentine Congress in 1911 and came into effect the following year. It was named for the president of Argentina at the time of its passage, Roque Sáenz Peña (1851–1914). See Rock, *Argentina 1516–1982*, 189–90.

41: Lugones Leopoldo Lugones (1874–1938) was the major literary figure in Argentina from the turn of the century on, the author of numerous books of poetry, historical fiction, and political and historical essays. His political ideas evolved from early socialism to an extreme nationalism of a fascist flavor in his last years. In 1924 Lugones gave his "Discurso de Ayacucho" (a speech on the anniversary of the Battle of Ayacucho in 1824) in which he proclaimed: "Once again, for the good of the world, the hour of the sword has sounded." On Lugones's subsequent involvement with the military plotters against Hipólito Yrigoyen, see Robert Potash, *The Army and Politics in Argentina 1928–1945*, 1: 19, 102.

42: Tute This is an Argentine card game.

48: La Tribuna A daily newspaper published in Buenos Aires in the latter part of the nineteenth century, directed by Héctor Varela. It was here that Lucio V. Mansilla published his famous *Excursion to the Ranquel Indians* in 1870: see Shumway, *The Invention of Argentina*, 257.

50: 1880 After the defeat of Tejedor's forces by Roca, a new national accord was established: Buenos Aires was made federal capital, La Plata was established as the new capital of the province of Buenos Aires, and the country was opened up to foreign investment and immigration. The "generation of 1880," including such figures as Miguel Cané and Lucio V. Mansilla, dominated the cultural sphere in the years that followed, while Roca and Pellegrini were president. See David William Foster, *The Argentine Generation of 1880* (Columbia: University of Missouri Press, 1990), and Gustavo Ferrari and Ezequiel Gallo, eds., *La Argentina del Ochenta al Centenario* (Buenos Aires: Editorial Sudamericana, 1980).

67: Justo José Justo José de Urquiza. See note to page 26.

68: the Tiger Normally a nickname for Juan Facundo Quiroga ("El Tigre de los Llanos" or "Tiger of the Plains"), it here seems to refer to Rosas.

68: Ramírez Francisco ("Pancho") Ramírez (1786–1821) was an important figure in the independence wars, later becoming the leader of the province of Entre Ríos: see Rock, *Argentina 1516–1982*, 93–95.

71: the Invasions In 1806 and 1807, British forces twice occupied Buenos Aires, only to be driven off by local resistance. The success of the resistance contributed to the strength of independence feelings in 1810.

71: Belgrano General Manuel Belgrano (1770–1820) won victories against the Spanish forces in Tucumán (1812) and Salta (1813). He was the subject of a great historical study by Bartolomé Mitre.

71: Santa Fe The province of Santa Fe is located along the Paraná River.

The reference here probably has to do with its swampy geography and subtropical climate.

73: Tigre Tigre, a resort area near Buenos Aires in the area of the Paraná river delta, is a labyrinth of islands separated by narrow channels. It was the scene of various important events in Argentine history, including the suicide of Lugones in 1937.

75: Cané Miguel Cané (1851–1905) was one of the most prominent members of the Argentine generation of 1880, and a close associate of President Roca. His *Juvenilia* is a classic account of schoolboy life at the Colegio Nacional de Buenos Aires, written while Cané was Argentine ambassador to Colombia and Venezuela.

75: Rivadavia Bernardino Rivadavia (1780–1845) was president of Argentina in 1826–27 and a leader of the Unitarian party.

75: Moreno Mariano Moreno (1778–1811) was an illustrious lawyer and a leader of the 1810 revolution against Spain.

76: Generation of 1837 The generation of 1837 was a group of young liberal intellectuals of Buenos Aires, exiled by Juan Manuel de Rosas (1793–1877), the dictatorial governor of the province of Buenos Aires from 1829 to 1852. The most prominent members of the generation as it first emerged were Juan Bautista Alberdi, Juan Cruz Varela, Esteban Echeverría, Vicente Fidel López, and Juan María Gutiérrez; Domingo Faustino Sarmiento's intellectual (and geographic) trajectory was different from those just mentioned, most of whom were from Buenos Aires, but in exile Sarmiento joined the group, though always with something like outsider status. See Romero, *A History of Argentine Political Thought*, 126–55 and Shumway, *The Invention of Argentina*, 112–67, for good accounts of the period; Tulio Halperín Donghi's anthology *Proyecto y construcción de una nación* (Caracas: Biblioteca Ayacucho, 1980) contains a wealth of writings by members of the group.

76: Facundo The title of Sarmiento's 1845 biography of Juan Facundo Quiroga, originally entitled *Civilization and Savagery*. For the moment the only available English edition is Mary Peabody Mann's 1868 edition, entitled *Life in the Argentine Republic in the Days of the Tyrants;* Kathleen Ross is completing a new translation for the University of California Press.

80: High in the sky This is a line from "Aurora," an anthem that is sung when the Argentine flag is raised.

80: Anahí　The legend of Anahí tells of a Guaraní Indian princess who is transformed into a red flower when she is about to be burned to death on a pyre. There is a Paraguayan song about the Anahí legend. The river region of northeast Argentina (the "Litoral" or Argentine Mesopotamia) is the region bounded by the Paraná and Uruguay rivers, consisting of the provinces of Misiones, Corrientes, and Entre Ríos.

82: the French blockade　The French navy blockaded the port of Buenos Aires from March 1838 until October 1840, and France allied itself with anti-Rosas forces in Montevideo.

82: the Terror　This refers to the most intense period of terror by the followers of Rosas, particularly those associated with an organization known as the Mazorca (corn-cob, but also a pun on "more gallows"); from 1839 to 1842 there was a particularly intense period of political persecution of suspected Unitarians and other dissidents. The best known literary representation of the period is José Mármol's novel *Amalia* (1852).

83: the General　The General referred to here is of course Juan Domingo Perón, who died in 1974. He was succeeded in power by his third wife Isabelita Perón (María Estela Martínez de Perón), who was overthrown in the military coup of 1976.

84: Leagues　The Rural Leagues were local grassroots groups organized by the Catholic left during the 1960s and early 70s. They were particularly strong in the river region of Corrientes, Santa Fe, and Chaco.

89: Martínez Estrada　Ezequiel Martínez Estrada (1895–1964) was an Argentine writer best known for his essay *Radiografía de la pampa* (1933; English trans., *X-ray of the Pampa*, Austin: University of Texas Press, 1971) and for his studies of Horacio Quiroga, José Hernández's *Martín Fierro* and José Martí. He also wrote poetry and short fiction; a volume of his short stories, *Holy Saturday and Other Stories*, is available in English (Pittsburgh: Latin American Literary Review Press, 1988).

90: Pueyrredón　Juan Martín de Pueyrredón (1776–1850) was leader of the Argentine forces that repelled the British invasions of 1806 and 1807, and led the Argentine Confederation from 1816 to 1819. He was the father of Prilidiano Pueyrredón, an eminent painter of the Rosas period, and uncle of José Hernández, the author of *The Gaucho Martín Fierro*.

92: Spinetta　Luis Alberto Spinetta is an Argentine rock musician.

92: First Triumvirate The first Triumvirate, led by Bernardino Rivadavia, ruled Argentina in 1811–1812. See Rock, *Argentina 1516–1982*, 85–88, and Shumway, *The Invention of Argentina*, 51–52.

92: I am the sister. This is a pencil This is in English in the original.

99: Angela 'admitted' "Admitted" was political slang for "disappeared" during the military dictatorship.

100: Raquel/Aquel *Aquel* was a codeword for Perón in the years of his exile. The incident referred to here was the massacre near Ezeiza airport on the outskirts of Buenos Aires in June 1973: see Rock, *Argentina 1516–1982*, 360, and, for more detail, Tomás Eloy Martínez's *La novela de Perón* (*The Perón Novel*, New York: Pantheon, 1988).

110: Gombrowicz The Polish writer (1904–69) lived in exile in Argentina from 1939 to 1963. His novel *Ferdydurke* was translated by committee in a Buenos Aires pool parlor in 1947, and he became a cult figure for many younger Argentine writers. His widow, Rita Gombrowicz, has collected testimonies about his quarter century in Argentina (*Gombrowicz en Argentine,* Paris: Denoël, 1984); his *Diary,* including extensive sections on his years in Argentina, is now available in English (Evanston: Northwestern University Press, 1988).

116: Soussens On Charles de Soussens, see Antonio Monteavaro et al., *Textos y protagonistas de la bohemia porteña: Antología* (Buenos Aires: Centro Editor de América Latina, 1980).

117: Hudson W. H. Hudson (1841–1922), the English writer born in the province of Buenos Aires, wrote a number of books on the River Plate region, including *The Purple Land that England Lost* (1885), *Idle Days in Patagonia* (1893), *The Naturalist in La Plata* (1892), and *Far Away and Long Ago* (1918). He was the subject of a book-length essay by Martínez Estrada, and of several essays by Borges.

117: Güiraldes Ricardo Güiraldes (1886–1927) was the author of a variety of fiction and poetry, the most important being his final novel, *Don Segundo Sombra* (1926), about a boy's apprenticeship to an old gaucho. Borges frequently notes that this novel is the Argentine version of *Huckleberry Finn* and *Kim.*

121: 9th of July This is Argentina's independence day, marking the conclusion of the Congress of Tucumán on July 9, 1816, which proclaimed the independence of the Argentina Confederation.

124 Groussac   Paul Groussac (1848–1929) was a French immigrant to Argentina who eventually became director of the National Library. He wrote a novel and several plays, as well as various works on Argentine history. His book on Don Quixote, *Une enigme littéraire,* was published in 1903.

127: Difunta Correa   In Argentine folklore, a woman who was found dead in the wastes of the northern province of Catamarca with a baby still suckling at her breast. She is the patroness of truck and bus drivers, and her followers leave bottles of water on her shrines in the northern deserts.

127: Strap   This plays on the literal meaning of Correa's surname, "strap."

128: On ne tue point les idées   For further discussion of this misquotation, see Sylvia Molloy's *At Face Value* (Cambridge: Cambridge University Press, 1991), 30–32.

132: Pibe Cabeza   Pibe Cabeza (a nickname from "pibe," boy, and "cabeza," head) was a thug in the employ of a ward boss, Barceló, in Avellaneda, one of the eastern suburbs of Buenos Aires in the 1930s. There are mementos of his criminal career in the police museum in Buenos Aires.

132: Castelnuovo   Elías Castelnuovo (1893–?) was one of the "proletarian" writers in the Boedo group in the 1920s and 30s.

132: Murena   The writer and critic H. A. Murena (1923–75) is best known for his essay *El pecado original de América* (The Original Sin of the New World), though he also wrote fiction.

135: The Flame Throwers   Los lanzallamas (1931) is the sequel to Arlt's anarchist utopian novel *The Seven Madmen* (1929), available in an English version by Naomi Lindstrom (Boston: Godine, 1984). In the preface to the sequel, Arlt mentions the crudity of some passages in *Ulysses* and the "spiritual delight" they cause in some of Joyce's Argentine readers, then adds: "The day that James Joyce is accessible to all [in translation], the representatives of high society will invent a new idol to be read by no more than a half-dozen initiates."

137: The Furious Toy   Arlt's *El juguete rabioso,* a 1926 novel, has yet to be translated into English. It is the story of a young man fascinated by the world of crime.

138: López Jordán   Ricardo López Jordán (1822–89) was a strongman from Entre Ríos who led the assassination of Urquiza in 1870.

138: Mallea   Eduardo Mallea (1903–?) was considered Argentina's leading novelist in the 1930s and 40s, though his stock has fallen in recent years. He was closely associated with the magazine *Sur*.

138: Gándara   Carmen Gándara (b. 1900) was a writer of fiction associated with the magazine *Sur*. Her books include *La habitada* (1948), *Los espejos* (1951), and *La figura del mundo* (1958).

139: Mujica Lainez   Manuel Mujica Lainez (1910–84) was a best-selling Argentine novelist perhaps better known as a dandy and socialite.

139: Wast   Hugo Wast, the pseudonym of Gustavo Martínez Zuviría (1883–1962), was the author of a long series of best-selling potboilers, many of which were widely translated as they seemed to provide "local color" about Argentine life. On Wast, see Francine Masiello's *Between Civilization and Barbarism* (Lincoln: University of Nebraska Press, 1992), 144–45.

139: Larreta   Enrique Larreta (1875–1961) was the author of a number of books, the best known of which was *La gloria de don Ramiro* (The Glory of Don Ramiro), set in the Spain of Philip the Second.

139: Nacha Regules   Nacha Regules is the heroine of a novel (1918) by Manuel Gálvez about prostitution and the Buenos Aires underworld. On prostitution in Buenos Aires, see Donna Guy's *Sex and Danger in Buenos Aires* (Lincoln: University of Nebraska Press, 1991), which includes discussion of this novel (164–70).

140: Banchs   Enrique Banchs (1888–1968) published several books of poetry at the beginning of the century, most notably a book of sonnets, *La urna*, in 1911. He then ceased publishing.

141: Ascasubi   Hilario Ascasubi (1807–75) was a journalist and gauchesque poet, best known for his two collections of *Paulino Lucero* (1853 and 1872), which focus on the period of the resistance to Rosas.

168: Fatoni   Vicente Fatoni was the author of numerous books on religion and philosophy, including *El budismo "nihilista"* (1941), *Introducción al existencialismo* (1953), and *El hombre y Dios* (1955).

168: Ortiga   This is a pun on the name of the Spanish philosopher José Ortega y Gasset (1883–1955): *ortiga* means "stinging nettle."

173: Ortiz   Roberto M. Ortiz (1886–1942) was a liberal president of Argentina from 1938 to 1942, though the government was mostly run by the much more conservative vice president, Ramón S. Castillo, from 1940 onward, due to Ortiz's sufferings from diabetes.

179: Café Tortoni   The Café Tortoni is a grand old turn-of-the-century café on the Avenida de Mayo in Buenos Aires, near the Plaza de Mayo. It is full of mementos of artists, musicians, and literati.

196: Mansilla   Lucio Victorio Mansilla (1831–1913), a nephew of Juan Manuel de Rosas and an eminent writer of the generation of 1880, is best known today for his *Excursión a los indios ranqueles* [Excursion to the Ranquel Indians], published in 1870.